RESTLESS

After a turbulent childhood, Emily Harrington has finally found peace living with her sister and brother-in-law on their Texas ranch. Betrothed to a good man, she teaches the ranch children and shares her happiness with her best friend, Cotannah. Emily believes her life could not get any better—until one sultry evening when the proud Choctaw brave, Tay Nashoba, rides into her life.

RECKLESS

As a leader of the Choctaw nation, Tay is honor bound to marry one of his own people—and he has come to Texas to claim Cotannah as his bride. But it is beautiful, bewitching Emily who enflames his soul—as forbidden passion unites them beneath a silver moon . . . challenging them to defy will, duty, and destiny in the perilous cause of eternal love.

GENELL DELLIN

SILVER MOON SONG

An Avon Romantic Treasure

AVON BOOKS ◆ NEW YORK

SILVER MOON SONG is an original publication of Avon Books. This work has never before appeared in book form. This work is a novel. Any similarity to actual persons or events is purely coincidental.

AVON BOOKS
A division of
The Hearst Corporation
1350 Avenue of the Americas
New York, New York 10019

Copyright © 1996 by Genell Smith Dellin
Inside cover author photo by Loy's Photography
Published by arrangement with the author
Library of Congress Catalog Card Number: 96-96477
ISBN: 0-380-78602-8

First Avon Books Printing: December 1996

AVON TRADEMARK REG. U.S. PAT. OFF. AND IN OTHER COUNTRIES, MARCA REGISTRADA, HECHO EN U.S.A.

Printed in the U.S.A.

RA 10 9 8 7 6 5 4 3 2 1

To my sister
Linda Ruth Smith
With much love and appreciation

Love is like the wild rose-briar;
Friendship like the holly-tree.
The holly is dark when the rose-briar blooms,
But which will bloom most constantly?

Emily Brontë

Chapter 1

Rancho de las Manzanitas
Nueces County, Texas
June 1874

The signal bell rang out just as Emily and Cotannah were putting the last touches to the cold supper Oleana had prepared for the travelers expected that evening. Instantly they looked at each other across the table and stilled to listen—every bell, every gunshot, every shout these days, could be a warning of *bandidos*—but this time the rings were short, quick ones and they paused after three to start over again, indicating the approach of friends.

Cotannah's face lit up with a blinding smile.

"They're here," she cried, doing a little twirling dance. "Oh, at last Tay's here! The handsomest man in all of creation has come to marry me!"

She whirled and started for the door, then whirled back again.

"How do I look, Mimi? Remember, he hasn't

1

seen me for four years, not since I've grown up."

"Beautiful beyond belief." She meant that sincerely. "You draw everyone's eye, just as Maggie does," Emily said. "You're beautiful and spirited and entirely irresistible, 'Tannah. Don't worry—Tay is bound to think so, too."

Cotannah's eyes misted over and she ran around the table to give Emily a hug, then she was gone. Emily lingered over this last moment of their old life, fighting back tears as she turned the platter of sliced melon on its bed of ice one more time and tucked in the edges of the napkins that wrapped the biscuit-ham sandwiches. Tay Nashoba was Cotannah's dream, and for her sake Emily was glad he was coming, but for her own sake, selfishly, she wished he had stayed in the Choctaw Nation. He was going to marry Cotannah and take her away from Las Manzanitas—dear, dear Cotannah, who called her Mimi just as Maggie did because she was as close to Emily as her own sister.

She left the dining room and walked toward the front of the house, toward the rest of the family gathering on the front porch to greet Cade and the guest he had gone to meet in Corpus Christi, Tay Nashoba. She would *not* be selfish and feel sorry for herself over the old life that was about to slip away; she would be happy and celebrate with Cotannah the new one she was beginning. That was the least she could do, especially when Cotannah had been so happy for her when she became betrothed to Lee.

"Aunt Mimi! Papa is coming!"

Miranda, who was usually called Randy, one of Maggie and Cade's three-year-old twins, called to her and came running out of the dusky evening toward the porch with her brother, Cole, hard on her heels. Emily bent down and held out her arms to them as they burst into the light of the lanterns hanging under the eaves. The children scrambled up the steps, gave Emily quick embraces, then raced to climb onto the balustrade of the porch.

"Papa will be s'prised to see us sit up here," Miranda announced.

Cole, who had never spoken, only nodded.

The drumming of the hoofbeats on the drive grew closer. Emily tried to keep one hand on each wriggling child to prevent a fall while she strained, like everyone else, to get a glimpse of Tay. Maggie, Cotannah, Aunt Ancie, and Uncle Jumper were all in the yard at the hitching rail beneath the live oak tree.

Suddenly the arriving party turned the bend in the road at a long lope, the silver on their saddles flashing in the light of the rising moon. Outriders broke away and scattered to the bunkhouse and corrals, and in another moment, Tay and Cade, riding alone, came closer and closer, looking very much alike in the dimness; two big men riding big gray horses long-trotting in step.

But it was easy to tell which was Tay. His horse was such a pale gray, it was nearly white,

and his wide-brimmed straw hat was of the
flat-crowned southern planter fashion rather
than Texas-styled, like Cade's. His hat, like his
suit, was white, as was the thin duster that the
breeze slapped against his long legs.

Even the way he rode was elegantly polished,
somehow. Without taking her eyes from him,
Emily steadied the twins on their narrow perch.

Cotannah waited between Aunt Ancie and
Uncle Jumper as the two men rode up, stopped,
and dismounted. Tay shrugged out of his duster and threw it over his saddle in one quick,
fluid gesture, then swept off his hat and came
forward to bow over Ancie's and Cotannah's
and Maggie's hands. They all stood in a circle
for a moment, talking. Emily felt a sudden,
sharp desire to hear what they were saying.

The big tree's shadows played the moonlight
over Tay's tall, broad body, which looked thick
with muscle. Giddily she thought that he probably played that Choctaw stickball game that
Cotannah and Cade always talked about.

Still talking, the group began walking toward
the house, with Tay and Cotannah just a few
steps ahead of the others. The stableboys ran
up and took the horses from the hitching rack.
Tay's hair, tied back at the nape of his neck,
gleamed blue-black, and his skin glowed like
copper against the white of his collar. He
looked as clean and crisp as if he'd just stepped
out of a bath, but as soon as he came within
earshot, Emily heard him contradict her
thought, as if he'd sensed it somehow.

"Miss Cotannah," he was saying as they

came nearer the steps, "when Cade met me in Corpus Christi, I told him I had to lay over a day to wash off my mask of trail dirt so I wouldn't scare you, and now here I am, dust-covered again."

His voice was like the sound of a river running slow and deep. It was beautiful enough to carry a person away. Emily thought she could listen to it all day and never even hear the words.

Cotannah stopped in the pool of lantern light at the foot of the steps and tossed her head flirtatiously, giving Tay that coquettish look of hers: the slight smile, the challenging glance from beneath her thick lashes. In the last few months, it had stunned six or seven men, made them crazy enough to dare Cade's refusal and ask to come courting her. Tay, however, must be accustomed to other women as bold and as beautiful, for he simply returned Cotannah's speculative look with an amused grin.

"I declare," she said, "I don't think you're ever going to ask me!"

Emily stared in shock. Good heavens, surely even the daring Cotannah couldn't be *that* blunt! She couldn't possibly be expecting a proposal of marriage the minute he got off his horse right here, in front of the whole family, could she?

But Tay didn't seem dismayed in the least. He only cocked one black brow and finished his perusal of Cotannah, looking her up and down, head to foot.

"No need to ask," he drawled. "Even without my spectacles I can see that you have finally grown up, Miss Cotannah."

Emily let out the breath she hadn't realized she was holding. Of course. Cotannah had told her that, after her childhood declaration to marry him when she grew up, Tay would teasingly ask her if she was grown yet every time their paths crossed. That had encouraged her to think that he'd taken her proposal seriously. From all Emily could see, Tay Nashoba would be a fine hand at encouraging any woman to think whatever he wanted her to think.

"I'm even putting up my hair now," Cotannah said.

She sounded like a little girl as she turned in a playful pirouette, but she certainly didn't *look* like one. The saucy movement let Tay see her new way of dressing her hair, but it also showed off her generous bosom and tiny waist in the tight-bodiced dress, as she obviously intended. She threw Tay an arch glance over her shoulder.

"Do you remember what you always said after you asked if I was grown up yet?" She didn't wait for him to answer. "You always said that you were still single, still waiting for me."

Emily thought for an instant he would ignore the remark, but he didn't. He broadened his grin.

"How could I forget," he teased, "when you always gave me *such* a look before you blushed and hid your face?"

"Because she knew she never should have

asked to marry you in the first place," Aunt Ancie said in her dry voice.

Cotannah blushed crimson and everyone around her laughed.

"Don't let her fool you, Tay," Cade said lightly. "She may look like a woman, but she still behaves like a child sometimes."

"*Cade!*"

Cotannah wheeled to glare at him, then she smiled when he flashed her his devilish, big-brother grin. Everyone laughed again. Then her gaze went right back to Tay.

"Could it be that Cade wants to keep you as his little sister forever so he won't feel that he's getting old?"

"Exactly! That's it!"

Amid more laughter, Tay started up the steps while Cotannah's admiring eyes clung to his every move. No wonder she was crazy about him—he was charming, and so smooth, he knew exactly what to say to make everyone feel good.

"Look at us!" Miranda called to the approaching audience.

Then she gave a frightened gasp and Emily wheeled around to see that she was standing on the banister, teetering, holding both arms out for balance. Dear goodness, *how* had the child scooted out of her grasp without her noticing? She caught Randy against her in one arm and scooped up Cole in the other so he wouldn't imitate Miranda.

"Tay, this is my sister, Emily," Maggie said, from behind her.

Emily turned and there he was, right in front of her. Vaguely she saw Cade and Maggie and Cotannah, too, but Tay Nashoba, up close, filled her vision. After hearing about him for weeks, the reality of him was startling somehow.

His eyes were *gray*! They were *light gray* and they sparkled and flashed in his dark face. The lantern light limned his high cheekbones as he smiled and inclined his head courteously.

"My whole name is Wynn Tay Nashoba," he said in his wonderful rolling-river voice. "'Wynn' and the color of my eyes are legacies of the Welsh trader blood on both sides of my family."

The heat of deep embarrassment flooded into her throat and cheeks, the old urge to stammer took hold of her tongue. She fought it and lost.

"I-I-I . . . I-I didn't mean . . . to st-st-stare. I'm sorry."

"No, no, not at all," he said gallantly. "We walked up behind you and startled you."

He sounded so sure, so sincere, so matter-of-fact, that she believed him.

He saw that, she knew he did, but he kept looking at her anyway as if to convince her. And she kept looking at him.

A slow buzzing began in her blood, a murmuring hum that sang and tingled just beneath her skin.

He saw that, too. His look grew more intense, and for the space of a heartbeat she thought he would take a step toward her.

Miranda launched herself out of Emily's grasp at that moment, and Tay caught her instantly between his big hands, brown, strong, capable hands. He settled the child into the crook of his elbow and smiled straight into her wide eyes. Randy smiled back.

"I saw you standing on the porch railing," Tay said, speaking to her in the same conversational tone he'd used with the adults, "and I thought you must be an acrobat or maybe a Comanche. They sometimes ride standing on their horses' backs, you know. Can you ride a horse?"

"Yes!"

"Then you are a Comanche," he said. "Are you a full-blood?"

"I am full-blood Texian," Miranda said, "on the Running M. M is for Miranda."

Everyone burst out laughing and Miranda beamed brightly at Tay, who shook his head in amazement. Then she turned to reach for her brother, motioning with her fat fingers for him to join her. Tay did come closer then, to take Cole as well, and Emily caught his scent, a heady mix of horse, leather, sweat, soap, dust and . . . Tay. Some aroma that she knew instinctively was his alone, something that drew her forward another half step to meet him as he lifted Cole's weight from her. His hand brushed her arm, and even through her sleeve it left a warmth on her skin.

"We'll give your aunt Emily a rest," he said, smiling at her and then at each twin. "You two together are as heavy as a bale of hay."

Then he turned his attention to Cole, holding him opposite his sister.

"You must be Cole. I heard about you from your papa during our long ride today. I'm your uncle Tay."

Randy reached across and patted her twin's arm, then stuck the tip of her forefinger into Tay's starched white shirt.

"Uncle Tay," she said.

"Uncle Tay," Cole repeated, speaking as clearly as his sister had done.

A shocked silence fell. Stunned, delighted, Emily clasped her hands together and looked at Maggie, who caught her glance and sent her a brilliant smile of victorious relief. Emily felt the same look reflected on her own face and saw it repeated on Mama's.

Cole looked at his father, pointed to Tay, and said again, "Uncle Tay."

"Those are the first words he's ever spoken," Emily told Tay while Cade and Cole beamed at each other amidst applause, gasps, and happy cries from everyone. "I'm glad you came."

Tay looked at her. She looked back at him. Again they connected; somehow, standing there close together, they remained separate from everyone else.

"That's a welcome worth the traveling."

He spoke the words low—for her only—beneath the noise all the others were making. The sound of them, the rhythm of them, entered her blood and flowed into the beat of her heart.

Cade touched Tay on the shoulder then, and

he turned away to be introduced to Mama. After that, he moved on into the house, still carrying the twins, who were obviously enthralled by him. Emily stared after him.

What he had said was probably nothing but an old Choctaw saying, a standard courtesy of every guest upon arrival. She would ask Cotannah or Cade about that. But the bigger mystery was what *she* had said to *him*. Wasn't this the same man she'd been wishing away not ten minutes ago?

Long after midnight Tay lay wide-awake, staring up at the dark ceiling, too tired to sleep. Too tired to think, too, but his mind refused to rest.

He ought to get up early in the morning and ride right back to the Nation, where he belonged. Cotannah was too young for him; she was like a baby sister to him, and he'd known the moment he saw her this evening that he would always love her in that way. *Only* in that way. While she loved him wildly—at least she believed she did.

He sighed. Dear God, there was no way he had the strength to cope with this situation. To tell the truth, he didn't even want to try. Dealing with the People and all his duties kept him drained; he had felt that way ever since the War. He should've known he had nothing left over to give to Cotannah or any other woman.

Damn it, why couldn't he have seen that before he came all this way? Of course, this trip would give him a holiday before the election

for Principal Chief, but he was a dishonorable
bounder and a cad for taking advantage of that
in view of what he was doing to Cotannah.

He took a deep, jagged breath of the night
prairie air and threw his arm over his eyes.
Everything would look different in the morning
or so his auntie Iola had always told him; all he
needed was a good night's sleep.

This time, though, he needed more than one
night, he needed days, too—a whole moon—
of no turmoil in his guts, no decisions to make,
nobody expecting, wanting, asking, demanding anything of him. What he needed was a
long, peaceful moon of gazing into Emily's
brown eyes.

The thought came to him unbidden, and
with it the bursting kernel of warmth deep
inside him; the feeling of something new and
tender coming to life that he had felt when she
first turned and looked at him. He had to stamp
that out. He couldn't let it live because whatever it was, it was far too dangerous. He had no
emotion to give to a woman. None.

Yet that moment when she'd turned to him,
her slender arms filled with the chubby, ram-
bunctious twins, had been a rare one. Her face
had been so . . . serene, so filled with love, in
the lantern light that it had brought him up
short.

He tried to drift away into sleep thinking of
the pretty picture she had made with her blond
head bent to the two dark ones of the children,
but a small voice in the back of his mind
wouldn't let him. A feeling for him had come

into her eyes the instant they met. Some power had connected them, fast as thought. He let himself ponder that mystery for the longest time until finally he slept.

Just before dawn he came awake with a start, wondering where he was. Once he knew, he lay without moving, listening, waiting for whatever sound had woken him to float back again. It never did—the whole, dark world was quiet.

But his mind leapt back to the War and the memories of waking on patrol, terrified, his pistol under his pillow and his rifle stock in his hand. Every muscle in his body tensed against the onslaught of memories, every part of his mind tried to push it away, but within three heartbeats he knew it was useless. He would never be able to go back to sleep.

Resigned, he threw off the sheet and swung his feet out of bed. The moon was down and the dark that preceded the dawn was filling the world—it was his usual time to get up, anyway. He might as well go for his run to greet the sun and clear his mind.

He found his moccasins, but he fumbled in his bags without immediately finding the buckskins he liked to wear for this ritual, so he pulled on the breeches and shirt he'd worn from Corpus, tied back his hair, and ran silently down the stairs. He got out of the house without making any noise and stood in the yard for a moment, stretching his body into full wakefulness.

Light was coming fast enough to show him

the way, but barely. Since he didn't know this country, he turned onto the driveway and began to trot in the direction of the road they had come in on the previous evening, hoping he could run fast enough to outrun the thoughts in his head.

But before his muscles had warmed up enough to really stretch his pace, before he even had passed all the outbuildings clustered within a hundred yards or so of the big house, he heard gunshots. There was only a passing instant, time enough to realize that the sound had come from up ahead and to his right, before the ominous drumming of hoofbeats shook the soles of his feet. Then he heard horses, coming fast across the grass off to one side of the road.

He veered off its packed surface and reversed his direction, heading back toward the stables, cursing himself for dressing in white to run in the dark, for not bringing along a weapon, for forgetting Cade's warning that there was a whole gang of *bandidos* who wanted revenge because Cade had killed one of their own. And he cursed himself for not taking care of his own horse the night before—his rifle would still be in the scabbard, but he had no idea where to find his saddle.

It was in the stable's tack room, surely, and if not, there'd be other weapons there and in every other outbuilding near the house as a matter of course. No doubt Cade and his men would be prepared for attack—they kept patrols out at all times.

More shots, closer now, rang out through the reddening dawn. Tay bent double and ran faster. A whole volley of shots, from both pistols and rifles, sounded louder now, and hoofbeats came pounding down the road. He dashed around the corner and in through the stable's double doors.

A horse whinnied in the darkness, another snorted and kicked the wall. Tay stopped still and looked around for the tack room, then he leapt toward the dark rectangle of a door in the white front wall of the long barn. His blood was up now, racing hot and fast, and he felt a wry grin twist his lips. A good fight, some dangerous action, would be even better than an early-morning run to help cure what ailed him.

Emily heard horses galloping and she knew, before she was even completely awake, that Cortina's bandits were attacking at last. She was up and snatching her dress from the chair, pulling it on over her nightgown, before they reached the house. Seconds later, Lee's voice was yelling from the front yard just below her window.

"*Bandidos, bandidos!* Hello the house! *Bandidos!* Rouse yourselves!"

She ran and looked out. In the dim half-light she saw Lee pull his horse to a stop, hit the ground running, and then leap over the banister up onto the porch. Thank God, the bandits hadn't hurt him.

The bell rang the alarm, rifle shots sounded from the lookout tower, and somebody began screaming in Spanish. Some yelling, yipping bandits raced into the yard on Lee's trail, firing wildly; then, as soon as the big Sharps guns roared at them from the lookout tower, they wheeled their horses and raced away again.

Another Sharps boomed from the first floor of the house—probably from Maggie and Cade's room—and the bandits vanished into the shadowy trees at the edge of the east pasture. The Running M horses inside it went crazy.

Sache! Oh, dear Lord, her own wild little filly would be throwing a fit. She'd be absolutely hysterical in her stall from the noise of the guns and the sense of danger in the air. All the hours spent trying to tame her would be wasted and she'd have the other stabled horses worked up into a frenzy!

Emily dashed back to the bed for her slippers, and as soon as she stuck her feet into them, she ran for the back stairs, trying to button her dress as she went. Lee, Cade, and the guards in the tower were here to defend the house, and so was Tay Nashoba. For that matter, Maggie could shoot as straight as any man, too, and vaqueros would be pouring from the bunkhouse and from their own houses to fight. They didn't need her here—she would do more good in the stable calming the nervous filly and the others.

She dashed down the stairs, let herself out the back door, and ran even faster across the yard, trying to keep in the shadows, to look in two directions at once—for shooters outside and for family inside who would come out to bring her back. Finally she reached the stable and darted into it through the wide doors, into the dim, early-morning quiet, a quiet so unexpected that it stopped her in her tracks.

None of the horses, not even Sache, was kicking or whinnying! A cold hand closed around her heart and she peered harder into the gloom. Were they *gone?* she wondered. Were the bandits who chased Lee only a distraction from other bandits who had been emptying the stables? Then her eyes adjusted and she saw a horse's head lift and turn to look at her, and then another.

She heard a . . . *singing?* Yes, it was singing, barely loud enough to carry to the front of the stable. She held her breath to listen.

Chapter 2

"*Uh–huh, uh–huh, kia yuhapa, kia yuhapa, yi a ha,*" a deep, rich man's voice sang, soft and low, "*yi, ya, yi, yaiya.*"

The breath went out of her in a long, ragged sigh.

"Tay?"

"Over here."

He was in the hay storage space next to her filly's stall, standing on something in order to look out the window that faced the house. The rifle in his hand glinted as he moved; his white clothes seemed to gather and hold all the light in the huge room.

Stunned, she started toward him. "What are you *doing* here—"

A fusillade of shots broke out again, sounding as if they came from somewhere between the stable and the house. More shouting came from farther away.

"Hurry! Get out of the aisle before some renegade rides past the doors and throws some rounds in here."

"Maybe I should close them," she said, half turning to go back.

"No! I have to be able to see out in that direction—the *bandidos* will be sneaking around our backs now that they've had a little taste of the Sharps head-on."

His voice held a hard excitement, an edge completely alien to the lulling tones of his song. She whirled and ran toward him and Sache, who had started nickering for her. Another spate of gunfire erupted; he glanced out the window again, then looked back at her with a flash of the whites of his eyes.

"What the hell are you doing coming out of the house at a time like this?"

"I asked you first, if you recall."

"I went out for a run and somehow ended up trapped in here with this witch-woman of a filly," he said dryly, glancing at Sache before he set his gaze on something outside the window again.

He fired the rifle and continued talking without taking his eyes from the action outside. "Is she a mustang?"

"Yes. She's mine and she's the reason I came out. I was afraid she'd tear the stable down and panic the other horses if there was a whole lot more gunfire."

He looked at Emily in quick surprise, then sighted on a target again.

"*Yours?* Surely not. She's mean as sin."

Emily laughed and reached into the stall. Sache turned in a fast circle, snorted, then kicked the side wall, before sticking her nose into Emily's hand.

"She's only mean to some people," she said defensively, stroking the soft muzzle snuffling into her palm. "She likes you enough to settle right down from your singing, so *you* shouldn't say she's mean."

"Just going by the look in her eye." He fired through the window again. "*And* by the fact that I had to resort to singing just to keep her on all four feet so she wouldn't come over the stall top after me."

"She's wary of people she doesn't know, especially men."

He turned to look at her and grinned. "Wary. That's an understatement."

"I'm just glad you were here," she said. "If you hadn't been, she might've really hurt herself."

His grin widened. "I'm the one who nearly got hurt." Then he glanced out the window again and his whole body tensed. "Emily, they've got more guts than I thought. They're going to try again—with torches this time."

Her blood froze. The house was wood-frame, not adobe like the stables, and if it caught fire, it would immediately be engulfed in flames. She dropped her hand from Sache and turned to him.

"Hand me that other rifle, please," he said. "Do you know how to reload this one?"

On shaky legs she picked up the long gun that belonged in the stable, which he had stood on the floor leaning against the wall. Then she managed to walk the rest of the way to the long wooden toolbox and climb up beside him. She looked out the window and chill bumps broke out on her arms: There were so *many* bandits! The four chasing Lee had been only a fraction of them.

Tay reached for the rifle, but instead she pointed the muzzle out the window and sighted on the movements in the trees along the creek. The *bandidos* were all milling around there, moving in and out of cover with complete impunity. At that instant one of them made a feinting dash toward the house. She fired.

"Hey—"

"You'll have to reload for yourself, I'm afraid. I'm busy, Tay."

He chuckled. "Gentle Emily," he said, shaking his head in amazement as he pulled fresh shells from his pocket. "Cade told me that's what the vaqueros sometimes call you."

She fired again. "The father of one of my very shy students started that name for me, but I'm not always gentle anymore. I've never been tough or brave, but I've been trying to learn to be more so, more like Maggie, since I've been here on the ranch. That's one reason I'm working with Sache."

"*Always*-gentle people have a hard time surviving," he said, looking up with a quick, slanting glance from his reloading.

Some part of her contracted, deep inside,

and she felt the strange pull toward him that she had felt when he arrived. Her eyes clung to his chiseled profile for a long moment before she looked outside again.

At that moment the bandits burst out of the trees completely into the open, more than a dozen of them, two carrying lighted torches, all of them riding fast across the grass. Behind them the rising sun turned the sky a mottled red.

"Th-th-they, they're coming, Tay!"

Fear formed such a knot in her throat, she could hardly speak. He looked out.

"Let's take out the fire carriers together," he said, as he put his gun into the window again. "Are you that good a shot?"

"Cade taught me. And everybody I love is in that house."

"Then your man is the one on the right."

He began sighting on his target as she did on hers. She fixed carefully on the bright flame of fire floating above the racing bandit and then moved her sights ahead of him before lowering the muzzle a fraction. She fired. The flame vanished, the bandits hit the road, and swirling dust obscured her vision, but she wasn't sure which happened first.

"I don't know if I got him or not!"

Tay fired.

A fusillade from the direction of the house filled the air, with the roar of the big Sharps rifles underlying the lighter noise of the other guns. More Sharps spoke from beyond the stable at the bunkhouse and from the outbuildings between the stable and the house.

"The vaqueros are awake," she said. "Now the *bandidos* are outnumbered and outgunned."

As the firing continued, several bandits fell or slumped in their saddles and the others started splitting apart, riding in all directions. The fire from the torches must have been smothered in the dust, for there was no more sign of flames.

"They're on the run," she said. "Thank God."

"But we'd better watch our backs because they're scattering everywhere—"

They were turning to look toward the door when something whistled between them and thudded into the wall. Faster than she could realize it was a bullet, Tay slammed into her, carrying her with him in one strong arm as he leapt headlong into the huge stack of hay.

A second shot hit the wall and he rolled with her, deeper and deeper into the storage stall, to get behind the chest-high adobe divider to the aisle. The hard muscles of his forearm flexed into knots against her back to hold his rifle away from her in a one-handed grip. Fragments of the raftered ceiling turned across her vision before he pulled her head into the hollow of his shoulder, his sharp cheekbone pressed against her temple, and the hay stuck prickly fingers into her skin as they thudded to a stop in a soft, hollow bed. Tay lay on top of her, holding her so close she could feel his pounding heart.

So close he set a fire in her blood.

For an instant they lay perfectly still, then, slowly, he pulled back and looked at her. She looked at him.

The silent acknowledgment shone between them like a shaft of silver light.

You feel it, too. You know it. Our spirits are drawn together.

Neither of them could even breathe.

"Hello the es-table!" a Spanish-accented voice shouted. *"Quién está aquí? Amigo o no?"*

Neither of them moved.

That has been true since the moment we met.

Tay smiled. Emily caught a long, trembling breath.

"Who was shoot-ing from here? *Un amigo?*"

The voice was closer still and it rang hard against the walls. Jingling spurs marked fast-approaching footsteps.

"We'd better speak up or we're liable to get shot," Tay drawled softly.

He slipped his arm from beneath her and stood up, reached out his hand to help her to her feet, all without ever breaking the look that held them bound. Emily could hardly find the strength to stand.

"I-i-it's me—Emily—Jorge," she called, at last, "and *Senor* Nashoba."

Jorge ran down the main aisle close enough to see them, close enough that they finally turned away from each other to look at him.

"You are not hurt, *senorita?*"

"No, Jorge, *gracias.*"

"Muy bien."

He gave them a brief salute and headed back

toward the open door as Lee appeared in the middle of it.

"*Es la senorita* Em-i-ly," Jorge called to him, "*y el senor del Norte*, shoot-ing out the window."

Lee ran into the stable and down the aisle, his gait awkward in his high-heeled boots.

"Emily, thank God! Are you hurt? They missed you upstairs and Cotannah came running down to tell us—"

He saw Tay then, and stopped in his tracks.

"I came out to calm Sache, and Tay was here. He had gone out for a run when the bandits came."

"A run? On *foot*? Before *sunup*?" Lee blurted the questions, frowning at her, then at Tay.

"It's a habit of mine," Tay drawled in an easy tone that, nevertheless, held a hint of challenge.

Lee didn't answer. He stared at him a moment longer, then shook his head slightly and came back to his usual, diplomatic self.

"Well, it's a good thing, I guess. Some part of this place would be on fire right now if you hadn't gotten shots at the torches."

"One of those shots was Emily's," Tay said.

Lee grinned as he came to the entrance to the hay stall and put his arm around Emily's waist. "She's a caution with a firearm. I'll have to be careful not to cross her after we're married, I reckon."

"Could be," Tay said.

The tension brought on an awkward silence, until the three began walking down the stable's aisle toward the door. Lee stayed between

Emily and Tay, and he put his arm around Emily's waist again when they stepped out into the full morning light of La Casa's backyard. Most of the family and several vaqueros were there, talking about the attack, but all Emily could think of was how strange Lee's embrace felt because he never had touched her in public before.

But that wasn't the only reason, she admitted to herself as Cotannah and Maggie came running to meet them. Lee's touch felt strange, alien, to her compared to Tay's.

She blotted that thought out, fast. That could not be. She loved Lee. She was betrothed to Lee. She was going to marry Lee. She gave him a shy, one-armed hug before she pulled free to go to Cotannah and Maggie, but he didn't return it because he was already absorbed in talking to Cade about the damage.

After Maggie and Cotannah had told of their consternation at discovering Emily gone at dawn, after she had promised to never do such a thing again without notice, they grew silent and looked at her curiously. She glanced down to see her dress gaping open and her breasts clearly outlined beneath the thin nightgown.

Shaking with consternation and embarrassment, she began buttoning her dress, which was fastened only at the waist.

"I-I-I didn't r-realize I was indecent, I-I was so w-w-orried about S-S-Sache."

"But how did you get hay in your hair?" Cotannah said.

Emily felt heat rise into her cheeks. "I-I-I . . . we . . . had to dive into the h-hay when somebody sh-shot in at the d-door. T-Tay saved my life."

And he held me in his arms. We looked at each other . . .

She bit her lip and muttered something about needing to get properly dressed. She walked right between them and headed toward the house. Tay Nashoba belonged to Cotannah. Cotannah had loved him since she was ten years old . . . and she would be his bride.

Three days later, on the weekend, the fiesta they had planned to welcome Tay to Las Manzanitas became a double celebration because the ranch had escaped serious damage and injury from the *bandidos'* attack. That Saturday afternoon, Emily's heart warred between wanting to be near Tay and needing to *never* be near him again. While she helped carry food out to the white-clothed tables set in the shade of the live oak tree, she decided she wouldn't worry: Cotannah would occupy Tay.

He would probably ask her to dance once or twice, just for courtesy's sake, but that would be all. And perhaps that would make Lee extra attentive to her, considering his slightly jealous attitude when he'd found them together in the stable.

She reached the table, pushed apart two napkin-covered baskets to make a place for the fruit tray, and set it down. Probably she had imagined what she'd seen in Tay's eyes during that early-morning attack—they both had been excited and worked up about the *bandidos*. Yes. Probably it was all in her imagination.

Restlessly she turned to search the growing crowd for Lee. Two more guitar players had joined the music-makers, and the number of vaqueros dressed in their best and with hair slicked down for the social was steadily swelling. So surely even a die-hard boss like Lee had ridden in from the range by now.

Three or four couples were beginning to dance to a lively Mexican melody. Maybe she and Lee could dance the whole evening together. Maybe, after supper, the musicians would play one of those slow, hauntingly sweet melodies that always filled her with unnamed, piercing longings and she and Lee would wrap their arms around each other and feel each other's body warm and close. Maybe—if they were dancing in the dark—they would kiss.

Especially since he had put his arm around her in front of the whole world that morning of the attack! She smiled to herself. Maybe Tay Nashoba's coming to Las Manzanitas would jar Lee out of his obsession with his work and set his attention on her!

She saw him then, tall and broad-shouldered and lean, standing a short distance away from a group of laughing vaqueros, talking to Ramon Guiterrez, the assistant foreman from the Saltillo section of the ranch. They were so deep in discussion that Lee obviously was aware of nothing else.

A fond smile touched her lips. He lived and breathed his work, not only because he was determined to be rewarded with more cows for his own herd, but because in the six months he had lived here he had grown to love this ranch as much as she did. Her spirit calmed at the thought. She and Lee were perfect for each other, they really were.

Lee loved her and he would be happy living here forever, safe in the bosom of her family where she wanted to stay. He had said over and over again that he didn't want his daughter, Katie, to grow up moving all over the country, the way he had done. The three of them and the children she and Lee would have together would be secure in this home for all their lives. And happy.

Suddenly, as she stood there watching Lee Kincaid, the man she had promised to marry, a rushing, hollow feeling filled her and she wished fiercely for something more. She wanted to *feel* something more when she was in Lee's arms, something like . . . like the heated excitement that had rushed through her when Tay had looked so deeply into her eyes.

A blush of guilt flooded up her throat and into her face. How could she entertain such a disloyal thought?

She kept watching Lee, willing him to sense her presence, to feel her eyes on him. Didn't lovers do things like that? Didn't they know instinctively when the other was near, didn't they know when the other was worried or in pain?

She felt her blood tumble through her veins.

Didn't lovers look into each other's eyes and know what their partner was feeling? Didn't they both feel the same emotions at the very same moment? Exactly as she and Tay had done . . .

Sweat broke out in her palms. No. Hadn't she just decided that she had imagined all that?

She willed Lee to look at her, but he didn't. He remained just as he was, talking and listening, head bent toward the shorter man, his mind a thousand miles away from her and their future marriage.

No, that wasn't fair. He was being the best foreman he could so their future would be the best; he had simply forgotten that this was a social occasion and a celebration; that he deserved a little time to be free of his responsibilities.

Heart thundering, she dried her palms on her skirt and started toward him. The music played louder, faster. The fragrance of delicious food floated in the air—Oleana's girls were bringing more stacks of tortillas and platters of sliced tomatoes and onions, dishes full of beans cooked with corn and onion and bacon, bowls of sweet oranges from Brownsville and more napkin-covered baskets of fluffy sopaipillas and freshly baked bread. People all around them talked and laughed, but nothing distracted her.

She was almost upon Lee and Ramon. She couldn't believe her bold behavior, couldn't think what was driving her to be so rude. It would annoy him if she joined them—women simply didn't interrupt men's talk for anything short of blood or fire. But to her own amazement, suddenly she knew she had to do it. She needed, desperately, to be with him, to be reassured, somehow.

When she touched his elbow, he jumped and swung around.

"Hello," she said, smiling up at him. "Since there's music and dancing and wonderful food, I'm thinking this must be a party."

Both men took off their hats. Guiterrez's dark face brightened in a flashing smile, Lee's darkened in a frown of annoyance.

"*Hola, Senor* Guiterrez," she said.

"Why, *Senorita* Emily, I have been trying to tell *Senor* Kincaid what you are saying, that this is fiesta," he said with a chuckle.

"We were talking business, Em."

Lee's voice filled with irritation. Inside, she cringed at his displeasure, but she resolutely kept her smile in place. She couldn't help herself. Oh, if only he would sense that and not be angry!

"I know, but it's a *purty*, Lee! Probably the only one we'll have time for until after roundup."

She glanced away, then looked up at him from beneath her lashes flirtatiously, her heart pounding. Never, ever had she behaved like this. Would he rebuff her in front of Ramon?

Finally, after a miserable, long moment, he smiled. "All right," he said, "I reckon you're lookin' so pretty this evenin', you get my mind off cows and grass."

Her trepidation turned to relief, then to a heady triumph. Maybe she should be bolder more often!

"I do hope so," she said, and slipped her arm through his.

"We'll finish this *mañana*, Ramon," Lee said. *"Bueno."*

Ramon bowed to Emily, turned, and strode away.

She tilted her head to one side and shot Lee another flirtatious glance, but this one he didn't see. He was looking toward the big live oak tree and the people standing in its shade. Cotannah and Ancie and Mama were playing with the twins while they talked with Pilar Lopez-Chapman, wife of the owner of a neighboring ranch. The Chapmans were one of the few neighbors who hadn't fled from the bandits to live in town, mostly because Pilar was Mexican and she had connections that could reach the raiders. Their ranch had never been hit.

Cade and Tay joined the women as Emily and Lee watched them. Emily tried not to let her gaze cling to Tay, tried to look at Maggie as she blew Cade a kiss and headed for the long picnic table to oversee the last-minute preparations.

"What do you think of Cade's new brother-in-law?" Lee asked, glancing back and forth between her and Tay.

A quick, sharp needle of . . . panic, yes, it felt like panic, stabbed her in the heart. But there was no need to feel that way, no need at all. She felt nothing for Tay, nothing.

"He seems . . . n-nice."

Then, to her own shock, she added, "I-I'm not s-sure, though, that he's the right man for C-Cotannah."

He swung around to look at her, his blue eyes wide. "How can you know a thing like that?"

For no reason at all, quick tears stung her eyes. "I-I c-can't. I d-don't know why I said that."

To her shock, he reached and took her by the hand. "Listen here to me, Em," he said gently. "Other people's courtin' and marryin' is something nobody else can know about nor meddle in. You'd best get your mind on your own and leave everybody else's alone."

The unexpected intimacy in his tone made her smile. "What should I be thinking of about my own?"

"Me. Just think about me. You're always worryin' over Cotannah or one of your school-kids or your mama or them twins or Katie, or even some horse or dog," he muttered, "and I might git a bit jealous now and then."

His eyes crinkled at the corners and he shyly ducked his head a little, but he kept looking into her eyes with a steady gaze.

Her heart grew warm and full for him. Usually he never, ever, would admit such a thing.

"Why, Lee Kincaid," she said, laughing a little. "Are you telling me that you need me? That you want my concern and attention on you?"

"I reckon," he said gruffly.

He smiled down into her eyes then, and she smiled back at him.

Lee had actually *said* he needed her! And before the night was over, he might even say he loved her! He had said it only the once, when he had asked her to marry him, and tonight she really needed to hear it again.

Chapter 3

ut then he said it too soon or too easily or too urgently or . . . something . . . Whatever was wrong, it wasn't what she needed at all.

He caught her hand and held it in both of his as he stepped in front of her so that she could see only him. That in itself was enough to make him seem like a stranger. Maybe that was what was wrong: He wasn't behaving like himself.

"I love you, Emily," he said, "and I want us to get married. I want you to be my wife."

He looked down at her with his washed-out blue eyes, solemn and serious. His gaze moved over her face.

Her heart gave a strange dip, then settled. Why wasn't it leaping with joy? Lee loved her and she loved him and she had just heard him say it.

"I have already accepted your proposal, sir, if you recall," she said, trying for a light, flirtatious tone.

"I mean *now*. There's no sense at all to us waitin' until October to tie the knot."

He tucked her hand into the crook of his elbow. "I've been thinkin' on this since the other mornin' when the *bandidos* attacked. What if they'd killed me instead of just chasin' me home?"

Her legs went weak at the thought. "Oh, Lee, it would've killed me, too," she said, "but life's always uncertain. We can't plan a wedding around bandits' attacks."

"Let's not wait until fall, Em. Let's marry tonight."

"Tonight!"

"The preacher's here somewhere, or else he's on his way. Everybody's gathered, including what neighbors we've got left. Why not?"

For the space of two heartbeats she thought she would agree. Why not indeed? Her life was already set in its course; why not go ahead with it?

But for some reason, the words of assent wouldn't come out of her mouth.

"B-because Mama would be horrified—she's already sent for a seamstress to come from Corpus next month to make my wedding dress. And Maggie wants to give me the wedding *she* never had and . . . and it would be a terrible shock to Katie."

"Katie loves you. She'd be thrilled."

The cold fingertip of panic touched her again. "She l-loves me, but her m-mother . . . Why, your w-wife has been dead less than a year, Lee! And Katie's only s-seven. Both of you need a little more time to make a place for me as a person, not as a substitute for h-her, in both your hearts and your h-home."

He ignored that. "We could marry now and in the fall you could find somebody else to teach the school . . ."

Her heart froze again. "No!" she cried. "*I* want to teach it. This ranch is the only place I could ever keep my school after I marry, and I need to do that. I love my teaching, Lee—"

"All right," he cut in, "I'll agree to that for a while because I want Katie to get an education and I don't want her to leave the ranch to do it. But I'm tellin' you now, Em, you'll have to find a replacement teacher by the time you have *our* children."

She bit her lip and held her rising confusion inside. That was what she wanted, too, wasn't it? So why wasn't she giddy with happiness?

"We must wait until fall," she said tightly. "I want Katie to get over her mother's death some more."

"Maybe so, but my house sure enough does need a woman in it right now."

"Are you saying that just any woman would do?"

He gaped at her. "What?" Then he took her meaning and his face flushed red beneath his tan.

"You know what I'm saying," he said angrily. "And you sure aren't acting much like you want to marry me at all. What're you doing—trying to drive me away? You want me to go back to the Texas Rangers if the new Governor Coke reestablishes them? Want me to ride off and join up again and leave you here with your precious school?''

He clung to her hand, though. Through the whole tirade, he held on to her hand. He loved her, he really did. And she had hurt him deliberately.

Shame overcame her. She did want to marry Lee and have a family of her own, her own house, her own children. She couldn't bear to lose him—or Katie, either.

"No," she said, covering his hands with her free one, "I don't want you to leave me at all." She smiled up at him until his frown faded away.

He pulled her closer, bent, and murmured into her ear, "You know, don't you, that you're the only woman I . . . love?''

His lips brushed her hair. His arm fell around her waist and squeezed her—right there in the middle of the yard, in the middle of fiesta!

"I love you, too, Lee," she whispered, going up on tiptoe to put her cheek against his. "October will be here before we know it."

He grinned and his face was absolutely handsome. "I won't quit trying to get you to marry me sooner," he said. "Now, I'll be along over to the table in a minute. Why don't you go on and help your sister while I see if I can spot Bob Sample anywhere. I need his crew to move some cows in the morning."

"All right."

She gave him another smile, picked up her skirts, and ran toward the table and her sister. Her head was dizzy with confusion, though, and she couldn't think what she was supposed to do when she got there.

"Mimi, will you pour the lemonade?" Maggie called as soon as Emily neared. "I'll go round up everyone and have them come and get their plates. The men are lifting the steer out of the ground."

Emily didn't trust herself to speak, so she nodded and took her place at the lemonade tray. As she poured, she took a deep breath and looked around her at all the familiar faces. She breathed in the smells of the sweet mesquite smoke and the roasted meat. This was home and it always would be. This was the safe home she'd always wanted.

Men were in the lookout tower and others were riding the perimeter to keep out the raiders. Some people wouldn't feel safe here—like the visitors they'd had a few weeks ago from the East—but she felt safer on Las Manzanitas in the worst times than she ever had in Arkansas. That was amazing when she remembered how she'd cried and cried and pleaded with Maggie not to ride into the wilds of Texas. Thank goodness Maggie hadn't listened or neither she nor Emily would have met the men they would marry.

Emily poured and Oleana's helpers carried the filled glasses. The family and the neighbors began gathering around the table to pick up their plates and drift into a ragged line, waiting to be served the barbecued meat. The musicians played a slow-moving, lilting melody, the twins ran to "help" their Aunt Mimi, and Lee came striding toward her, smiling. The air was softening as the afternoon sun dropped down and the breeze was springing up.

A great rush of happiness shook Emily, drowning, for a moment, all her confusion about her incoherent feelings. For now, Lee was coming to have supper with her, and Cotannah was still home with them. For now, everybody Emily loved was together in one place. For now, for one evening, the old life she loved was still holding intact.

Her warm feeling stayed wrapped around her even after Maggie seated her and Lee next to Tay and Cotannah, even after Cotannah insisted that Mimi sit beside Tay so they could become better acquainted. It remained intact until he sat down in his chair and his arm brushed hers. The warmth shattered as heat shot through her like a fire arrow.

It was her imagination again, she told herself. He was handsome and exotic and different, that was all that created this attraction to him. In fact, it really wasn't an attraction, it was more of a fascination with the unknown. She had never known a man like him.

"Miss Emily," he said and inclined his head, "I haven't seen you all day. How are you this evening?"

His tone was so intimate, she felt as if he had stroked her skin with his hand. It sent a strange thrill shimmering through her whole body.

"Fine, thank you," she murmured.

She tried not to, but she had to glance up at him, had to see the expression in his incredible

gray eyes. As soon as she did, she couldn't look
away.

He flashed her a grin. "Been practicing your
rifle shots? Or have you spent the day catching
wild mustangs and starting them under
saddle?"

She grinned back. "I did all that before
breakfast. The rest of the day I've spent cooking
this welcome feast for you."

He chuckled and the low, warm sound made
her go weak inside, took her back to lie in the
soft hollow of the hay with his arms around
her. The heat in his eyes and their bright
intensity deepened—he was thinking of the
moment in the stable, too.

Oh, dear Lord, she thought. And then she
couldn't think at all.

Lee bent to say something to her, and she
heard him, but she couldn't turn to him. She
tried to answer, but she couldn't yet.

Fortunately, Cade chose that moment to
stand up at the head of the table. He tapped on
his glass to get everyone's attention, and finally
Tay's gaze let hers go. Suddenly she felt as if
night had fallen. She turned toward Cade, glad
of an excuse not to talk to Lee until she could
think again.

"I want to thank our neighbors and friends
who have come over to Las Manzanitas to meet
our guest today," Cade said. "Tay Nashoba has
traveled by ferry, train, stagecoach, and horseback all the way from the Choctaw Nation for
his first visit to Texas."

Cade motioned for Tay to stand up. Emily

didn't dare so much as glance at him again, but
the air around her simmered with his presence.
Her very skin felt sensitized because he was
standing near.

Cade said dryly, "Don't be surprised if Tay
comes up and shakes hands with you and starts
telling you why you ought to vote for him. He's
running for Principal Chief of the Choctaw
Nation, and he doesn't want to get out of
practice campaigning while he's here."

Everyone laughed and Cade sat down.

"My only regret is that you all aren't members of the Nation," Tay said, "because this
sumptuous hospitality that the Chisk-Kos have
provided for us today would, without a doubt,
bring me every one of your votes."

He made some other remarks that turned the
attention from himself to others, including Cotannah, who was blushing happily. He *did*
always know what to say to make everyone feel
good—he had a silver tongue to match his
silver eyes.

But his words floated past her, for the most
part. She couldn't really think about them, for
his voice had pulled her out of herself again,
out of her mind and into her senses. It carried
her along in its rhythmic flow like a bird
floating on the wind.

Tay spoke for a moment or two longer, but he
had no idea of what he said. It must have been
all right, because his audience responded with
general, good-natured applause as he sat
down. Beside Emily.

His arm brushed hers again and he turned,

but Lee was leaning near, talking to her. The man was jealous. Tay had noted that as soon as Lee had run into the stable and found them together that morning of the attack. The man was betrothed to her, but some devil inside him wouldn't let him leave them be.

"I'm sorry, Miss Emily," he said, "I didn't intend to knock you right out of your chair."

The touch, even through his sleeve and hers, had sent heat singing through his veins, had made him need to look into her warm brown eyes again. But they were more wary than warm when she turned to him.

"You haven't unsettled me one bit," she said crisply. "Please set your mind at ease about that."

So. She was feeling the heat, too, and it was scaring her.

"You do *sound* a bit unsettled, however."

His drawl seemed like a taunt, even to his own ears, but he really didn't mean to tease her or make her angry. Or maybe he did.

"I am not."

He smiled. The way she snapped the words at him, the latent tremor in her voice, showed the feeling ran deep in her as well. Good.

"Excuse me, please," she said, and turned abruptly away.

He felt his smile broaden, then Cotannah touched his arm and said something he didn't catch. He swung around, away from Emily, and looked down into her beautiful, trusting face, which was turned up to his like a flower to the sun.

What the *hell* did he think he was doing? He had no emotions to give to a woman, any woman, and that was that.

All through the supper, Emily could feel Tay beside her, even when she wasn't touching him or looking at him. She tried, but she could barely eat with such a hot, peculiar turbulence filling her. Lee was attentive and he talked to her, but she had trouble keeping her mind on him, trouble understanding what he said.

Her whole body kept trying to turn to the right, to turn to Tay; her tongue kept wanting to talk to him, to get his attention somehow. She was restless, so restless that she wanted to jump and run, her feelings so riotous that she couldn't give them names, much less control them. Who was this wild woman coming to life inside her?

Lee didn't even notice that the wild woman was there. He talked about Katie and the ranch, mentioned their wedding again, talked about the cattle and the weather, and she replied as best she could. Then he leaned across in front of her and spoke to Tay.

"Cade said he took you over some of the ranch today. What did you think of it?"

She and Tay turned toward each other, and their eyes met with the force of a runaway train slamming into a wall. *He* saw the wild woman, his intense gray gaze told her. *He* knew she was there.

Every nerve in her body shattered into shards and she looked down at her plate, forced herself to take a forkful of food. She lifted it to her mouth and took a bite without tasting a thing.

Cotannah leaned in front of Tay to join the conversation.

"I've been asking him the same thing, Lee," she said. "I want to know his impression of Texas."

"The ranch is great and Texas is everything I expected," Tay said, his voice musical enough to cast a spell. "I had heard that Texas is a land of outlaws and beautiful women, and I've found that to be true."

He smiled at Emily and then at Cotannah, who blushed and gazed at him even more worshipfully, if that was possible. He put down his fork, leaned his broad shoulders against the back of his chair, and looked at them both.

"You ladies are proof." His easy smile was nothing short of contagious. "Don't you agree with me, Lee?"

"You bet your saddle I do."

"That was terrible, those *bandidos* attacking on your very first morning here," Cotannah said, boldly clasping Tay's muscular arm with both her small hands. "They could've killed you, Tay, if you'd been farther from the house on your run."

Tay smiled down at Cotannah, then turned that silver gaze of his full on Emily.

"Fortunately, Miss Emily protected me," he drawled. "I was just glad she was gunning down the bandits instead of me."

Emily smiled back at him, her gaze fixed on his mouth, his sensuous, smiling mouth. His lips were full and they curved lusciously over his white teeth—shockingly, the new wild woman in her fairly ached to trace the shape of them with the tip of her finger.

Lee's voice came from behind her and made her jump. "Reckon you won't go out before daylight anymore without a weapon."

Tay Nashoba's bold gaze left her. She slumped a little, as if he had taken her breath along with it, and let herself rest against the back of her chair. She felt as if she'd just run a long, long way.

"I won't," Tay said to Lee. "That was stupid of me that morning. From now on, I really should take along a gun *and* a partner to watch my back."

"Oh, I can't bear it for you to be so modest," Cotannah cried, with her hands still resting on his arm, "when you were such a hero in the War!"

Tay's face darkened so swiftly that Emily could hardly believe it; she felt him go stiff beside her, although they weren't touching at all. He set his jaw, and his wonderful mouth fell into a hard, hurting line. Then, instantly, as if he'd caught himself revealing too much, he forced a slight smile and shrugged his massive shoulders.

"Wars and attacks by bandits aren't good subjects for dinner or for mixed company, I'm afraid," he said smoothly. "But I thank you, 'Tannah, dear, for your confidence."

Cotannah's hand still clung to his arm. He patted it dismissively and then reached for the crystal bowl that stood directly in front of his plate.

"Let me try some of this great-looking potato salad," he said. "Cotannah, did you make it?"

"Yes, and I made some corn fritters, too, because I remembered from the wild-onion feasts back home that you love them better than any other kind of bread," Cotannah said, looking up and down the length of the table for the napkin-covered basket that held her other creation.

But Tay Nashoba didn't hear or see her. He offered the dish and its serving spoon to Emily, on his left, without glancing at her, either. He was staring off into the middle distance, his face dark again with memories of the War.

Cade soon got his attention by speaking to him from across the table. He took the bowl back from Emily and served himself before passing it on to Cotannah. He smiled again, laughed and joked with Cade and Maggie, and the moment passed. But Emily couldn't forget it.

Tay had suffered a great deal, she realized, with a sharp twinge of sympathy that surprised her with its force. The War had been horrible, the eight years since then had not erased the pain of it, and she was sorry that Cotannah had mentioned it at all.

"Did Cade show you the horse yearlings?" Lee asked Tay as he passed a delicious-smelling platter of sliced tomatoes, cucumbers, and onions to Emily. "I'm as proud of them as if they belonged to me."

The two men talked horses, but she had no idea what they said. All she knew was that she needed to concentrate on Lee and try to keep her mind on him. Somehow she managed to get through the rest of supper and join in the general talk and revelry without speaking directly to Tay Nashoba again.

As soon as the musicians began to play once more, she leaned nearer to Lee and whispered that she would love to dance. He got up immediately, held her chair, and took her into his arms when they were barely away from the table.

"We make a fine pair in any company, don't we, Mimi?" he said, dancing her across the grass to the lively rhythm of the guitars. Well, almost to the rhythm—he was always a half beat too fast, as if to force the music to catch up to him. "You're a woman any man could be proud of."

A trickle of calm came back into her heart, cooling the heat of the wild woman a little. "Thank you, Lee. I'm proud of you, too."

He pulled her closer into his embrace. "That sweet smile of yours never fails to make my heart beat faster."

He placed a callused knuckle underneath her chin and tilted her face so he could look down into her eyes. "Smile for me, Emily."

She did as he asked, and he smiled back at her with his blue eyes lit with love.

"Think about a quicker wedding, Mimi . . ."

"Let's not talk, Lee," she said. "Let's just enjoy the music and not talk about anything."

Silently he folded her closer and tucked her head into his shoulder as the fast song flowed into a slow one. She tried to lose herself in the warmth of his embrace, tried to smother the new realization that had just hit her. But the stubborn thought wouldn't go away.

Lee always had to feel *he* was in control—that was the reason he wanted to change the wedding date *she* had chosen. He thought about work all the time because *he* had to tell everyone else what to do. Why, he couldn't even dance to the music because he wasn't going to let the guitarists set the rhythm for *him*.

But wasn't that true of all men?

No, it wasn't true of Cade. Of course, Cade had more than the average woman to contend with in Maggie. But also, Cade and Maggie shared a passion that was enough to erase all issues of control. They were unusual, true partners. Lee was no more dictatorial than the average man. He certainly wasn't anywhere near as bad as her father, Pierce, had been.

She danced closer to him as they moved across the grass—but not so close as to be outrageous—and she waited for the deep sense of safety that she used to feel when she was in his arms. It never came.

The music stopped and she looked up to see Tay Nashoba standing at Lee's shoulder.

"My partner has requested a dance with you," he said in his smooth, gallant way.

Lee turned to speak to him as Cotannah slipped past the men to take Emily's hand and pull her a step or two away.

"I want you to dance with Tay so you all can get better acquainted before the men go off by themselves and start talking cattle and politics," she whispered. "Oh, Mimi, you're going to like him . . ."

The music started up again, the guitars accompanied by plaintively lilting fiddles this time as Lee danced away with Cotannah in his arms.

"Miss Emily," Tay said in his unforgettable voice. "Would you do me the honor of giving me this dance?"

He touched her, just once, in the small of the back, and a fire sprang to life in her belly.

If she had one shred of sanity left in her, she would refuse him.

Instead, she turned into his waiting arms.

Chapter 4

⌒⌒◯◯⌒⌒

Lowering her lashes so as not to see his face—or perhaps so he wouldn't see hers—she placed one stiff hand on his shoulder and the other on his huge palm. A tremor ran through her.

The scent of him filled her nostrils, the smells of starched, ironed cotton and bay rum, with faint undertones of horses and sweat and leather. And soap, plain, strong soap. The image of him naked in a copper bathing tub the same color as his skin, with his muscles rippling, assaulted her and made her palms itch to feel its wet silkiness.

She closed her eyes to banish the image from her mind before his sharp, knowing gaze saw it. She held her breath to make herself smaller so as not to feel the hard, sure clasp of his fingers burning into the flesh at her waist. She tried to draw back from the long, graceful motions of his powerful horseman's thighs, brushing against hers even through the layers of petticoat and skirt. Cloth had never been so thin.

Nor had the air ever been so fragrant with sweet flowers, or the coming dusk so deep and soft. The music floated out into it, found the rising breeze, gathered it up, and brought the twilight freshness swirling in from the prairie to surround them, to hold them apart from everyone else in a dance all their own.

Tay guided her with a firmness that floated with the rhythm, the melody, with the new night itself, a sureness that urged her to give in to the awakening of her senses. A man's chest had never been so broad, his muscles had never been so strong, moving beneath her hand.

She fought to hold her body the correct distance from his, fought to remember that he belonged to Cotannah and she to Lee. Most of all, she fought to keep her eyes away from his powerful face.

"We should talk," she said abruptly, "about Cotannah."

He was silent for so long that she looked up to see whether he had heard. His silver-gray eyes captured hers all over again.

"Why?"

His intent look sent a thrill down her spine. She couldn't answer at first, couldn't *remember* why, couldn't think what she'd said in the first place.

Finally she made her brain work again. "B-b-because she w-wants us to g-get acquainted," she blurted.

Then she bit her lip and held her tongue,

determined not to speak again until the stuttering left her. She hated how it crept into her voice every time she felt a little panicked.

"We *are* getting acquainted during this dance," he said. "Communication doesn't always have to be with words. Wouldn't you agree, Miss Emily?"

Her cheeks burned and she tore her eyes from his. He had already sensed everything she'd been feeling! Dear goodness, he had the power to look right into her mind; he had probably seen the image of himself in the bathtub as soon as she had.

"I do enjoy a good conversation, however," he said easily as he pulled her gently into a turn. "Perhaps you'd like to talk about your wedding plans."

Startled, she glanced up at him again.

"When are you planning to have the ceremony?"

She looked at him narrowly. Had he somehow divined what was in Lee's mind as well as in hers? "We've agreed on early October."

"Something in your tone suggests that isn't quite definite."

Hot annoyance stabbed through her. Was nothing hidden from this man? "Nothing in this world is definite. Plans often change in the most unexpected ways, wouldn't you agree?"

He smiled and cocked one black eyebrow as he looked down into her eyes. "A wise man once said, 'The universe is change.'"

"Marcus Aurelius," she said crisply. Then

she could not resist the temptation to best him by finishing the quotation: " 'Our life is what our thoughts make it.' "

His smile broadened, his eyes gleaming with pleasure as if he'd taught her that himself. "So *your* thoughts have led you to marriage," he said. "Will you tell me what thoughts they are?"

"They must be much the same as yours. Aren't you here on a mission of marriage, yourself?"

"The reasons to marry are legion."

"Perhaps. But only one reason is the right reason, and that is love."

"Ah," he said, grinning as if she had left a chess piece open for capture. "But what is love, Miss Emily?"

He guided her into another turn, which brought her body nearer to his and made her long to dance even closer in spite of all her efforts to hold herself farther away. His silver eyes glittered with challenge.

"Now, don't quote me some meaningless drivel like 'Love is heaven and heaven is love.' "

"I wouldn't think of it. No one can tell you what love is—you find out only by experiencing it for yourself."

"Hmm," he murmured, "wise words. Wise woman. Thank you, Teacher."

The sarcasm scraped her raw nerves. She stiffened within the circle of his arms. "I will not permit any disrespect of my profession. I consider my work as important as yours or

Lee's or Cade's or any other man's—as important as that of the President of the United States—not because it is mine but because it so deeply affects my children."

She tried to stop in her tracks and pull free of him, but she never had a chance. His strength carried her on and on in the steps of the dance as easily as if she weighed no more than a will-o'-the-wisp.

"You're misunderstanding me, Emily—I respect your profession above all others. Teaching, done well, is the most difficult and the most invaluable pursuit on the planet, and I admire you greatly for doing that work."

He was utterly sincere; she knew that in her very bones. "How do you know I do it well?"

"Cade told me so, and he said you're holding classes even in the summer to make up for your students missing them during roundup. I'd like permission to visit your school one day, if I may."

He truly meant it. His feelings were entirely genuine, and they took her breath away as completely as if he'd doused her with a deluge of cold water. She searched his face.

"Most men think of school as simply a place where a woman is caring for children—that is, when they think of it at all. They consider it too uninteresting to talk about, much less to visit."

Lee, for one, never wanted to hear about it. And someday he would insist that she give it up.

"I find it fascinating. The process of transferring information and attitudes and judgment from one mind to another is one of the most mysterious on earth."

A thrill, a shuddering, delicious tingling, rushed through her. He was, indeed, a rare and exotic specimen of a man.

The song came to an end, the dancing stopped, but he didn't let her go. Instead, he squeezed her hand as if to make sure she was listening.

"Our children need good educations if they're to survive—I want every idea, every observation, every insight, every teaching method you have, to take back to the schools in the Nation," he said, with a fervor that aroused her emotions as much as his touch and his scent aroused her body.

"I'll help you any way I can."

"Thanks, Emily," he said, "and thanks for the dance."

Suddenly she realized that her fingers were clinging desperately to his hard, strong ones and she couldn't let go. His admiration was intoxicating, a revelation to her. Usually everyone took her work for granted. No one, ever, not even the appreciative parents of her students, had made her feel so good.

The other dancers walked around them. Finally, slowly, their hands opened and their fingers trailed apart.

The lanterns being lighted in the trees behind Tay glowed like giant, glittering fireflies, brighter than she had ever seen. The fragrance of the prairie grasses floated on the night breeze, sweeter than she had ever smelled.

She clasped her sweating hands, squeezing them together as if that could stop her rampaging thoughts. The only one she could capture, the only one she could hold still to examine, was the scariest one of all: Never, ever, in her entire *life* had she felt so many sensations in every one of her senses, and so many different, *deep* emotions in her heart and her soul, as she had gone through in the paltry few hours since Tay Nashoba had stepped down off his horse onto Las Manzanitas.

This must be what the poets called being truly *alive*. All the midnight thoughts she'd been having of late came rushing back to her, and for the first time she looked them right in the face: She, quiet, gentle Emily Harrington, wanted more than a life that was comfortable and secure.

She wanted a life filled with passion, passion of every kind. She wanted to feel this alive all of the time.

The dance wasn't over until long after midnight, and all that time she felt that intense desire strumming through her body like the vibrating strings of the tinkling guitars. She had sensed it before, and it had floated in and out of her mind at night when she couldn't sleep, especially since she had become betrothed to Lee, but now she knew she'd never be able to hide it away from herself again.

Nor from Maggie, apparently. As she walked

beside her sister toward the house, each of them carrying a sleeping twin, she felt Maggie's sharp gaze in the moonlight.

"Mimi, it seems to me that you're reacting a bit strongly to Tay Nashoba."

Emily felt her blood thicken in her veins. Her arms tightened around Cole's sleep-heavy little body. "What do you mean?"

"You know what I mean. You were dancing so close to him, it was impossible not to notice, and when the music stopped I thought you two would never step apart."

Emily's face flamed with embarrassment. Surely that couldn't be true. They had not done anything that anyone would pay attention to; surely they hadn't.

"We were not! And, anyway, what were you doing staring at us?"

"Who could help but stare at you? Everybody had to walk around you and Tay as if you'd taken root and grown into the middle of the dancing ground."

Emily's breath stopped. Cotannah. Dear God, had Cotannah noticed anything?

"I . . . w-we only danced one dance."

"One dance was all I needed to see."

Heat came rushing up into Emily's neck and face. "And just *what* did you see?"

When Maggie stopped walking and faced her, Emily stood still.

"That you and Tay are attracted to each other. That if you aren't careful, the two of you will break Cotannah's and Lee's hearts and both of your own in the bargain."

Emily wanted to lay Cole down on the ground, cover her face, and run away from Maggie's shrewd, blue-eyed stare. Maggie never missed a detail; she saw everything, always.

"I'm not trying to take him from Cotannah," Emily whispered. "I'd never . . ."

Maggie stared at her for another long moment, then she shifted Randy onto one shoulder and came closer to put her arm around her sister.

"I know that, darling," she said, keeping her voice low so no one else could hear. "But some feelings are so strong, they override everything else. Just be careful, Mimi. Stay away from him. You and Tay could never have anything that would last—you could never go back to the Nation with him and be the wife of the Principal Chief, you know that. Nothing good can come of this, so leave him alone."

"It isn't Tay, Maggie," she said, in a rush of words that came pouring disjointedly into her head and onto her tongue. "It's just that I've discovered I want *more* somehow, from life, more feeling and excitement than I've had. I want more from loving Lee. I've been feeling that for a while now. It comes to me sometimes in the night when I can't sleep."

She stopped and swallowed hard, trying to find the right way to say what she needed to make Maggie understand. "You know . . . I-I g-guess I just w-want a love more like what y-you and Cade have."

Maggie hugged her. "I hope you find that, oh, I hope you do, Mimi. But not with Tay. I love you and I want you to have every happiness, but I love Cotannah, too."

"So do I. I love her. I'd never hurt her!"

"I know that. But she noticed at the same time I did that you and Tay couldn't seem to tear yourselves apart."

Emily's blood stopped flowing. "Maggie, what did she say?"

"She said, 'Oh, look! Tay and Mimi are talking, they're going to be friends just like I wanted them to be!'"

"We are. She's right. He's the first man I ever met who respects my work and appreciates what I do. He and I shared some poetry and—"

"And a strong physical attraction." Maggie's tone was so flat and sure that it brooked no contradiction. "Mimi, I saw the way the two of you looked at each other the moment you met. I, like Cotannah, saw the hay in your hair when you came out of the stable together."

They stood close together for a moment, leaning on each other, the sleeping children heavy in their arms.

"'Tannah's young and she's so sure that Tay loves her and intends to marry her that it doesn't even cross her mind that he might be attracted to you. She trusts you completely and she wouldn't think that you might be attracted to him. So far, she doesn't see this pull between you."

"Oh, dear God, Maggie, I don't want her ever to see it. She's loved him ever since she was ten years old."

"And whether Tay loves her in return, only time will tell," Maggie said. "But in the meantime, don't come between them, Mimi."

"I won't."

And she wouldn't, Emily vowed, as she and Maggie walked side by side the rest of the way across the yard and into the house. No passion, not for life and not for a man, could ever be strong enough to make her betray her friend.

A few hours later, Tay stepped out through the front door into the pale predawn light and breathed in great heaps of the fresh morning air. Then he blew it out again, with force, to expel the bad dreams from his body and from his mind. The nightmares had followed him all the way to Texas.

But why had he even dared to hope they wouldn't? Hadn't they ridden with him every mile he'd traveled since the white man's Civil War?

He breathed in and out again, shallowly and much too fast, as he crossed the wooden planks of the porch, leaped the steps, and began to run. It was more than the old, familiar *shilups* and goblins of the War that had haunted him last night, and he might as well face that fact right now so he could free himself from it.

The dream that had shattered him was of Emily. Even now, just remembering it, it seemed more real than the sun rising out there ahead of him. The sweet taste of her hesitant mouth clung to his lips, the soft shape of her full breasts pressed against his chest . . . In the dream, he had kissed her desperately while they danced.

He took a deep breath, blew it out slowly and thoroughly, then began to run faster as he forced his practical side to take over. It was silly to attach so much significance to such a dream, a dream born not of hidden feelings in his heart but, no doubt, of the frustrations of his body.

That would be another good thing about this plan Uncle Kulli Hotema had cooked up for the arranged marriage to Cotannah. Not only would it assuage Tay's loneliness, it would give him physical relief as well as children.

Surely, if a child were the goal, he would not have that awful sense of emptiness that sexual encounters with every woman had always brought him—that he had given away a piece of his soul to someone who was not his soul mate. Cotannah would *be* his wife and help-meet, after all.

But why couldn't it have been Cotannah and not Emily in his dream?

He ran faster. He looked to the eastern sky as he tied his beaded headband tighter around his forehead. Watching the sun rise for a new day would make the past recede—he knew that because he learned it all over again every morning of his life. It would make the foolish dream recede, as well.

Softly he began his chant.

This day. This day is dawning.

This day. This day is all we can live while this sun rides the sky. The past is gone.

This day. This day we live by truly being in it, heart and soul.

He sang low as he ran out of the yard and onto the rolling prairie, feeling through the thin soles of his moccasins to find the shape of the face of Mother Earth here in Texas. A tremulous morning mist, so thin it was barely there, so nearly invisible that it looked like a spirit moving, shifted and drifted in the low places. And he followed it, drawn to its moisture floating in the dry air, pulled to its mystery as he always was in the mountains of home.

As he had been drawn to the mystery of Miss Emily.

The thought of her reached for him, caught him again. She was a very unusual woman: serene on the surface, and deeper perhaps, yet volatile and passionate at the core.

Still, there was a balance in her, a sympathetic steadiness that drew at his heart. Looking into her brown eyes when she'd turned to him that very first time, there in the light of the lanterns, had been like falling into a friendly forest pool.

On the other hand, looking into Cotannah's dark eyes agitated a man like glimpsing the inside of a whirlwind. What a child/woman she had become at eighteen! She deserved a young man driven by the same bright lust for life, not a jaded old one, twice her age, burdened with responsibilities that would decide the fate of the Nation.

This marriage is going to be a great, good thing

for the People. The alliance of such old Choctaw families will remind them of the past and give them pride; it will give them an example of unity for the future and perhaps discourage so much of this intermarrying with whites.

That had been Uncle Kulli Hotema's admonition to Tay on the eve of his departure for Texas. No amount of explaining that Tay and Cotannah must get reacquainted, now that she was a grown woman and not a little girl, no amount of repeating that the two of them would have to take some time before making the decision whether to marry, had dented the old man's thinking. To his mind, the marriage was a done deal.

As it obviously was, also, to Cotannah's. She was a beautiful bundle of expectations set to marry him, and he never should have invaded her world.

He shook back his hair over his shoulder and lifted his face to the morning, tried to empty his mind by opening his eyes more fully to the pink-and-red-streaked sunrise and his ears to the waking calls of the birds. The wind washed his bare chest with a cool caress. But Cotannah's look of joyful anticipation stayed with him.

Anger surged into his blood, speeding through his veins. He ran faster and faster, pumping his buckskin-covered legs up and down, slapping his feet against the earth in a desperate, furious rhythm. Why should he feel guilty? He had made no promises, none at all.

On the other hand, why shouldn't he fulfill Cotannah's and Uncle Kulli's expectations? Why shouldn't he simply court her and marry her and take her home with him?

It would help him win the election and it would help him survive being Principal Chief. He had been lonely for too many years now. He would love to have the comfort of a wife and children to surround him when a long day of negotiating and hard decision making was done. The feel of Miranda's small, chubby body, the warm, trusting weight of it between his two hands, came back to him. It would be even more of a pleasure to hold his own child. What a thrill that would be!

He swerved around a low-spreading clump of mesquite and kept going, running toward the sunrise at that same desperate pace. It was stupid to put himself through the tortures of the damned and to say he couldn't marry her just because he hadn't fallen madly in love with the grown-up Cotannah.

He had known ever since he'd been elected to the Council that he would have no deep emotions left over to give to a wife and a family. But if he had a woman to call his own, he might surprise himself.

So why shouldn't he marry Cotannah? He might even be saving her from some foolish heartbreak. Left to fate, she might think she'd found love with some man who, after marriage, would beat her or otherwise mistreat her. She would certainly be better off with Tay.

What was it Cade had said on the road from Corpus Christi? *Whatever happens between the two of you will come naturally.*

What had come naturally was an uncanny affinity between him and Emily.

He smiled. She had felt it, too. He had seen it in her eyes in that first moment and in the tumbled hay, and he had known it for sure when she'd spoken to him with that uncharacteristic sharpness at the supper table.

They had both known it when they were quoting lines of the same poem. It endeared her to him that she'd not shown a flicker of surprise that he, a Choctaw living in the Nation, could quote Marcus Aurelius and Sir Walter Scott. She hadn't fluttered her eyelashes and exclaimed that he was so unusual for an Indian, nor had she wondered where he had gone away to school as did many white women he met socially. Of course, he had to admit, Emily was close to both Cade and Cotannah, and knew that the members of the Five Civilized Tribes were not ignorant savages.

Emily was close to him, too. Already. He didn't understand that, but it was true. Intellectually. Spiritually.

Suddenly he could put a name to what he had seen in her, what had unsettled him enough to have that dream. She was the embodiment of love—the way she had been holding and tending the twins when he'd first seen her, the delight in her face when Cole had spoken for the first time, the way *she'd* spoken to *him* in her soft, pleasant voice to say she was glad that he had ridden onto Las Manzanitas.

His hungry body had simply confused the *kind* of love she embodied. That was all that had caused the dream.

No need to worry about his heart here. None at all.

He began chanting again.

This day. This day is dawning.

His run into the dawn would settle his mind. Never had it failed him.

Chapter 5

Emily ran down the stairs, through the hallway, and let herself out the front door. She stopped to close it slowly, silently. Maggie and Cade's room had windows along this side of the house, and she didn't want to wake them as they'd been up late last night. But, for her own sake, she wanted to slip out secretly, and she didn't need to be interrogated about taking a solitary sunrise ride when raiders were still infesting the whole border country.

There was no way she could look Maggie in the eye and explain why she couldn't stay in the house for one minute longer, no way to say why she wasn't still asleep. How could she sleep with her heart pounding a runaway beat, her blood racing in her veins, and her thoughts whirling in a vortex of confusion?

A long ride out onto the prairie would help, she thought, as she tiptoed across the porch and down the low steps, then started along the walk toward the stables. Fresh air always cleared her head.

Not only that, but a ride on skittish Sache's back would take even a vaquero's mind off his troubles. She tried to set her mind on the filly and keep it there.

But the sound of laughter close by, *very* close, stopped her in her tracks. Somebody else was awake! Who? What was she doing? It sounded as if someone was hiding in the snowball bushes that grew thick between the stone-paved walkway and the long porch.

She parted the bloom-laden branches and stepped off the walk onto the soft earth between two bushes, looking right and left along the porch.

The laughter came again, its tone now so deeply provocative, so blatantly sexual, that it took her a moment to recognize it was Maggie. She'd never heard her sister sound that way before—she'd never before heard *anyone* sound so . . . earthy, so . . . shamelessly . . . well, lustful. There was no other word for it.

Emily froze. Surely Maggie and Cade weren't *outside* . . . No. Their bedroom was directly in front of her, their open windows separated from her only by the width of the porch.

"A man couldn't resist you if his very life hung in the balance," Cade drawled, his words floating out through the window in a tone thick with desire.

Emily started to back out of her hiding place,

to head on her way to the stable, so she wouldn't hear this intimate conversation that was clearly not meant for others' ears. But somehow she couldn't move.

Cade's voice held a tantalizing cadence that slowed her frantic heart and set it to a pulsing, throbbing rhythm. Instead of walking away, she stood transfixed, staring through the bushes and across the porch to the windows.

The curtains billowed out, then blew back into the room and fluttered around Maggie and Cade. With a shock running through her, she realized she could see them, standing just inside the wide windows, facing each other, only inches apart. He towered over her, huge and dark; she stood in her white nightgown, looking up at him, with her head tilted flirtatiously and the breeze stirring her curly hair.

Maggie laughed again. "I can remember, once upon a time, when you resisted me," she teased, "and your life *was* hanging in the balance."

"Ah," he said, "but that was before I knew what I was missing."

Slowly, deliberately, his eyes never leaving hers, he lifted his hand and pushed her gown off one shoulder, ran his palm over her skin all the way down her arm. Maggie arched her whole body toward him, shook back her hair, and smiled up into his eyes.

They came together then in a tense, hungry movement, a quick, desperate reaching of raw greed for each other, yet in that same instant, Emily realized that it was a motion entirely sure of fulfillment. It looked like a part of a primitive dance, a sexual dance, and it burned its image into Emily's brain.

Amazed, astounded, filled with wonder and longing, helpless to move or even to breathe for that instant, she watched their endless, deep-drawn kiss until, finally, her eyes blurred with tears. Letting the flowered branches fall, she turned and ran for the stables.

Dear Heaven above, *she* had to have that, too. She longed for it, she *ached* for it. She needed a man to love her like that.

That was what she had been trying to tell Maggie last night. *That* was what she needed that she didn't know how to name.

She reached the open archway of the stable, stopped and leaned back against the doorpost, gasping for breath, staring blindly deep into the gloom of the huge barn. She breathed in its sweet, pungent scents while she saw and heard *herself*, not Maggie, with her naked man in the pale, early morning.

He reached for her, swept his hand down over her back, circled his palm hard in the small of her back and cupped her buttocks to pull her to him. He made a guttural sound, deep in his throat, as he bent his head toward her upturned lips, then traced the curve of her throat with his thumb before he cradled her head for his kiss. And then he stopped to tantalize her, to brush his lips back and forth,

back and forth, across hers, driving her to
complete distraction before his mouth settled
over hers.

And then his kiss took her spiraling out into
the hottest winds of desire; it set her blood on
fire and sucked the strength and the breath
from her body. His lips were full and sensuous,
his face darkly, dazzlingly handsome; he had
eyes burning silver as the stars.

The sight of his face stopped her hard-
beating heart: Her fantasy man was not Lee. It
was Tay Nashoba.

She closed her eyes and shook her head,
making a strangled little sound. No. She had it
all wrong; this couldn't be.

But when she opened her eyes, she saw him
again. Try as she would, she could not make
him be Lee.

At last Emily stood away from the post, set
her feet a little bit apart to steady herself,
and turned her body, stiff as a toy soldier's,
toward the tack room. But she couldn't take one
step until she'd come to terms with her imagination. Tay Nashoba holding her again, even
closer than when they'd danced. Tay Nashoba,
Cotannah's man, kissing her, was a thought
she simply would not entertain. *He* was not
what she'd meant, not at all, when she'd told
herself last night that she wanted a life full of
passion.

Now, he might seem to have *caused* her to
want more than a safe, secure, comfortable life
because she had had that thought right after
she danced with him, but it was simply coinci-

dental. She had been intellectually stimulated by the conversation with him because none of the other men on the ranch ever read poetry or thought about the art of teaching or talked to her about such things.

That was it, that was all. He *was* handsome and interesting and very different from any other man she'd known in all her life; *that* was why she was having hallucinations about him. That and the fact that she hadn't slept, hadn't rested all night.

Slowly, carefully, she moved her head, looked around the stable as if she'd never seen it before. The muted munchings and stirrings of the horses always made her feel warm and cozy and safe. The smells of hay and horses and manure and sweet feed always pulled her close to the earth and to this place, Las Manzanitas, which had become her dear home.

The way the light slanted through the wide doors into the aisle between the stalls always gave her a feeling of peace and sent her floating off into daydreams. Now, though, none of it touched her.

From the back of the barn, Sache whinnied to get her attention, and when Emily didn't respond, she kicked the wall. Riding Sache would straighten out her mind.

She marched to the tack room door, and reached blindly for the first saddle on the rack. Its weight made her stagger as she carried it out to the hitching post. Lack of rest had made her so physically weak that it was no wonder her imagination was playing tricks on her. A long ride in the fresh morning air would make her feel better, truly it would.

And it did, for a little while. She longed Sache first, until the filly was blowing a little, then she threw the saddle on her and took off. The filly still had so much energy, though, that she kept dropping her head and shaking it playfully as if to say she was thrilled to be with Emily and going somewhere.

Emily tried to fix her mind on her mount, tried to focus on what she might do next. Or on the rooster crowing from Oleana's chicken yard or on the other horses whinnying from the east pasture as they rode down the fence. For a while, she nearly succeeded.

After they crossed the line of live oaks that grew along the creek, so dry now that they didn't even raise a splash, she lifted her face to the new sun and moved the mare out at a long, slow lope. The only sounds in the world were Sache's hooves striking the ground and the breeze, gusting now and then into a wind— and the raucous thoughts clamoring in a closet in the back of her mind, demanding to be let out. Resolutely Emily shut them up tighter and locked the door.

When she reached her special place on the caprock, after she had feasted her eyes and her spirit on the sight of the land spread out below her, only then would she try to sort out her feelings. *Not* until then.

Again she turned her face to the sun, now fully up and already promising a hot day ahead. The breeze contradicted that thought, though, touching her cheeks with cool fingers, playfully ruffling her hair. Quail called again and again from deep in the mesquite thickets.

But the loveliness around her wasn't enough to hold her attention. As the land began slanting upward and the filly picked her way around thicker clumps of brush and through the scattered rocks, the confusion broke across Emily's mind again, chafing it as sorely as the unfamiliar saddle chafed her legs.

Grabbing the wrong saddle had been an incredibly stupid thing to do, she thought, as she rode out onto the caprock. She must settle herself, here, this morning, right now, and get back to normal, back into her mind, back into control, or she might do something even more stupid that would have worse consequences.

She stood in the stirrup and swung herself down to the ground, then threw her reins over Sache's head for a ground-tie. The sky still held some pink, and she watched it fade as she walked on a little way to the rock where she usually sat. Below her, the grassy prairie rolled forever and ever without pause, dotted here and there by cattle and brush, drawing her gaze on and on until it reached the horizon.

Her eyes filled with stinging tears. Everything looked the same as always, yet somehow it wasn't the same. No, *she* wasn't the same.

This strange dissatisfaction, this unreasoning *wanting*, longing for something more, had in-

vaded her body and her mind, and she had to
get rid of it. Lee. She must think about Lee and
about their life together and all that they had
planned. Half the women in the world, probably more than half, never had lives as good as
hers was now or men as good as Lee.

But the difference in the way she'd felt last
night dancing with Lee and the way she'd
felt—

Sache snorted and threw up her head, looking back the way they had come, whuffling a
warning deep in her throat. Emily froze.

Could it be the big cat, the cougar that had
come into the schoolyard at the end of the
winter? The men had trailed it off and on all
through the spring, after it had padded through
the ranch headquarters so boldly, but none had
ever even gotten a shot at it. It was too fast and
too cunning, they'd said.

Fear sent her blood surging. She was
trapped. The caprock jutted fifty feet or more
above the prairie, the only way off it was the
trail she had taken to it, the one that led in the
direction that Sache was staring.

The brush cracked and popped. Or was it
rocks rolling down and hitting more rocks
below?

It couldn't be raiders. They wouldn't bother
to come up a rough trail where there wouldn't
be many cattle to steal. But it was somebody—
or some animal—moving fast, straight toward
her and her mare.

She never knew how, but instead of huddling against the rock as her body begged

her to do, she scrambled to her feet. Poor Sache wouldn't move as long as she was ground-tied—she had taught her well not to do that—so Emily had to pick up the reins and throw them over her neck. Maybe there'd be time to jump into the saddle, too, but if not, she would at least give the filly a running chance.

Sache whinnied. Emily glimpsed something coming around the side of the hill and flung herself toward her horse. Her hand tangled in the reins, and as she jerked at them to free it, she forced herself to look over her shoulder.

It was a man—a big, wild, naked Indian—and she screamed. Her rising fear spiraled crazily, riding on her voice up and up, then plunged into her feet. It was Tay Nashoba.

Relief claimed her.

But only for an instant. Another fear came over her, a stronger one than fear of the cougar, rising inside her like a tidal wave, then rolling out of her toward Tay, sucking the heart right out of her chest. Hollow, she collapsed against Sache's warm shoulder before her legs went out from under her.

How could she stop these wild *yearnings* that sprang to life every time she saw this man?

His long, loose hair swung forward on his shoulders, held by a beaded band that circled his forehead. Only a sheen of sweat covered his muscular upper body, but she'd been wrong in first thinking he was naked all over, for his legs *were* covered by leggings of buckskin.

"Emily!" He strode toward her, closing the distance between them fast with his blazing, bright eyes fixed on her face. "I'm so sorry I startled you," he said. "I made as much noise as a herd of wild horses so you'd look down and see me coming."

"I-I-I wasn't listening."

He stopped right in front of her, close enough to touch. Easily close enough to touch.

He balanced on the balls of his moccasined feet set slightly apart, with his long, horseman's muscles flexing in his thighs. "What were you doing that you didn't hear me?"

The muscles of his chest were beautifully sculpted, rising and falling from the effort of his uphill run. She wanted to run the palms of her hands over them, to feel his skin. Her nostrils quivered, caught the sharp smell of his sweat.

He had asked her a question, but she had no idea what. "Y-y-you s-s-scare m-m-me s-s-so . . ."

She stopped, mortified that she hadn't said "scared," past tense, as she had intended, stunned by the flame that flared deep in Tay's eyes. He, too, had noticed that she was no longer talking about his sudden arrival on the caprock.

They looked at each other for the space of two tumultuous heartbeats, then he placed his hands on the horse behind her, one on each side of her, and bent his head to kiss her. Her heart stopped. So did the world. The caprock dropped away from beneath her feet and the horse from behind her. His lips tasted like spicy cedar and they were hot as afternoon sunshine.

Hot and knowing, sure and demanding. They moved her, spoke to her, deep, deep inside, calling to that wild woman whom she'd discovered last night.

She answered with her own heat, her lips moving with his, beneath his, in a growing hunger that scared her more even as it thrilled her.

How could a kiss . . . a kiss really be like this?

It could. It was.

And then he parted her lips with the tip of his tongue and sent a sharp shock at such an intimacy shooting through her. She grabbed his shoulders and clung to him.

The shock faded beneath his tantalizing tracing of the shape of her mouth. He explored, slowly, suggestively, the seam of her lips, dipped into it and out of it.

She let him do it once, and again. Then she opened to him and met him in kind.

He stepped closer and cradled her head in both his hands, running his fingers into her hair as if to make sure she couldn't get away, then he thrust his tongue deeper, twining and teasing with hers. The inside muscles of his thighs brushed the outside of her legs through her riding skirt.

He took her, fast and deep, into the fascinating, sensuous delight, stroked her tongue with his and then took it away, only to slowly, enticingly, give it back again. He groaned, deep in his throat, when, instinctively, she closed her lips around it and drew on it for a gratification that spread through her whole being and burned in her blood.

He pulled her closer and her breasts brushed his bare chest. She pressed her palms harder to the hot, sleek skin of his back, innocently, thoughtlessly trying to get closer yet, and brought the hard shaft of his manhood against her.

With a strangled moan, he tore his mouth from hers. She looked up at him through a pink haze.

His silver eyes burned through it, blazing like stars in his dark face. "Now *you've* scared *me*," he said roughly, "so we're even, Miss Emily."

He was still so close that his breath whispered against her lips. Its cedary fragrance mingled with the smell of his sweat.

"You don't *look* scared."

His eyes darkened. "I am. And so are you. But that won't matter."

He was still so close that she couldn't think. Except that she wanted another kiss, *another*, she wanted him to kiss her forever, and that wasn't thinking, it was purely an instinct like drinking cool water in the heat of the day.

Her lips parted, ready for his, but he was looking at her with a bright, hard knowing in his eyes.

"Matter? Won't matter for what?"

His hands on her arms burned into her skin.

"For us. You know it as well as I do. Admit it, Emily."

"Ad-m-mit wh-what . . . ?"

"We're meant to love each other."

That bald, flat statement brought her back to reality as fast and as completely as if he'd slapped her across the face.

"But we *can't!* Th-there's C-Cotannah . . ."

"And I'm sorry about that. But I don't love her in this way. We can't choose who we love . . ."

"Maggie warned me! After the dance, she warned me to stay away from you. I-I have to get away!"

She tried to act on her words, but even though he dropped his hands, he stood where he was like a rock, his legs still straddling hers, his eyes holding her in the vise of his will. The languor of his kiss left her body, and panic raked across her nerves to leave her tense and trembling.

"Admit it, Emily. Say it."

With a strangled sob, she twisted around to Sache, pressed her face into the silky neck, warmed by the sun.

"You can't deny this thing between us, Emily."

Tay's voice was soft, yet strong, so strong it had a thread of steel running through it. The thread of truth.

She whirled back around to confront it. "All r-right, I c-can't!"

His eyes locked with hers. "Good." The corners of his mouth lifted a little in the ghost of a smile while his eyes burned into hers. "Think about it, Emily. Just think. And remember how hard it is for you to lie."

He bent toward her then, and she thought he was going to kiss her again. But he only touched her face, just once, in a feathery caress that nevertheless left the track of his callused fingertip across her cheek.

"Think about it," he whispered.

And then he stepped back from surrounding her and he was gone.

For the longest time she couldn't even move. Finally she slumped against the faithful Sache and braced her elbow so she could manage to touch her fingertips to her mouth. Her hands smelled of Tay's sweat, her lips were swollen and they felt bruised, her hands were shaking.

She was shaking all over. She was as drained of strength and sense as she'd ever been. And all she could know was the taste of his kiss.

At that moment she couldn't have said one word except *More! Tay, please, more!* even if the cougar had jumped out from behind a mesquite bush right then.

But Tay was gone.

And she wanted him back, oh, dear God, how she wanted him back again!

What had they done? Tay Nashoba was the man Cotannah loved! And she herself was in love with Lee!

But Tay didn't love Cotannah. Not in that way.

That made no difference. Cotannah loved him, or she thought she did.

Heaven help her! She, Emily Harrington, was in love with Lee. She was betrothed to Lee. She was going to *marry* Lee in only a few months' time. Why, she had never kissed Lee . . . and Lee had never kissed her . . . like that!

She whirled and walked away from Sache, strode to the edge of the rocky precipice, and stared out across the rolling land below. To no avail. The old, familiar dreams of living here safely with her family proved helpless to block out the new sensations in her body.

She traced her lips with the tip of her tongue, tasting Tay again. Her blood raced, yet her heart still held that hard, steady beat to which he had set it. Her whole body pulsed with an excitement she had no words to describe, with a wanting for Tay Nashoba, no, a *need*, a true need.

She was twenty-three years old and she had never known a kiss could be like that, and now she knew it. Of course, she had never kissed a man at all until she became engaged to Lee. Did Lee know a kiss could wipe out the world?

Maybe Lee could learn to do that. She could teach him, perhaps, to throw himself into loving and playing and living with her as passionately as he already gave himself to his work. After all, she was a teacher, wasn't she?

She touched her throbbing mouth with her fingertips and sank into a trembling heap, sitting flat on the ground with her knees drawn up to rest her forehead. Her hands curled into fists and she beat them against the uncaring caprock.

Perhaps she should give in to Lee's pleas and marry him before October, probably she should—then she wouldn't be tempted to give in to this we-are-meant-to-love-each-other that Tay insisted was between them, pulling them together by a spiritual force.

She should. She should get herself well and truly, safely married and get out of Cotannah's way, as Maggie told her to do. Because one fact had to override everything else: There was no way she would do anything to hurt Cotannah, never, not in her whole life long. She would rather die than betray her best friend.

In spite of everything else, she must hold that thought.

Finally, after a long, long, time, she managed to get enough strength to stand up and walk back to Sache, who was still waiting, head hanging, dozing off in the quiet heat of the sun.

"I-I can't b-believe you didn't s-spook right here in the middle of all those g-goings-on."

Emily hugged the filly's neck before she gathered up the reins and stepped back up into the too big saddle.

"I-I g-guess you're t-truly tamed. I should've named you Dove or Honey instead of Huisache, after a prickly old cactus. Isn't that right? Now, isn't that right?"

She petted Sache's neck and crooned to her all the way down the side of the caprock; she tried to hold the vision of Cotannah's happy, hopeful face when she'd stood in the circle of lantern light, looking up at Tay on the evening he arrived. But none of it helped, none of it could make her mind stronger than her body—it just kept on crying out for Tay again, only for Tay.

Chapter 6

Two hours later, Tay stepped out of the house onto the front porch for the second time that morning. He felt as if a year had passed since dawn . . . since he had momentarily lost his mind and done what he'd wanted to do from the minute he'd first stepped on to this very veranda—which was to kiss Emily. Thank goodness Cade was waiting for him or he might not be able to restrain himself from riding out to find her and kissing her again.

God help him. Now he had to sit down and talk about Cotannah, and the devil of it was that he had no room in his life for *either* woman. Nothing of his soul to offer a woman. How could he when the Nation demanded his all? He tried not to think as he walked the length of the house to the shady corner where Cade sat.

"So, old friend," he said, "those tall Texas tales of *rancheros* working from first light to no light are nothing but lies."

Cade, sitting in a cane-bottomed chair with his legs crossed at the ankle and his booted heels propped up on the railing, turned to look at him. He grinned lazily and lifted his coffee mug in salute.

"Lies and gross exaggerations," he drawled agreeably. "I spend my days right here listening to the quail calling and watching the sunlight play on the prairie."

"Sure you do." Tay chuckled and crossed the porch to take the chair on the other side of the low table that held a tray filled with coffeepot, mugs, cream, sugar, and sweet pastries.

"Jorge brought me your invitation just as I finished my bath," he said, "and I could tell by the awed tone of his voice that, even if it is Saturday, coffee on the porch with *Senor* Cade in the middle of the morning ranks right up there with other usual occurrences on Las Manzanitas like blizzards in June and broncs that don't buck."

Cade laughed. "You're right. Cows and fences and raiders and such have no respect for Saturday and Sunday. I haven't started work this late since the day Maggie and I rode onto the place—but when we woke up this morning, we said, hey, after all, there *was* a fiesta last night."

"I'm honored."

"We can't work. We're entertaining the next Principal Chief of the Choctaw Nation."

Tay chuckled. "I need you to come home and campaign for me if you're that sure I'm going to win," he said lightly as he pulled back the chair and dropped into it.

"You *have* to win," Cade said, suddenly serious as he turned and set down his chair and then his mug to pick up the coffeepot and pour a cupful for Tay. "You're the only candidate who can save the Nation from the coal interests and the railroad interests and the other assorted white intruders."

Tay's gut contracted. He didn't want to hear it. Not yet. Right now, with Emily's sweet taste still on his lips, he didn't want to even think about his responsibilities or what he should do for the good of the People. The People ruled his life.

"The Nation survived for hundreds of years before I was born," he said.

That should be his motto; he should hold that thought. Maybe he didn't *have* to let the People rule him, maybe they could live and prosper without his services.

"Yes," Cade said, "but the Nation was never threatened with extinction the way it is now. If we let them completely overrun us, it'll be the same in the end as if we'd all been killed before we left the Old Country."

Tay snapped back defensively before he thought. "*You've* assimilated. You're not doing anything to stop it."

Cade's face hardened as he handed him the cup and he met his eyes straight. "True. But I still care."

Tay accepted that along with the coffee. "Sorry." He reached for another topic. "I ran several miles across your ranch today—you're living in a wild and beautiful land here."

"Hard and hot and with no heart for a man," Cade said, his tone light again.

"A wanton strumpet of a land."

Cade nodded, smiling wryly. "But *I* love *her*."

"And you love Maggie. Together she and this land have settled you down at last." Tay took a sip of the hot coffee, surprised that he'd spoken of love so freely. He was trying not to think about love.

Cade's whole face lit up. "Maggie's a marvel," he said, shaking his head in wonder, "and a fascination. I see something new in her every day."

Tay's heart twisted—he couldn't talk about this. He grabbed for another subject and found that the Nation was all he knew, after all. "People in the Nation still expect you to come riding in alone one of these days, the way you used to do."

Cade chuckled. "People in the Nation don't know Maggie," he said, and took a pastry from the plate. "She'd be right beside me with one twin in front of her in the saddle and the other in front of me."

"From what I've seen, the twins would be mounted on their own steeds and galloping several lengths ahead of you and Maggie."

He managed to keep his tone light, but thinking again about the sweetness of holding the twins made his heart heavy as stone. "I think they're great," he blurted. "I've never seen children quite like them. I could sit and watch them all day."

"Both of them liked you immediately," Cade said. He chuckled and added, "Cole's first words are proof of that. Maggie and Emily were ecstatic that he spoke for you, and we're all relieved that nothing's wrong with him. But privately I think they're a bit jealous, too, that you got him to talk when they've spent months coaxing him with no success."

The offhand mention of Emily struck Tay like a surprise blow. He ought to ignore it, ought not to take the opportunity to talk about her . . . but it was such a perfect opening . . .

"That's the teacher coming out in Emily, no doubt. She's frustrated that her little student didn't perform."

Cade grinned. "Yes. Did you get a chance to talk to her about ideas for teaching English to take back to the Nation?"

"A little bit, during the dancing. She said it's fine for me to visit her school when it takes up again."

The Nation. He needed to keep his mind on the Nation. On what was good for the Nation.

"Good. Her methods with the Spanish-speaking children will surely work with the Choctaw children who don't use English at home." He finished his pastry and took another, motioning for Tay to do the same. "Everybody on this ranch loves Miss Emily, and she loves everybody. The twins adore her."

Tay grasped at the subject of the twins again to get away from talk of Emily and who loved her. "Much as I enjoy Miranda and Cole, it must be even more of a thrill when you look at them, when you hold them."

"They are miracles," Cade said. "There's no other word for the feelings they give me." He smiled at Tay over the rim of his coffee cup. "You'll find out what I mean if you decide to marry."

"I'd like to have children." Tay took a sip of coffee and then a deep breath. He had to say something; if he didn't, he'd be even more of a bounder. "I ought to mount up and ride out of here this morning," he said.

Cade stopped his cup in midair, halfway to his mouth, and fixed him with a disbelieving look.

"I don't love Cotannah, Cade, except as a little sister. I always have, and I knew the minute I saw her again that I always will love her only in that way."

It felt good to say it, but he didn't want to look Cade in the eyes. Cade surprised him.

"Maybe so," he said, his tone light, "or maybe you'll change your mind in a few days. But whatever you two decide, there'll be no hard feelings with me, Tay."

"Thank you for that. I hate to disappoint Uncle Kulli, though—not to mention Cotannah's feelings."

"Don't worry about all that. The way I see it, it's too soon to tell. You don't know Cotannah as an adult, and that'll take some time." He sipped at his coffee and laughed. "Why, the first time I ever talked to Maggie, I'd have sworn she'd be the last woman in the world I'd *ever* marry. It wasn't ten minutes later that we were standing in front of the judge."

They both laughed and then sat in companionable silence for a moment, until Tay, to his own consternation, asked about Emily instead of Cotannah.

"Are Maggie and Emily close?"

"Yes," Cade said, "Maggie has always tried to protect Emily, and that's made them unusually close."

"Big sisters often do feel protective."

"Actually, Emily's a year older than Maggie, but she was always much more timid."

"I called her Gentle Emily and she said she's become a lot less timid and gentle since she's come to live at the ranch."

Cade threw him a sharp glance. Instead of meeting it, he took another drink of coffee.

"That's true. Emily and Cotannah both have changed a great deal in the three years they've been here. Emily *is* a lot more confident, but she still has that need to try and make everybody happy—she just loves everybody."

Tay drank some more coffee and nodded. He didn't quite trust himself to speak.

"Cotannah, on the other hand, just wants to try to make *herself* happy," Cade said wryly. "She, too, has definitely lost her childhood shyness and learned to speak up."

"Yes, last night your little sister was moving us all around like a general on a battleground, arranging the seating and telling me to dance with Emily so I could get acquainted with her best friend. She was entirely artless and charming."

Cade chuckled and nodded. "If we'd only known that her blurting out a marriage proposal to you when she was ten years old was a hint of bolder things to come, we could've tried harder to raise her right."

Both men laughed.

"She's a pistol," Cade said proudly. "I always think she's a whole lot like Maggie in some ways."

"They're both strong women," Tay said, "and unusually beautiful ones, too."

That was an understatement. Cotannah's dark beauty was dazzling, stunning enough to strike any man in the world half-senseless—it was far more powerful than even she yet knew. And she carried her head with such pride on that long, slender neck of hers, and her huge, almost black eyes flashed such a drop-dead look, that no man breathing could resist the challenge.

Maggie had blue-sky eyes blazing her feelings to the world, pale porcelain skin, and the face of a wild, naughty angel framed by masses of curly black hair. She wore it down, loose and free like a girl's, despite her status as a married woman and mother of two children. Yes, Maggie was an original, and she was marvelously beautiful; there was no doubt about that.

In his opinion, though, neither of those fiery belles could compare with Emily—they could not compare with her at all—for hers was a quiet beauty that she didn't even know she possessed. Her heavily lashed eyes were the color of warm chocolate, and her long, wavy hair was sun-streaked with every shade of blond.

Brown eyes and blond hair made a fascinating combination, one that he could look at forever. He didn't recall ever seeing it before, but then he didn't see many blondes of any description.

But somehow her physical beauty didn't even enter into the feelings he had for her. He'd felt that spiritual connection with her before he had even ever looked at her face or her body.

"Why do you think she has a need to try to make everyone happy?"

He took a drink of coffee, swallowed, and then held his breath. What the hell would Cade think? He hadn't even used her name, he'd just assumed that Cade would know which woman was on his mind.

"Emily and Maggie's father, Pierce Harrington, was one mean son of a bitch," Cade said. "A dictating, cruel-hearted bastard. All four daughters and their mother were terrified of him, and the house was full of tension all the time. Maggie says Emily always tried to lessen it, tried to prevent confrontations, tried to make everybody be happy so everything wouldn't get worse."

A fury swept through Tay that surprised him with its strength. His fists clenched and his heart beat fast at the thought of Emily as a helpless child, and Maggie and their sisters, small and vulnerable, living in fear of their own father.

"It's a good thing the bastard's already dead." His voice sounded so hard and cold, he hardly recognized it himself.

Cade nodded, then looked at him. "My sentiments exactly."

Tay forced himself to lean back in his chair and relax. "Well, we need someone like Emily in the Nation," he said. "Heaven knows *I* can't make everybody happy."

"Neither can Emily, but she hasn't quite learned that yet. She's always been especially determined to make life wonderful for Maggie and the twins and her mother, and now she's added Lee Kincaid and his little girl to the list."

Lee Kincaid. That strutting little bantam rooster ought to be the one trying to make *her* happy.

That wasn't fair, Tay admitted quickly. Lee appeared to be nice enough—but he still felt a stab of jealousy that went right through his heart.

He couldn't say a word, for the rush of that feeling was too strong and swift. It caused a heated, blinding agitation within him.

Cade didn't seem to notice Tay's silence. He got up, tossed the last of his coffee into the snowball bushes, and stretched the kinks out of his legs.

"Well, I have to get to work now," Cade said.

"You want to help us move some cattle? Oh, and tomorrow afternoon, it being Sunday, we do generally slack off a little. Let's hunt some quail over in the canyon. Cooked over a mesquite fire, they make a Texas treat you won't want to miss."

"That'd be great," Tay said.

Work and hunting both would be a distraction, and distraction was for sure what he was going to need.

When Cotannah finally woke up on the day after the fiesta, she lay in bed for a long time thinking about it. Thinking about Tay, about dancing with him, about being in his arms.

He had seemed huge, towering over her as they danced, hugely tall with his shoulders hugely broad. Actually, he was bigger than she'd remembered. And he was more handsome, if that was possible.

She gave a little squeal of delight and threw herself onto her stomach with her face in the pillow, hitting it with her fists as the thrilling realization went spiraling through her all over again. He was here! Tay Nashoba was actually here, on Las Manzanitas, and he had come to court and marry her!

It was unbelievable. It was a dream come true. She shivered and pinched herself to make sure she was awake and that it was all real.

This all seemed as unlikely as if one of Aunt Ancie's old traditional tales had suddenly come to life and started playing itself out. She might as well have journeyed to the sky like the legendary brothers Tashka and Walo, and had the Sun and Moon speak to her.

She threw herself onto her back again and stared at the ceiling. Yet, on the other hand, she had always known this would happen. She had made it happen. She had loved Tay and overcome her ten-year-old shyness to ask him to marry her; she had written to Uncle Kulli to find out whether he'd stayed single the minute she had turned eighteen. It was her destiny to love Tay, and his to love her.

And she couldn't wait to see him again. Maybe he was pacing the veranda, waiting to see her! Maybe he had dreamed of her last night as she had dreamed of him and he was aching with longing to see her, too!

She threw off the sheet, leapt out of bed, and dressed in one of her most fetching dresses—one made of a deep rose-colored calico that brought out her dark hair and eyes. She brushed her hair until it shone and tied it back with a ribbon that matched her dress exactly, then ran downstairs and through the house, looking for Tay.

She found Maggie instead.

"Maggie, have you seen Tay? I thought he might come and talk to me while I have my breakfast. I guess he's already had his?"

With a laugh Maggie looked up from her task of sorting the silverware used for the fiesta and putting it away in the buffet. "Oleana quit cooking breakfast hours ago. You've slept through dinner, too, 'Tannah, but it was just leftovers from last night. Run out to the kitchen and ask Oleana to give you something."

Disappointment stabbed at Cotannah. The house was too quiet, she heard no men's voices. "Where's Tay?"

"Gone to move cattle with Cade and the men."

The disappointment deepened. "For the rest of the day?"

"I think so."

"Did Tay ask about me?"

Maggie glanced up at her. "What would he ask? He knew where you were. He was dancing with you only a few hours ago."

Cotannah laughed and hugged herself. "Oh, Maggie, wasn't it the most *beautiful* fiesta? Wasn't it wonderful?" She ran to Maggie and hugged her. "Maggie, Tay is perfect! He's perfect!"

Maggie hugged her hard and then stepped back and looked at her as she let her go. "No man is perfect, 'Tannah."

Cotannah laughed as she turned toward the back door on her way to the kitchen, a small outbuilding separate from the house. "He's the next thing to it, then," she said. "Really, Maggie, you'll see."

When she ran out the back door and down the steps she scanned the grounds of La Casa to see if by some rare chance the men had finished with the cattle and come in early. They hadn't. Emily and Katie were in the round pen with their horses, Old Casoose was sitting in the door of the stable in the sun, the twins and

Mama Harrington had walked down to the chicken yard to feed the chickens. Nobody even looked up to notice her, so she ran back to the kitchen.

"And here is my 'Tannah," Oleana greeted her, "come to eat while I am washing the very last dish."

She was smiling, though, and only teasing, so Cotannah took a plate from the shelf and began helping herself to tortillas and spicy sliced beef. She added tomatoes and sat down to eat.

"Here are the on-ions and peppers for you, *Senorita* Lie-Abed-All-Day," Oleana said, bringing her a bowl of chunked vegetables in a picante sauce.

"No, thanks, I don't want to smell like onions when Tay gets back."

"They will be gone until long after dark, *Senor* Cade said. Your on-ions will be gone by then."

That news hurt her feelings and it made her mad. Great goodness, didn't Cade know that Tay would be anxious to see her, that he didn't want to ride around out there in the sun working as a vaquero for hours and hours? Didn't Cade realize how *rude* it was to treat a guest like that?

"I don't want to chance it," she said.

Oleana left the dish on the table and went back to her work, putting away the huge cooking pots her older daughters had cleaned.

"*Mañana*," she said, "for the supper, we will have quail, *Senor* Cade tell me. He and *el senor del Norte,* they will go hunting *mañana*—in the afternoon."

Cotannah dropped her fork and glared at her. "His name is Tay!" she cried. "Or *Senor* Nashoba. Not the *gentleman from the North!*"

Her voice echoed angrily in her own ears. Oleana stared at her, wide-eyed.

"I'm sorry, Oleana," she said contritely, "but I just cannot believe this is true. Tay has come all this way to court me, yet he's gone today, and now tomorrow too! He could have taken me for a buggy ride on Sunday afternoon!"

Oleana made a soothing, clucking sound and came to pat her on the shoulder. "He will be here for many weeks," she said. "Do not fret, *senorita*. You have many, many Sundays to come."

Chapter 7

The longer Lee rode on the same crew with Tay Nashoba, the more irritated and cross he became. The man was a horseman, he had to give him that, and he knew something about cattle, because he caught on fast as to how to keep from losing them in the brush when they broke away from the herd, but for some reason, just being around that Indian got his bristles up something fierce.

Well, to put it plain, he knew what the reason was, he finally admitted to himself. There'd been something in the air that morning of the raid between Tay Nashoba and Emily, no mistake about it. *And* he'd be hog-tied and branded if that same *something* hadn't been there in the air again last night at the fiesta.

But it was not Emily's fault, he thought, slowing his horse and setting him into a rollback so he could ride around the rear of the herd. She was only interested because the arrogant yahoo could talk books and poetry with her. At least that's what she said they'd been talking about when they'd stayed so close together long after the music and dancing had stopped.

Well, damn it, he'd had enough of breathing the same air as the educated redskin. They could move the rest of the cows without him.

"Mr. Chisk-Ko!" Lee called to Cade.

Cade slowed his horse, and Lee went trotting up to him.

"Reckon I oughta get on over to the fencin' crew and then ride back to La Casa. I'll send some boys out to make contact with the patrols."

Cade pushed back his hat and wiped sweat from his forehead with a bandanna. "Right. We've got plenty of hands to handle this here."

Lee nodded and rode off at a long lope. He reached the fencing crew within half an hour and took their order for more supplies, then he pointed his pony toward headquarters. There was still half the afternoon left to spend with Emily, plenty of time to make her forget all about last night.

When he reached the outbuildings of La Casa, he slowed to a walk and came in between the bunkhouse and the stables. At first he didn't see anyone, then Emily came around the near side of the round pen, leading the pony with Katie in the saddle, clutching the horn with both hands while they moved along at a brisk jog. The bigger miracle was that they were both laughing. Katie was hanging on for dear life, true, but she wasn't pale as death and she wasn't screaming to get off. She was *laughing!*

He rode right up to the pen before either one of them knew he was there. Slumped in the saddle, he rested one arm on the horn and relaxed.

He had nothing to worry about, nothing at all. Emily loved Katie with a passion and she loved him, too, he was sure. Tay Nashoba belonged to Cotannah, and Emily loved Cotannah, too. He had let himself get all worked up over nothing.

"You girls seem to be having a fine time," he called.

"Look at me, Papa, look!" Katie called back. "I'm not scared anymore."

"I see you're not."

Emily led the pony straight up to him and halted, smiling, no, *aglow* with happiness.

"Whoa," she crooned to the pony. "Whoa, now, Topper."

"We *are* having a fine time, Papa," Katie said. "Miss Emily has got us nearly running now."

Lee laughed. "Next thing I know, you'll be racing Juanito and his sister across the prairie."

"And I'll beat them, too!" she cried, beaming at him in a perfect imitation of Emily's expression.

"Katie's a natural rider," Emily said. Standing beside the little girl at the stirrup, she reached up and patted Katie's leg. "She's only seven now, and by the time she's seventeen, she's going to ride all the way into Corpus Christi all by herself."

Katie nodded, smiling, and said, "I made that plan this morning."

Lee chuckled and got down from his horse. He walked around to the gate and went into the round pen to join them. "You'd better hope that Cortina and all the other *bandidos* are long gone to Mexico by then," he said, lifting his daughter out of the saddle.

Katie's face went solemn and she stuck out her chin. "I ain't afraid of Cortina," she said firmly. "I ain't afraid of him or of riding horses or of anything else."

"I'm *not* afraid, remember?" Emily said softly, correcting her. "Saying 'ain't' is not a good habit to have."

"I'm not afraid," Katie repeated. She brushed Lee's hand away and kept her seat. "Now I'm going to ride Topper all by myself to the stable. Papa, you don't come with me. I can side-pass him to open this gate, and Juanito will help me unsaddle."

"But maybe I should just—" Lee stopped when Emily laid a hand on his arm.

"She can do it," she murmured.

"I can do it," Katie parroted as she took the reins Emily handed her. "Watch me, Papa," she said.

She turned the pony and headed out of the pen. Once she had maneuvered the gate, they applauded hers and Topper's skill at side-passing, and giddily she kicked the pony into a trot and headed for the stable. She looked back over her shoulder to see if Lee had noticed that bit of bravado.

"Ride 'im, Katie!" he called. When she was

out of sight he turned to Emily. "You've done this for her," he said, "and I don't know how."

"Neither do I," she said, laughing a little, her eyes shining, "because, as you know, I'm not known for my courage. Maggie's the one who should be teaching the lessons in how to be brave."

"*You're* the one who loves Katie, though," he said, "and that's what worked this miracle. After her mother was killed on that runaway, I didn't think she'd ever ride horseback by herself again."

They smiled at each other and his heart filled. "I only hope you love me as much as you love my daughter," he drawled. "I'm thinking that you do or you wouldn't be here." He reached out and brushed her hair back from her face in an uncharacteristically intimate gesture. And he didn't even feel awkward about it.

"Want to know how I persuaded Katie to ride?"

"Tell me," he said, taking her elbow in a loose grip.

"I told her a woman can't always be waiting on a man to take her everywhere, that sometimes we have business of our own to conduct. Therefore, we need to be able both to drive and ride horses."

"You'd better watch yourself, Miss Emily," he said teasingly, letting go of her arm to drop his hand to the small of her back, "or I'll have to be setting a guard on the two of you to see what you're up to."

"We women are up to more interesting things than what you men worry about, like pushing the cattle and worrying about grass and water holes," she said. She gave Sache a pat. "We're gathering samples of all the flowers on the ranch to dry and show everyone when school takes up again, and we're looking for different kinds of rocks, too."

He slipped his arm around her waist and pulled her awkwardly against him. "Marry me long before October, Mimi, will you?"

He tilted her chin up, and Emily looked up into his eyes. But hers held a little shadow and she didn't smile at him.

"Let's not talk about that now, all right? Let's give Katie a chance to get her life back together one piece at a time."

"All right. But I'm taking you on a picnic tomorrow afternoon, just the two of us. What do you say to that?"

That made her smile. "I say fine. I'd like that. Will you take me where I can gather some flowers?"

"I'll take you up into the canyon. There'll be a dozen kinds of flowers up there."

"Then it's a date," she said, still smiling. "I'll ask Oleana to pack us a basket."

Soon after that, he left her to go back to work. He went to find riders to send out to check the patrols; he wrote out the order for fencing supplies and told three men they'd be riding into Corpus for them on Monday. He hated to spare that many men from the work, but the road was so dangerous, he couldn't send any fewer. All the while his step was light and he hummed or whistled a tune.

He would talk Emily into it yet. He'd talk that girl into marrying him long before fall rolled around.

Emily worked valiantly at keeping her mind on Lee and on what he was saying during their Sunday afternoon ride up to the canyon. Most of the time she succeeded fairly well.

And she tried just as hard to have a good time. But she felt restless. And she missed Katie.

"We should've let Katie come with us," she said, as they climbed the last rolling rise of the land that led up to the canyon's mouth. "I feel bad because she wanted to so much."

"But *I* wanted to be alone with you so much," Lee said lightly.

He rode his horse closer to Sache and smiled at her. She smiled back.

"It's too dangerous to bring Katie very far from La Casa," he said. "We may have to make a run for the hills—bandits could pop out from behind a rock any minute now."

Emily shivered. "Thank you so much for reminding me of that."

He laughed and leaned out of his saddle to put one arm around her. "I'll protect you, darlin'. I promise I will."

She laughed with him, but when he put his arm around her, she felt nothing nearly as thrilling as when Tay touched her.

"There's a spot near the springs where the

river heads up," he was saying. "We can spread our blanket on the grass in the shade under those trees and take a little nap."

He was riding right beside her, no longer touching her, but she could feel him looking at her.

"I thought we were coming out here to eat all this lunch instead of napping," she said. "You can't imagine what all Oleana has packed in this basket."

"We can do both." His tone was comfortable and easy. "Don't worry, darlin', together we can do anything. Anything you want."

He rode ahead of her then, to lead the way down into the brushy canyon. "Just watch the basket so it doesn't get hung up on a branch," he called back over his shoulder.

As if she didn't already know that or couldn't figure it out for herself.

Soon, too soon, they reached the spot he had chosen, which really was a pretty place. They swung down off the horses; Lee untied the basket and lifted it down, then helped her spread the blanket beneath the scattered oak trees.

"I wish it would rain," she said, as he led the horses a few yards away and left them ground-tied. "Look how slowly the spring's flowing."

"Yeah. We're gonna have to move all the cows from the pastures without creeks or ponds."

They talked about the ranch work while Emily gathered a few dusty flowers here and there. Then they opened the basket and settled beside each other on the blanket to enjoy their feast. Lee ate three pieces of fried chicken and reached for a fourth.

"Life on the Running M took a definite turn for the better the day your mama decided to take up raising chickens," he said.

"And when she taught Oleana to fry it southern style."

"Even if I did have to bring in a milch cow so she could have buttermilk to dip it in," he said. "I'd do it again any time."

"Even if Old Casoose quit on you and you had to milk her yourself?" She laughed at the pained expression that her teasing brought to his face.

"Even then."

"You're so brave, Lee! I am impressed."

He finished eating and wiped his hands on one of the huge cloth napkins Oleana had sent. "Come here and let me *really* impress you."

He pulled her closer to him, half into his lap, and tilted her chin up for his kiss. She fought the instinct to pull away.

This isn't Tay, some part of her screamed, *this isn't Tay.*

But it isn't supposed to be, another part screamed back. *I am betrothed to Lee.*

She made herself relax in his arms. Hadn't she resolved to find what she needed with him? Wasn't she planning to teach him to live with the passion she had realized she needed?

She lifted her arms and put them around his

neck. But he felt strange and slight against her body, as unfamiliar as if they'd never held each other before. Tay was so solid, his body so powerful, so thick and substantial under her hands—he was like a rock to cling to in the midst of a cold, blowing storm.

Oh, dear God, why had she ever let him touch her? Now she was ruined for anybody else.

She pressed her body against Lee's, willing the entrancement she had felt with Tay, praying for that excitement to flood through her again. They loved each other, she and Lee. Truly they did. So why couldn't he make her feel those wonderful sensations?

But even when he held her closer and kissed her harder, all she felt was a cloying closeness. His teeth were hurting her lips, his arms were crushing the breath out of her.

The fault must be all in her—she had never hated his kisses before. Before . . . Tay.

She moved her mouth beneath Lee's, boldly parted his lips with her tongue.

He gave a little grunt of surprise, but then he responded eagerly. Still she felt no excitement. No thrill. Her whole body just shouted that if he didn't let her breathe pretty soon, she would smother to death.

Finally she managed to break the kiss. She dropped her arms to her sides and buried her face in his chest, trying to hide it from him, trying to hide the fact that she wanted nothing so much as to burst into tears.

Never, never in all her life, not even when

Papa had drowned the kittens, had she ever felt so totally empty, so entirely without hope. This was all Tay's fault, and when she gathered up her strength again she was going to hate him with all her being. She was never going to let herself want him again.

"Emily, baby," Lee said, and began stroking her hair, "I knew it. I knew you'd think it over and agree that we should marry sooner. You want me, honey, and you've just proven it to me."

She bit her tongue. No matter what she could say at this moment, it'd be wrong. Tay's kiss had taken away her ability to think straight as well as her ability to enjoy Lee's caresses.

Tay's kiss. She could taste it right now on her lips, feel the thrill it had sent through every inch of her body. She could be one hundred years old, she knew now, and she would still remember that kiss exactly as it had felt at that moment there in the early-morning sun on the caprock.

Why? *Why* couldn't it be Lee who made her feel those sensations?

"*Now* what do you say?" he murmured, his voice full of significance. "Do you still want to wait all that time until October?"

The happiness, the hope in his tone made her want to jump and run. And it broke her heart. But if he felt so much for her . . . wouldn't she eventually feel it for him, wouldn't it be contagious if she tried, really tried, to make it so?

And wouldn't he make her feel the way Tay

had if they learned together how to live a life of passion?

"Let's . . . let's not make any decisions right now, Lee," she said, still hiding her face. "Why don't we just enjoy this afternoon together, since we have so little time alone?"

If she spent enough time with him, if she kissed him again and again, if they could be alone and relaxed and talk about their plans, she could find those thrilling sensations with him. Surely she could. She loved him. She had loved him for months now. He was a good man, Lee Kincaid. He was the best man for her.

He froze suddenly, and held her closer to him, his one arm crushing her against his chest while he reached for his pistol with the other. He cocked his head to listen; she held her breath and listened, too.

"There," he whispered. Lee pulled her even closer to him.

She heard it: the sound of a shod hoof striking stone. Near them, very near.

And with no more warning than that, two horses' heads appeared, coming out from behind a big oak tree. Two gray horses carrying Cade and Tay.

Heat welled up in her like a spring of hot water; it spurted up and up, climbing her neck and flooding her face. She was turning a bright, burning red, she knew it, but there was nothing at all she could do about it.

"Mr. Chisk-Ko!"

They walked the horses up to the edge of the blanket, and just sat there, looking down. Cade smiled. Tay's face flushed and filled with thunder.

"Sorry to disturb you two," Cade said. "We had no idea there was anyone around."

Lee turned Emily loose and clambered to his feet. She sat where she was without moving. She couldn't move if she tried, too mortified to move. Too horrified.

Too filled with unreasonable guilt. Tay's burning eyes had not once left her face.

But now they shifted to Lee. "*You* should've known *we* were around, Kincaid," he said, precisely in the tone he could've used had he, not Cade, been Lee's boss. "What do you think you're doing bringing a woman way out here if you can't even protect her?"

Lee sucked in his breath and took a step toward him, his fists doubled up. "You better watch your mouth, you arrogant sidewinder. Watch your tone and what you say to me."

Amazed, Cade looked from one of them to the other. "Hold on now, boys," he said, letting his gaze rest on Tay. "Hold on—there's no call for trouble here. We had no notion at all that we'd be interrupting your Sunday afternoon, Lee, Emily, and we're sorry. We just rode down in here looking for quail."

Emily dropped her gaze to the blanket and picked at it, her hands trembling, her face burning even hotter.

If only they'd go on, ride away, get on with their quail hunting!

But Tay couldn't rest, couldn't let well enough alone. "Emily should come with us," he said. "There could be bandits thick as cactus in this canyon, not to mention between here and the house."

Emily threw up her head and stared at him, glaring at him to be quiet.

"I don't mean to speak rude to your guest, Mr. Chisk-Ko," Lee said, speaking between clenched teeth, "but if he don't shut his mouth and stop insultin' me right now, I aim to drag him off that horse and shut it for him."

Tay stood up in his stirrup and started to step down.

Cade leaned over and laid his hand over Tay's on the saddle horn. "I'd consider it a favor if you didn't take him up on that, Tay."

For a long, incredibly tense moment all three men stayed exactly as they were while Tay and Lee tried to stare each other down.

"I'd appreciate it," Cade murmured.

Tay turned and glanced at him, then dropped back into his saddle.

Cade exchanged a few words with Lee that Emily didn't hear, and all the while Tay looked at her, boring his steely gaze of accusation straight into her. She knew she was blushing red as the blossoms of the flowers she'd picked, but she glared back at him anyway.

What are you doing here with him? In his arms?
It's none of your concern. You don't own me.

"We'll be heading on off for now, Emily," Cade said, carefully keeping his tone calm and easy. "See you at the house."

They turned the horses, Tay looking back at her over his shoulder the whole time, and then, thank God in Heaven, they rode away. Instead of feeling better, though, she felt worse.

She felt horrible. She had never felt so guilty in all her life.

Chapter 8

ay turned in the saddle and looked back toward the spot where they'd left Emily as he and Cade rode on down the canyon. His blood was roaring in his ears, his stomach churning. He had never felt so betrayed in all his life.

"We ought to keep an eye on them," he muttered. "Any tenderfoot who can't hear us coming wouldn't know a bandit was there until he galloped away with Emily thrown over his saddle." When he turned, Cade was watching him, frowning.

"Lee's a pretty good hand and an ex–Texas Ranger. I reckon he can take care of himself and Emily, too." The coolness in his voice came through loud and clear. "Maybe you'd better tell me what your problem is with him, Tay. If it's warranted, I'll fire him, but if not, I sure would hate to see the man quit the Running M right now. That'd put us in a hell of a bind."

Suddenly Tay remembered himself talking to Lee, heard the cold fury in his tone and the insulting words he'd said. He must've sounded crazy in the head.

"Uh . . . no, it's . . . nothing to fire a man over." He turned his head away from Cade and looked down at the ground. God help him, he was losing his mind!

"Well, what is it?"

"Nothing. We just don't like each other's looks, I guess, that's all."

They rode in silence for a while and he used it to try to whip his raging heart into shape. She didn't belong to him, she was betrothed to Lee. He had no right to feel possessive of her.

Oh, yes, he did. That kiss on the caprock gave him every right. *Damn it, what's she doing out here in the middle of nowhere wrapped in another man's arms?*

The turmoil kept roiling inside him the whole time they were hunting and all the way back to La Casa. He finally gave up trying to talk to Cade and just put all his effort into staying beside him and not turning back to look for Emily.

Finally, after a ride that seemed to take years, they rode into the yard at the ranch. Even taking care of his own horse and cleaning and dressing his own birds couldn't calm him, couldn't keep him from looking up every time he heard the noise of hooves, and at last he strode across to the house and threw himself up the stairs, four at a time. He would bathe and dress for supper, and if Emily wasn't home by then, he was going back for her, no matter what kind of trouble he caused.

Fortunately, that turned out not to be necessary. He was putting on his pants when he heard her voice outside his window in the yard, and by the time she came running up the stairs he had pulled his shirt over his head and had one boot on. Holding the other one, he opened his door and stepped out into her path.

She gave a startled cry and stopped short.

Her expression changed from surprise to anger in a heartbeat.

"*What* were you doing out there, insulting Lee like that? Insulting *me?* I can take care of myself, thank you, and so can Lee, if I need him to."

He heard, but he didn't even take in what she said. All his raw nerves could comprehend was that she had started in as if they were in the middle of a conversation already, as if they'd known each other forever. And the fact that her emotions were running at a fever pitch just like his.

It made him grin. He couldn't help it.

"Maybe I was a little out of line . . ."

She set her fists on her hips and advanced on him. "It's not funny! You very most certainly *were* out of line! I do not appreciate you carrying on like that—and in front of Cade, dear goodness, what must he think, and setting Lee into a jealous fit of quizzing me within an inch of my life about you when I don't even *know* you—"

A door slammed, somewhere behind him.

She threw her hand over her mouth and

leaned around him to see. "Be quiet!" she whispered. "That may be Cotannah!" No one appeared, so she glared at him again. "We can't risk Cotannah overhearing us," she murmured. "Leave me alone."

She moved around him after throwing him one last, furious glance. He turned to watch her go, and stopped her.

"Emily!"

She whirled and answered his stage whisper with one of her own. *"What?"*

"Have you been thinking about it?"

She hesitated for one beat too long, telling him that she already knew the answer to the next question she asked. "Thinking about what?"

"Admitting the truth. About us."

Even in the pale afternoon light that reached into the hallway he could see the color rise into her cheeks again.

"No!" She turned and fled to her room.

He dropped his boot to the floor and smiled as he put it on. Yes. She felt it, too.

As she bathed and dressed for supper, Emily alternately racked her brain for an excuse to escape it and lectured herself that she couldn't let anything keep her away from the table. Never, ever, could she let Tay think she was trying to avoid him.

And she had to show Lee that there was nothing between her and Tay. She had to *prove* it to him—she could not tolerate going through another inquisition like the one he'd put her through this afternoon when Tay and Cade had left them.

She finished washing, snatched up her fresh dress, and jerked it down over her head. He *had* to believe that he had no effect on her whatsoever, that she was in love with Lee. Dear God, he *had* to leave her alone! The way he had behaved in the canyon proved that beyond a doubt. Why, he would rip apart the whole fabric of their lives if he didn't get hold of himself.

She put the finishing touches on her hair, threw down her brush, and lifted her chin to her reflection in the mirror. She would. She would do it for Cotannah's sake, no matter how much she wanted to go into his arms and have him kiss her again.

And, she thought, as she left her room and started down the stairs, she would not compare any more kisses! She loved Lee and she loved dear little Katie—they were depending on her; it was her duty to take care of them. It was completely unworthy of her to compare physical sensations when deeper, more delicate feelings were much more important.

From the middle of the stairs she saw through the open front door that Cade, Tay, and Lee—keeping a definite distance from Tay—stood in a loose circle outside on the porch in the darkening evening, talking to a dusty vaquero who was still sitting his horse. Something about the way they listened to the man, an alertness in the way they held themselves, struck fear in her. He must be carrying word of more *bandidos*.

When she reached the entry hallway she stood and watched them all for a moment, then ran through the house and into the dining room to find Maggie.

In one glance, Maggie recognized the look on her face. "He was riding at a long lope even though his horse is nearly done in," Maggie said, negotiating her way toward the table with full dishes from the kitchen in both hands. "I just hope we haven't lost another hundred head today."

"I just hope they won't dare come near La Casa again," Emily said, lowering her voice as Maggie made a face at her and glanced over her shoulder to signal that Oleana was close behind her. "We were really lucky last time—"

Oleana, who usually became hysterical at the very mention of raiders, burst through the doorway carrying an enormous platter of fragrant grilled quail. Emily smiled at her instead of finishing the sentence.

"*Senorita* Mimi," the cook cried softly, "can you keep *Senorita* Cotannah out of *mi cocina mañana, por favor?* Take her out for a ride or some-thing?" She clamped her lips together and glanced over her shoulder as if imitating what Maggie had just done.

Emily laughed. "You all remind me of a row of clowns . . ."

Cotannah came in behind Oleana carrying a tall, decidedly lopsided stack cake, so lopsided that she had to support it with one hand to keep it on the plate. She went straight to the sideboard, set the cake down, and glanced furtively toward the hallway before bending over the open sideboard's door to rummage around inside with her free hand.

"I can't let him see this," she wailed. "Maggie, Mimi, don't even mention dessert at supper. Oleana and I have decided to serve some oranges instead, and I'll make a cobbler tomorrow. Tay likes blackberry cobbler better than cake, anyway."

Oleana made a face at Cotannah's back and rolled her eyes at Emily in a pleading look. *Por favor?* she mouthed.

Emily smiled and nodded. "But Katie and I want you to come riding with us tomorrow," she said brightly. "You don't even like to cook, 'Tannah, so please say you'll come with us."

Cotannah whirled on her, horrified, waving the tin cake cover that she'd found in the sideboard.

"Shhh!" she hissed, looking toward the hall again. "Don't let Tay hear you say I don't like to cook."

When Tay didn't immediately appear in the doorway, she dropped the cover over the falling cake and ran to Emily. "I have to do *something* to get his attention," she murmured. "He's ignoring me completely."

"He is not," Maggie said, arranging the dishes on the table. "Good heavens, 'Tannah, he had supper with you at the fiesta, he danced with you all evening . . ."

"But he must not have liked me, because he

hasn't spent one single minute with me yesterday or today!"

"Give him time. He and Cade have a lot to talk about," Maggie said.

The men's voices sounded in the hallway and Cotannah shushed the women again. The men fell silent, too, as they entered the dining room.

Tay's huge frame seemed to fill it up. Emily tried not to look at him, but she couldn't not see him—it was like that first moment when she turned and he was there beneath the lantern on the porch, looking at her with his hot silver eyes.

And now—as then—they lingered on her. She found it hard to breathe.

"Ladies," he said, and acknowledged them all before he went to the place at the long table that Maggie absently indicated to him, stopping on the way to hold Cotannah's chair for her.

Good. Maybe sitting beside Cotannah would remind him why he was here. Thank goodness Emily was all the way across the table from him tonight.

But even there she wasn't safe, for when she turned away he brought her attention back to him again.

"And how are you this evening, Miss Emily?"

He spoke pleasantly, in his deep rumble of a voice, in a parody of pretending a politely distant relationship—after the way he had behaved in the canyon! She gritted her teeth.

"Did you enjoy your ride back from the caprock the other morning? Let's see, that was yesterday, wasn't it?"

Cotannah said quickly, "Did you see Mimi out there?"

"Yes. I was running, she was riding, and our paths crossed on top of the world. We shared the beautiful view from up there."

Emily's heart jumped, racketing, up into her throat. Why didn't he just tell them everything? Next he'd be describing the *kiss* that they'd shared.

Cotannah turned to look at Emily. "Mimi, you didn't mention that you'd seen Tay."

Emily felt as if every eye in the room was fixed on her face. Her hot face, which must be extremely red by now. "Of course not," she said coolly. "I attached no significance to the meeting."

There. That should put him in his place.

"At the time she seemed to think it surprising, at least, that I had found her private hideaway," Tay said, a teasing edge in his tone.

Dear Lord, what was he *doing*? She had to get control of the conversation. "I-it offers a beautiful view," she said formally. "How d-do you think it compares with your mountains at h-home, Mr. Nashoba?"

He looked directly at Emily, the corners of his mouth—his beautiful mouth—lifted in a bland smile. She, however, saw the teasing glint deep in his eyes.

"The two places are so different, they're hard to compare. But you know that from traveling through the Nation on your way here. What do *you* think?"

"Each is wild and beautiful," she said, "b-but in different ways, as you say."

What a stupid remark. How was it that only two days ago at the fiesta they had been quoting poetry to each other and matching wits? His kiss had shattered not only her body, but her brain.

He nodded slowly, however, as if she'd said something truly sage. His body was so thick and substantial, it seemed almost muscle-bound, heavy with muscles in the shoulders, chest, and thighs. But he moved with the grace of a wild animal, a raw power that contrasted sharply with his starched, full-sleeved white shirt and finely made breeches.

"Emily?" Lee said. "I reckon I'm supposed to sit here beside you."

With a start of surprise, she turned to look at him, but instead she saw Tay, naked to the waist as he had been early yesterday morning, his coppery skin covered with a shining sheen of sweat. Sweat popped out on her own face— she absolutely, positively, was losing her mind. What was *wrong* with her?

Lee sat down beside her and threw her an irritated glance; she realized she hadn't even answered him. She didn't even remember what he'd said. She looked down at her plate and tried to slow her heartbeat, tried to get her breath.

Maggie broke the tension. "Cade, what did that vaquero say?"

"That all of you ladies need to stay close to the house for the next few days."

"Sounds like a challenge to me," Maggie said in a tone that mimicked his, but hers had an edge to it and she looked up at him with worry in her eyes.

Just as everyone was seated, Mama came in. "The twins are asleep already," she announced, "and I deserve a medal on a ribbon."

"You also deserve a civilized dinner conversation," Cade said, "but I'm afraid we have to talk survival instead, while we're all here together."

"*Bandidos?*" she said tersely as she slid into the chair he held for her.

"Yes, we've just had news."

"Then tell us."

Emily looked at her mother in wonder. Three years ago she could not have imagined southern gentlewoman Amanda Louise Harrington living on the wild border between Mexico and Texas, much less talking so calmly of its dangers. Life on Las Manzanitas had changed Mama as much as it had changed her and Maggie.

She would think about *that* during supper and forget about Tay; she would completely forget that he was there and give all her attention to Lee.

"A band of eight or ten Mexicans tried to take our horse herd on San Fernando Creek today," Cade said and accepted the platter of quail.

"Our *good* horses!" Maggie gasped.

Emily looked around for Oleana and was thankful to see that she'd gone back out to the kitchen.

"We only had four men anywhere near there, but they started a running gun battle and finally drove the raiders off. We lost about twenty head of horses and one man was slightly wounded."

"Is he at the bunkhouse?" Maggie asked.

"Yes, but you needn't go out there. Luis's wife has already dressed the wound."

"San Fernando Creek is so close to the house," Maggie said. Suddenly she sounded completely forlorn.

Emily reached out and patted her arm. Besides the recent attack, raiders had invaded La Casa Grande, had even gotten inside it, four years ago—just after Cade and Maggie had arrived. Maggie would never let it show, but she was nearly as afraid of the bandits as Oleana.

"San Fernando *is* way too close for comfort," Cade said, "so I'm asking all of you women to stay near La Casa, within the perimeter of the outbuildings, while we mount more patrols and ride out to look around a little."

"I'll ride with you, of course," Tay said.

"Right," Cade said briskly. "Lee, after we eat we'll plan on how many men we can spare from the artesian well and the fencing." He looked from Lee to Maggie and gave her a reassuring smile. "We'll be a lot more careful this time and they won't get anywhere near headquarters again." He waited until Maggie smiled back at him before he spoke again. "You ladies aren't touching your food," he said. "Better eat—you're going to need your strength."

Emily felt a sudden, deep kinship with Oleana. If she let it, this roaring fear in her blood—which certainly was not all caused by the thought of *bandidos*—could easily bring on a fine bout of screaming hysteria.

Cotannah sneaked out of her room and down the stairs, tiptoed through the back hallway to the pantry, and felt around in the semidarkness for the basket she had left on the meal box. She held it stiffly in her hand instead of sliding the handle over her arm so it wouldn't bump against the wall as she crept on her way toward the back door.

She set her jaw, held her breath, resisted the voice inside her head screaming for her to *hurry*, and put her mind to maintaining the sleeping silence around her. It was a long way from here to Maggie and Cade's room, but Cade had ears like a fox, he always had, and he'd be getting up soon to go on patrol. If he caught her disobeying his order to stay near the house, she wouldn't have to wait for the bandits to kill her.

She smiled to herself and touched the handle of her knife, riding deep in her pocket. *Bandidos* had better stay out of her way—all the bad men in Mexico couldn't keep her from picking blackberries and making a cobbler for Tay. She would have to practice some more to learn to make cakes, but she had made cobblers before. Uncle Jumper always said her pies were better than Aunt Ancie's.

But Cade wouldn't hear her, and bandits could never catch her once she was mounted on Pretty Feather. That mare had outrun three different racehorses.

Cotannah moved no more than an inch at a time as she opened the back door without making a sound. *Nothing* would stop her from finding the berries so she'd have something to talk about with Tay, something to get his attention. She might even get to see him a few minutes from now—on his morning run as Emily had done—because he might run early before riding on patrol with Cade. If not, at supper this evening he would praise her for her cobbler and she would tell him all her adventures of going to get the berries.

Luck was with her all the way across the yard and into the stables. She didn't disturb the silence of the sweet-smelling summer morning at all, and she found Cade's and Tay's favorite gray horses out in the catch pen. So when they came out to go on patrol, they probably wouldn't notice that Pretty Feather was gone from inside the stable.

No one was about yet except, of course, for the men in the lookout tower, but it was still far too dark for them to see her in the black cloak she'd worn. It was making her sweat, but she had to keep it on until she was out of the yard and into the trees, at least.

She shushed the sleepy horses, giving extra

pats to Emily's rowdy, noisy Sache. She saddled Pretty Feather, then led the filly out the back door and away from the lookouts. As soon as she had trees between her and the house, she mounted, and as soon as she'd crossed the creek, she risked a short trot.

Luck stayed with her as long as the darkness did. She was within a mile of the blackberry patch when the sun came up and she crossed the trail that the Mexicans were traveling.

Chapter 9

Emily threw on her wrapper and went downstairs as soon as she heard Cade and Tay leave the house. If she knew her sister, Maggie would be sitting on the veranda now, thinking about Cade riding into danger.

The best thing for Maggie and for her was to keep each other company. She could help Maggie get her mind off the bandits, and Maggie could help her get her mind off . . . Tay. In fact, they might just plan some more of the details for her wedding to Lee.

That was a good idea, she told herself as she tightened the knot of the soft belt at her waist and ran down the stairs. There were so many plans still to be made and carried out that they couldn't possibly have the wedding early, so when she and Maggie were done she would make a list and show it to Lee so he'd stop all that talk about marrying sooner.

Sure enough, when Emily opened the door and stepped out onto the porch, which was washed pink and yellow with light from the rising sun, Maggie was there, pacing up and

down. She had already dressed in a riding skirt
and boots and a blue cotton shirt that exactly
matched her eyes.

"Oh no," Emily teased, "does the fact that
you're dressed to ride at sunup mean that we'll
all have to get to work before breakfast?"

Maggie whirled, and welcomed her with a
hug. "It means I need to be ready for anything," she said. "Cade's on patrol and I'm
holding down the fort." She gestured toward
the low table that held a coffeepot and mugs.
"Oleana's so nervous over the bandits coming
all the way in to the San Fernando Creek that
she's not only dressed but has made pots and
pots of coffee, and now she's out in the kitchen
cooking enough food to feed everybody in
Texas."

"I just hope it's not tamales for breakfast,"
Emily said lightly. "You two need to calm
down—we have lots of defenses, and Cade
and Tay out on patrol."

"But they can't be more than one place at a
time, and there're thousands of *bandidos*," Maggie said, starting to pace again. "And when I
woke up this morning I just had a feeling—"

A shout from the lookout tower stopped her
words.

Then they heard thundering hoofbeats off in
the distance. Maggie ran down the steps and
toward the tower as the shout from the top of it
came again.

"*Caballo sin jinete!*"

Horse without a rider.

Cold fear clutched Emily's heart. Tay! Could
something have happened to Tay?

That was insane. He was a big, powerful man, well armed, no doubt, and he was with Cade. If one of them was hurt, the other would be bringing him in.

The noise of the galloping horse sounded closer. Emily ran to the corner of the porch to look to the south of the house. The lookouts had used field glasses, no doubt, for the horse was no more than a small object, moving fast on the side of the trees lining the creek, too far away for her to see whether it carried a saddle or a person or both.

Something must have terrified it, because it was coming fast, running flat out. The seconds seemed to take hours to pass, but finally it was past the east pasture and heading for the house. Emily stared, closed her eyes, and looked again.

Pretty Feather? Who had taken her out? Cotannah was still asleep . . .

A small, very fast horse with bright bay and white markings was coming straight to the house as if coming home. It had to be Pretty Feather.

Maggie rushed back toward the live oak tree and stood near the hitching rail. But Pretty Feather was having none of that. She came straight toward Emily, who ran down the steps and into the yard, then stood still so as not to spook her.

The filly's eyes were wide open and rolling, foam dripped from her muzzle, her blaze face was black with sweat. The mare was terrified— no telling how far she had run.

She came to a sliding stop within a yard of
Emily and stood there, trembling, trying to get
her breath. That was Cotannah's saddle, all
right, but Cotannah would have had to leave
the house in the black dark. She wouldn't have
done such a thing . . .

Then the filly dropped her head and Emily
started walking slowly toward her, crooning
comforting sounds of nonsensical words to
calm her, holding out her hand to let the filly
smell her. She hadn't taken two steps when she
saw the berry basket.

"Cotannah's the one hurt," she called out to
Maggie, who was approaching from the other
side. "Dear Lord, she went after those blackberries—"

Then she saw the piece of paper tied to the
handle of the basket and stopped dead in her
tracks. With a strangled cry, she pointed at it.
"Oh, Maggie . . ."

By the time Emily could make her feet move
again, Maggie had torn the paper loose and
was holding it to read, her shaking hand making it flutter as if in a wind. She was as pale as
buttermilk and pressing her lips together as if
fighting valiantly not to scream.

When she looked up at Emily, she didn't
even try to talk. She slapped one hand over her
mouth and offered the ragged note to Emily.

Emily smoothed the note out on the saddle
and tried to read the ornately beautiful pen-
manship, written in the blackest of ink. And in
Spanish. She had learned a lot of that language
in the past three years, but this was different

somehow, it didn't make sense to her. She did, however, recognize the last word of the signature: Cortina.

When she glanced up questioningly, Maggie nodded.

"Cotannah," she said in a grim voice so thick it could have choked her to silence. "Cortina has her. He wants to trade her for ten thousand American dollars. In gold." She gave a quick gasp as if desperate for air. "At sundown tomorrow at the spring in the Canyon Borrecitas."

Emily and Maggie stared at each other through a roaring silence.

"What does that mean, the phrase at the end, *la ley de fuga?*" Emily asked.

"That they'll kill her at the first sign we're attempting to rescue her."

Emily felt her blood drain from her. Her lips turned so cold, she could hardly speak. She couldn't even *consider* that Cotannah might be killed.

"What'll they do to her before we can get there, though, Maggie? This isn't fair. It just absolutely is not fair that Cotannah is in their clutches . . ."

"Cade," Maggie whispered, her lips barely moving. "We must call Cade in."

For the first time, Emily became aware that people were coming from every direction, vaqueros, children, Mama, Oleana. Maggie began shouting the news and then a rapid series of orders: for the men in the tower to fire the trouble signal; for Jorge to ride to *Senora* Pilar's

ranch and ask her to try to communicate with
Cortina; for the stableboys to take care of Pretty
Feather and saddle some other horses; for
Oleana to pack provisions.

The booming of the big Sharps rifle that the
guards kept in the tower roared her down. The
sound would carry for miles: two shots, then a
long pause, then two more.

"I wish she had woken me!" Emily cried. "I
wish I'd gone with her."

Maggie grabbed Emily's hands and nearly
squeezed off her fingers. "No! If you'd gone,
then you'd *both* be hostages!"

Oleana shrieked and began sobbing. "I
should have forbidden her *mi co-cina*," she
wailed. "I should have said not to make a pie
because she could not bake it in my o-ven!"

Maggie turned on her. "The packs!" she
shouted over the sound of Oleana's weeping.
"Stop crying and go make the packs, Oleana,
pronto!"

Her voice sounded brisk and nearly steady,
but her eyes still shone with terror. She met
Emily's gaze and then turned instantly away—
it must have been like looking in a mirror.

Emily's heart split open. What an idiot she'd
been, whining to Cotannah about losing her,
her best friend, when she married Tay and went
to live in the Choctaw Nation. *This* was what it
meant to truly lose her friend.

Within twenty minutes Emily had dressed
and found a child of Oleana's to get food while
she saddled Sache, found a pistol and a rifle,

and had them loaded and ready. All the while she kept her mind racing, trying to think exactly what to say to Cade so he would let her ride with the men to Cotannah's rescue.

When Cade and Tay rode into the yard at a gallop, Emily looked out the window and saw Maggie look up from her personal inspection of the freshly saddled horses and run to the men, waving Cortina's note. Sache was standing, saddled, ground-tied at the foot of the steps.

Emily strapped the pistol holster's belt around her waist, picked up the rifle, and walked out onto the porch. The whole house and yard was one big beehive of activity, and she took advantage of that to fix the rifle in her scabbard, tie her packs to the saddle, and mount Sache unnoticed.

Thank goodness Mama was keeping watch over the twins upstairs so they wouldn't be aware of what had happened to Cotannah or she could never have escaped Cade's attention this far. She picked up the reins and turned Sache around so she could watch Cade.

Surely he couldn't refuse to let her go when she was all fit and ready.

He looked up, saw her start toward him, and snapped at her. "Where do you think you're going?"

She forced herself to hold his black, burning gaze. "I'm riding to help rescue Cotannah," she said, proud that the words came out so evenly, that her voice sounded so calm.

She walked Sache forward.

"We don't need that responsibility," he said.

"Taking care of Cotannah will be all we can handle."

"She may need a woman's help."

Cade's eyes never wavered, but a twitch at the corner of his mouth proved she had struck a nerve.

"That's right," Maggie cried. "Mimi, *I'll* go in—"

Emily kept her eyes on Cade's. "No. Miranda and Cole need at least one parent with them," she said.

Maggie said nothing, and Emily knew she had spoken the thought that had stopped Maggie's words in midsentence.

"Forget either one of you going," Cade said in a dismissive tone. "You both know it's impossible."

He crushed Cortina's note in his hand and stepped down off his horse to speak to Maggie. But there was no hope there. Maggie wouldn't plead with him to change his mind because she thought Emily's presence would hinder the men, and she feared for Emily's safety. That was why she had volunteered to go in Emily's place—Maggie thought she'd be a help, not a hindrance, and could look out for herself.

And that was true. No matter how scared she was, Maggie always did what she had to do, which was why everyone always said she was brave. But this time Maggie couldn't protect her sister. Emily had to do this herself.

She squared her shoulders and took a deep, ragged breath. So. There was nothing else for it: She would have to enlist Tay's help. She hadn't even looked at him since they rode into the yard. But now she looked straight at him.

"I have to go help her," she blurted, believing somehow that he would understand. "She's my best friend and it's my fault she took this chance and went out alone this morning."

His eyes narrowed in his shadowed face. He was wearing one of Cade's Texas-styled hats, a tan-colored one, and a tan vest over a white shirt. His jaw was set at a determined slant and he looked as dangerous as any hardcase that had ever ridden through Las Manzanitas.

And he *didn't* sympathize with her. His chiseled face tightened into even harder lines, and she felt a sinking inside that dragged her toward despair.

"How can you think we'll let you go?" His tone was as hard as his face. "And how could such a stupid decision on her part be your fault?"

"I didn't tell her I met you on the caprock," she said, and somehow, upset and worried as she was, she suddenly could taste his kiss again.

Resolutely she pushed the memory away.

"Why would not telling her that make her leave the house in the dark of night after Cade specifically forbade it?" he shot back, completely disbelieving.

"We're best friends—we tell each other everything," she said desperately. "And at supper when you mentioned we saw each other, she commented that I hadn't told her about it, remember?"

"You explained at the table that our meeting was of no importance to you," he said coldly. "Why would it be important to her?"

"Because everything about you is important to her," Emily said stubbornly. "She wants your attention. She was on her way to pick blackberries to make you a pie when Cortina captured her, I just know it."

"I thought you were saying Cotannah's foolish behavior was your fault. Now you're trying to blame it on me."

For one horrible second she thought she'd gone too far, that she had lost whatever chance she had with him.

"Cotannah alone made that decision," he said. He spoke roughly, almost carelessly, but Emily had a strange, fleeting feeling that he was trying to comfort her.

She didn't know what else to say, so she watched him and waited. He didn't move a muscle, didn't say a word, and while she waited for his decision, the truth hit her in a huge wave that threatened to wreck her utterly and wash away the pieces. Cotannah's own decision or not, Emily had hurt her and she had to tell her she was sorry.

"I have to go," she said simply. "I have to go help Cotannah or I'll die."

He looked at her for the length of one more heartbeat, then turned to Cade, who was telling the stableboys to hitch up a team to the coach. When they ran for the stables, Maggie touched her husband's arm and gestured toward Tay.

"Let Emily come with us," Tay said when Cade looked at him. "I'll be responsible for her."

The words put Emily back together again, filled her with relief. He had saved her.

"I know she can shoot—we fought the bandits together before."

"I know, because I taught her," Cade snapped. "All right, let her go if that's what you want. There's no time to argue it, we have to get moving." He turned and signaled for one of the vaqueros, then reached out and put his arm around Maggie to draw her closer while he talked to Tay. "I'd bet the ranch that Cortina's men are watching us right now," he said. "So we'll have to outfigure the horse-stealing hide peelers. I'll take an army of guards and the coach and extra horses and set out on the Corpus Christi Road so it'll appear that I'm going to the bank for the ransom money."

"Where will you stop to double back?" Tay asked.

Emily marveled at how completely they had both turned to the business at hand. Their voices held an edge of steel that sent a surge of excitement into her blood. They sounded incredibly confident and cool and dispassionate now that their first shock and anger had cooled.

They would get Cotannah back. Cade, she knew, was as tough as they came—he had survived a rough rogue's life for a lot of years, and now he was holding this ranch while the neighbors were running for the protection of town. Tay had been through the horrors of the

War of the Rebellion and had come out a hero. They would save Cotannah. And Emily would help.

"I'll slip away from the coach at Seguro Bend—remember where we saw the deer on our way up from Corpus?"

Tay nodded.

"The Mexicans will see the coach rolling on toward town and they won't be as much on guard for us to sneak up on them."

"In the meantime, I'll pick up Cotannah's trail," Tay said, "and you'll catch up to me."

And me, Emily thought. She didn't say it, though; she was afraid to push them.

"Right. Keep lots of extra guards posted," Cade told Maggie. "There's no telling what Cortina may do."

"Don't worry," she whispered. "We can hold the ranch. Just bring our 'Tannah back."

"We will." Cade stood looking straight into Maggie's eyes, his hand resting lightly at the nape of her neck. The way they looked at each other made Emily feel a hollow ache inside— she could see the communication flashing back and forth between them as clearly as she could have heard it if they'd spoken. Yet somehow it went deeper than words and it flowed stronger.

As it had done more than once between her and Tay.

She pushed that thought away as Cade bent his head and kissed Maggie one time, hard and quick, and then he let her go. The coach drove up and he tied his horse to the back of it, then motioned to his guards to gather around it. They were all alert and ready to ride.

All of them together would save Cotannah before anything bad happened to her, Emily thought, as Tay moved out, too, in the opposite direction, and Sache started to follow. She waved good-bye to Maggie, her throat so full suddenly that she couldn't speak.

Tay silently cursed himself for a fool as he led the way around the north side of the house and started across the back of the place, keeping to the cover of the outbuildings and trees. Why, *why* had he let his infernal heart drive him into such an untenable position? Why had he not told her to stay home, as any sane man would have done?

But he felt better having her with him, protecting her himself, rather than leaving her to chance here at the ranch. *He wanted her with him.*

His blood was rising hot and his skin was going cold and nerveless; his senses were opening in all directions; he could feel himself focusing in for battle. Here was something he could do to make one thing right in the world, and he could do it and protect Emily at the same time. He needed this challenge. The muscles in his calves itched and burned with the desire for action, the urge to lift his horse, Eagle, into a lope and ride to the rescue.

They reached the stable and rode up the west side of it. At the end of the building, he spotted the track of Cotannah's mare that Cade had described to him. Emily rode up beside him.

"I know the way to the blackberry patch," she said. "I think I can save us some time."

He caught her scent—sweet roses mixed with her own warm woman-fragrance—and suddenly he tasted her lips again, as surely as if his mouth had just left hers. He clenched his hands around the reins.

What was he *doing*, bringing her along? Any wet-eared boy would know better than to bring another woman into this kind of danger, yet he couldn't help himself.

"We hope they'll follow Cade and the coach and not see us at all," he said abruptly, "but as a precaution we'll stay to cover as much as we can. I'll lead."

"How can you lead when you don't know where you're going?"

"Ah! How can *you* when you don't know what you're doing?"

She flashed an angry glance at him. "Some men have a terrible need to control everyone around them," she said haughtily. She smooched to the mare and rode out a little bit in front of him.

His anger flared suddenly. He sped up, reached out fast and grabbed one of her reins, and pulled Sache closer to his mount.

"In this case I fully *intend* to control everyone around me," he said harshly, "and you will cooperate. You begged me to bring you along. Therefore, you will do exactly as I say."

To his consternation, Emily's brown eyes filled with sudden tears. "Why did I ever think that you're different from the rest?" she cried.

"The rest of what?"

"The rest of the *men,* always bossing people."

She swallowed hard, and he could tell that it took a herculean effort for her not to cry. One large tear trembled on her thick lashes, but she held it back.

"Get your hand off my mount!"

He tried to turn loose of her mare's bridle, but his fingers refused to move. If he let go of her now, in this state, no telling what she would do.

"We're letting our emotions carry us away," he said. "We're so worried about Cotannah, we aren't thinking straight."

She sat back in the saddle and relaxed a little bit. "We never think straight when we're together, Tay. Haven't you noticed that?"

"I've noticed."

He set his jaw grimly and picked up the pace. That was true and it was one more reason why he should have left her at home.

Chapter 10

They rode in silence. Tay finally let go of Sache's bridle and dropped his hand to his side while he glanced down at the ground to make sure they were still following Pretty Feather's trail.

Suddenly Emily felt lonely for the sound of his voice. "I'm so glad you spoke up for me so I could come with you," she said. "Thanks, Tay."

He glanced up at her with a look in his eyes that tore at her heart. "I only hope that it really was the right thing for you. It's more dangerous out here than back at La Casa, and I knew that better than you did." His voice was rough with a tension that made him tighten one of his hands on the reins and make a fist with the other. "I'll do my best to protect you, Emily. I'll die if I can't because I couldn't live with another regret like the one I already carry."

He said that quickly, as if he had to, as if it were a relief to get it out. But then he stopped. Whatever this was that he was telling her was

not something he talked about often; she knew
that.

"What is the one that you already carry?"

"Seven brave boys who are ten years dead."

Astounded, she gaped at him. He gave her a
quick, sharp glance before he looked ahead
again, motioning to the trees lining the creek
where he wanted to go. They rode into them
single-file, crossed the creek, and then rode out
of the big yard that surrounded La Casa and its
outbuildings and onto the prairie, keeping to
the brush as much as possible.

When they rode side by side once more, Tay
took up his tale again.

"They died in the War," he said bitterly, "in
the white man's Civil War, and I'm the one
who gave the order that sent them to their
deaths." His voice became raspy and then it
grew rougher still. "Since I can't bring them
back, I'm bound to trying to make life better for
the families they left behind—and for all our
People."

On the last word, his voice broke. He looked
at her straight, as if daring her to react to that
show of emotion, then glanced at the ground
again. With one sparse gesture, he helped her
spot Cotannah's trail—she marveled that he
could be so emotionally wrought up and still
be so intent on their purpose.

"Tay, you can't blame yourself. Those boys
went to war. People get killed in wars."

He gave a skeptical shrug. "It was the Battle
of Honey Creek," he said, "and I was new to

command. I was trying to be Jeb Stuart, so I
formed them into a scouting band to harass the
enemy and I sent them straight as shot arrows
into an ambush."

He picked up his horse into a faster trot.
Emily smooched to Sache and kept up with
him.

"If it's been ten years," she said thoughtfully,
"then I doubt that anything I say will help heal
the wound. But I can tell you that you're going
about it in the right way: Anything I ever do to
help erase another person's hurt erases some of
my own as well."

He looked at her, startled, as if that were an
answer he hadn't been expecting. Then he
smiled.

She smiled back.

So *that* was why he'd ordered her so harshly
to do as he said. He couldn't bear to see her *or*
Cotannah hurt or killed while they were his
responsibility. He would die if he couldn't
protect them; he had said that and he had
meant it.

Her heart lifted a little. Tay *wasn't* like other
men, like her father or even like Lee, who
needed to control people and situations. At
least he had a reason.

They rode in companionable near-silence for
half an hour at a fast, long trot. Finally Tay
reined in.

"Here," he said. "Here's where they caught
her."

The ground was sandier there, along the
edge of an arroyo, and even she could pick out

at least three distinctive tracks among the many
hoofprints trampled into the earth. Cotannah
had tried to run, but the dry creek bed had
stopped her.

"I can't stand it," Emily cried, beating her
saddle pommel with her fist. "I can see it all
happening!" She pulled Sache around. "Let's
go. Hurry, Tay, we've got to find her. I can feel
her fear in my own flesh and bones."

"Hold on a minute. We don't know which
way to go."

He swung down off his horse and knelt in
the dirt to feel some of the tracks, then stood up
and squinted into the distance, walking back
and forth a short way to look at several scattered hoofprints.

"They caught her here, wrote the ransom
note, and sent her filly home. Now we don't
know Cotannah's track anymore. The bandits
split into three bunches here and we can't
know which group has her."

"Is there one very deep track?" she asked,
riding Sache around to look at the confusing,
overlapping hoofprints. "Cade says that means
a horse carrying double."

"It might. But it might also mean one heavy
bandit. Cotannah doesn't weigh much,
anyway."

Emily pulled up. "I know! The blackberry
patch where she was headed is near the
Suarezes' ranch house—they're one of the
neighbors who have fled into town to escape
the raiders. Maybe they took her there."

He pushed his hat back on his head and

squinted up at her. "How far is it from that Canyon Borrecitas where they're supposed to meet Cade tomorrow?"

"Half a day's ride southwest."

"Are there pens there to hold cattle?"

"Yes! It's a working ranch, only abandoned this spring."

"I don't know whether you noticed," he said, "but some of them held a bunch of cows right over there near that oak motte while the others caught Cotannah. They may send a couple of men back to Mexico with the herd now or they may not."

Warmth spread through her insides, which were so deeply cold with fear for Cotannah, warmth at the way he spoke to her as if she were his equal at reading sign. He respected her, her abilities, her opinions.

He reached for his reins. "It's a good possibility. Point the way."

Sure enough, one bunch of the bandits had struck out in the direction of the Suarez Rancho.

"Cotannah *was* brought this way, Tay," Emily blurted. "I can feel it."

He only nodded and kept his eyes on the ground, riding a length ahead.

She sucked in a desperate breath and prayed: *Oh, dear God, give Cotannah strength. Keep her safe. Give her strength.*

"H-h-how many of them are there, can you tell?" she called.

"Looks like six or seven."

She slumped in her saddle, then turned to

look over her shoulder for Cade. But he couldn't possibly be anywhere near them yet— the coach wouldn't travel as fast as a single horse, and the ride back from the Seguro Bend would take some time. She shivered. Even when Cade joined them, they would be only three against six or seven.

Six or seven in the one bunch. By the time she and Tay found Cotannah, all the bunches might be back together again. Suddenly she was as cold as if the sun had vanished behind a cloud, as if winter had come. And she was thankful that Tay Nashoba was with her.

Dear Lord, bless Cotannah, who was all alone when they swept down upon her. Please hold her in the hollow of your hand.

"They've split up again, but it's probably only to try to fool any pursuers," Tay said, as calmly as if he were discussing the weather. "Let's swing out in an arc and try to cut their trail farther on."

Numbly she let Sache follow him, but she did pick up her reins. She tried to watch where they were going, tried to see and read the trail, but everything blurred in front of her. She had to get a grip on herself, had to stop imagining what was going on up ahead and get her mind on the here and now. Tay might miss something. She might find something that would lead them to Cotannah.

But he saw it first.

He made a quick, incoherent sound, just a swift intake of breath, but the urgency in it brought her back to herself. She stood up in her stirrups and stared past him.

"Oh," she cried, "oh, Tay!"

Up ahead, a stone's throw away, Cotannah's cloak lay on the ground like a huge, black, fallen bird. Half in and half out of the shade of a small, gnarled mesquite tree, it rose and fell in sun-streaked hills and dark, shaded valleys. Her breath wouldn't come. Was . . . could it be . . . that Cotannah was under it?

The instant she had the thought she knew it wasn't true. And she knew, in a way she hadn't known even in her worst imaginings, that it might be better if she were. The whole world around her suddenly became as clear to her as that knowledge—every sense she possessed sharpened and grew keener still.

She and Tay were Cotannah's only hope. She must overcome this horror so she could find her friend.

Tay rode to the cloak, bent from the saddle and picked it up, looked it over carefully.

"She surely couldn't have dropped it for a clue for us without their noticing," Emily said, forcing her mind into motion so it could fight down her fear.

"No," he said. "Even in the dark, if they caught her before sunup, it would've gone billowing down and scared the horses." He threw the cloak across the front of his saddle. "Let's go on a little farther and see if there's anything else."

It wasn't five minutes until they found one of

her boots, and then, a few seconds later, the other.

"Dear Lord," Emily said, as Tay got down and picked them up, tied their laces together. "Oh, dear Lord, Tay, what if they've taken all her clothes . . ."

She couldn't even finish the sentence, but she held out her hand for the boots, and he gave them up for her to hang across the horn of her saddle.

"I doubt that they have," he said too quickly. "Probably they're trying to discourage her from attempting to escape—trying to make her feel vulnerable."

A rude sound, something between a snort and a choking, burst out of her mouth. "They ought to know they accomplished that the first minute they touched her," she cried. "They don't have to treat her like this!"

He said nothing, just walked back to his horse and got on. *Stripping her of her shoes may be nothing compared to how they are treating her now.*

The thought hung in the air between them, but neither of them said it. They just made the horses move even faster as they continued farther on the trail.

Then it was a banner of white cloth, caught on the thorns of a huisache bush, waving in the wind like a beckoning hand. Without a word, both of them put their heels to their horses and loped toward it, although Emily wanted nothing so much as to turn and gallop the other way. She could not bear any more of this. What, *what* would be the next thing they would find?

A scrap of color caught at the corner of her eye as she went by, and she turned to look, but then it was gone. And so was the heart within her, because they passed the turnoff they always took to go to the Suarez place with its garden and berries. The berries sweet enough to make a pie.

The white, flapping flag was Cotannah's petticoat.

At least it wasn't her chemise, Emily thought, as Tay gathered it up. She had to think so her heart wouldn't feel. They could have taken her anywhere.

"I wonder if we should leave these things where we found them," she blurted. "What about Cade? Would they lead him to us?"

He didn't pause in removing the cloth from the thorns. "Cade will find us. He can track a mosquito through a thunderstorm. And we'll find Cotannah, so we need to take her clothes back to her."

His voice was rich and low, sure and serene. Comforting. But it didn't comfort her. He didn't know where Cotannah was, either. She reached out and took the wadded, soft cloth from his hands.

He turned restlessly in the saddle, sweeping his gaze across the land. "Cortina fixed that petticoat on that bush like a flag, trying to draw us straight to the west. Where is the Suarez place from here?"

"South. Back there's the turnoff."

"Come on. Let's give it a try."

Her heart was beating now like Casoose's hammer on the forge. "I may have caught a glimpse of color when we passed the turnoff back there."

"Show me."

She tucked most of the petticoat beneath her and sat on it to keep it from fluttering in Sache's line of vision, then turned the mare to follow. He was already on his way.

"A deep, rich yellow," she said. "It may have been a blossom on a cactus or a bird or a flash of sunlight, but it may have been Cotannah's yellow hair ribbon."

But when she turned off the main trail and started down along the brushy coulee where the Suarezes' trail ran, she couldn't find the color again. Her heart sank. They had been riding fast as they passed. Had she only imagined it?

"I don't see it now," she said as a sick emptiness spread through her.

"There."

The breeze freshened from behind them, cooled her back where the sunshine already lay heavy below the shade of her hat, and stirred the leaves on the heavy brush. It picked up something yellow and waved it.

"Yes! There!" she cried.

They worked their way around a reaching branch of mesquite and half slid down a steep little drop in the ground. Tay took hold of the strip of yellow and lifted it from the thorn that had caught it, held it out to Emily: a long piece of yellow satin ribbon with tatted lace edging.

"It's hers," she said. "I have one off the same bolt."

Tay's eyes were hard as gray granite. "We've got them now," he said, and pulled his horse around to start down the trail. "It's good you spotted the ribbon, Emily. I missed it the first time."

She smiled to herself. He *was* different—he wanted her to share the victory.

"As I recall," she said dryly, "we were already heading in this direction. But why were her clothes on out there farther?"

"To decoy us past this place. The petticoat was carefully fixed like a flag." He lifted into a trot. "Stay behind me," he ordered. "They may have guards out. Just tell me when we're getting close."

She clung to her saddle horn on the downhill slopes and prayed. They had to save Cotannah any more humiliation and harm, physical harm.

But when they finally got there and dismounted to hide in the oak motte on the little rise and look down into the Suarezes' yard, she saw that they were too late on both counts. Cotannah sat slumped on a horse in the full glare of the sun wearing only her torn chemise and pantaloons, her hands tied to the high, curving horn of the saddle. Blood was running down the outside of her thigh, more blood streaked her arms, her head hung forward, face toward the ground. She was the absolute picture of despair.

Emily stared, frozen, unable to bear the sight, yet unable to tear her eyes away from it. Several bandits, some mounted, some on foot, moved around in the yard and corrals of the Suarez house, apparently making preparations to leave. The good horses stolen at San Fernando Creek were being moved slowly, so as not to spook them, out of the pole corral, and a herd of a hundred or so head of cattle were being held by three men a quarter mile or so farther down the grassy valley.

One man finished tying his packs onto his saddle, then mounted and rode over to Cotannah. The taunting sound of his voice floated to Emily and Tay, but not the words. It came to them just as he reached out and brushed her loose hair back and then slapped her bare cheek so hard that the sound echoed against the stone of the house. Her head rocked with the blow and then dropped to hang hopelessly again.

Hot, sickening rage filled Emily to bursting. She wanted to kill him, she had no doubt that she could kill him.

"Obviously they don't plan to trade her," Tay drawled in a tone so cold with hard purpose that it eased her a little. "They're heading out for Mexico with 'Tannah, the cattle, and the horses, leaving two or three of them behind to ambush Cade tomorrow at Canyon Borrecitas."

"I can't believe that's really Cotannah down

there looking so listless and hopeless," she cried, nearly strangling on the words. "Oh, Tay, they've killed her spirit and they're about to kill *her*."

"They're about to get a big surprise."

His granite confidence consoled her tremendously in spite of the fear trying to cool her hot blood, which was roaring for vengeance through her veins.

"What's our plan?" she said.

For the first time, he took his gaze from the scene below and looked at her, his pale eyes blazing in the dark angles of his face. "You'll have to help make the plan, because I'm not sending any more troops into battle."

"I said I'd die if I don't help her, and now I'm even more sure of it. If they shoot me, so be it."

He grinned. "That's my partner," he said. "Are you as good with that sidearm you're wearing as you are with a rifle?"

"Yes."

"Then we're a real threat to banditry on the border," he said, moving carefully backward toward the horses. "Here's what I'm thinking."

"Tell me," Emily said, starting for Sache, being careful to keep down and not to show herself against the sky.

"You could ride down that side of the rise and spook the cattle into stampeding onto the heels of the horse herd while I get to Cotannah from the opposite direction."

"Sounds good," she said, in the same matter-of-fact tone he had used.

They sounded as calm as if they rescued helpless maidens from evil bandits every day of the week. Her breath caught just a little, but he appeared not to notice.

"It's impossible to predict how things will fall out in the confusion we'll create," he said. "Just keep calm, shoot at the center of whoever's shooting at you, and above all, *keep moving.*"

"If we get separated, there's a bend to the north in the creek that runs along the back of this place that's marked by a huge live oak," she said as they reached the horses and picked up their reins. "Shall we meet there?"

"Fine." He stopped still and turned to her. "You're a cool-headed woman, Miss Emily," he said, the corners of his mouth lifting in the trace of a smile.

"And you're a fair-minded man, Tay Nashoba."

His eyes narrowed to sparkling slits in the dust on his face. He reached out and touched her hair. "Ride safe," he said.

"You, too."

Their eyes held for a moment longer, then they moved apart and mounted their horses like mirror images, like partners in a dance. Tay's words made her roaring blood leap. Did he actually think that she could do this? He did. She could, for she had no choice.

They turned and rode their separate paths down the side of the hill. When she reached the bottom, she didn't let herself stop and look for Cotannah again as she wanted. She could see the cattle through the brush and she knew what to do—Cotannah was Tay's responsibility.

So she set her heels to Sache, pulled the petticoat from beneath her, and shook it in the mare's line of sight. It would take a miracle for her to keep her seat once she really started waving it, but miracles seemed to be happening today. Thank God she wasn't on a sidesaddle.

Sache spooked and charged out of cover at a gallop, moving so fast that Emily's head snapped back and she couldn't lift the petticoat in front of her. She held it to one side, pulled it as high as she could to make it wave in the wind, and charged toward the cattle, trying to scream and yell but unable to make a single sound.

Her eyes and her mouth filled with dust, and her ears with shouts and yells. Then she heard the beginning of rumbling hooves. Pray God the cattle would run quickly—fast and hard to scatter the horses. She lifted the petticoat higher and leaned forward to flap it in front of her. The bandits would ride to save the horses; they'd hate to lose them nearly as much as they'd hate to lose Cotannah.

Shots sounded behind her, and Sache doubled her speed. Emily grabbed the saddle horn and the whole world turned to swirling dust. She ducked her head and twisted to one side as the wind parted the cloud of sand for a moment. In that instant one of the bandits, riding at a gallop after the cattle with his gun held high, looked directly at her from a stone's throw away. He was shooting into the air to try to turn the cattle, and when he saw her, he jerked the handgun down to level it on her.

His face engraved itself on her memory: a dark oval with small, shocked black eyes and coarse features suddenly frozen fast in a mask of surprise. Surprise, no doubt, that she was a woman. She smiled against the force of the wind.

Bawling and thundering hooves of cattle filled the air, and closer to her, the sound of Sache's running feet roared in her head, but she still heard the other shots when they began. There were so many, fired so fast, that she ached to turn and look. But, instead she was leaning forward against Sache's neck and she couldn't straighten up at the speed they were going.

The sharp crack of a rifle shot came very near her and then a whole volley sounded behind her. Tay? Was he shooting or was he hurt? Did he have Cotannah yet or was he fighting to take her? Emily's very flesh and bones were burning with the need to know, but she couldn't stop, couldn't turn, couldn't go back. She could barely guide her own horse—Sache was running full-out—but she finally headed her in the way she thought was north.

The wind tore Emily's braids loose from their bindings and whipped her face with them. She clung to the saddle horn so hard that the knot in her reins bruised the palm of her hand, drove the other hand into Sache's mane, and rode until she could not hear any noise behind her. Then she started pulling the mare in a circle to slow her.

Her arms were shaking with fatigue and so weak they felt detached from her body, but she finally stopped the filly and looked around. They had passed the bend with the live oak a hundred yards back, so as soon as she had the strength, she turned Sache around and started back toward it at a walk.

Heaving a sigh of relief that she'd survived and that she knew where she was, she stood in the stirrups, shaded her eyes with one trembling hand, and looked for Tay and Cotannah. They were coming! At least it was a gray-white horse and a man wearing a tan hat in the lead, and a horse behind him, so who else could it be?

She started at a trot to meet them—the exhausted Sache refused to go any faster than that—and Emily wasn't sure she could stay in the saddle because her legs were so weak. They came closer. Her heart leapt and then fell like a stone.

Tay had Cotannah, yes, but she wasn't riding the second horse, she was a limp bundle in Tay's arms, her head resting in the cradle of his elbow and her long hair swinging like a black banner back and forth with the rhythm of the horse. Oh, dear God, was she dead? Had they killed her?

Fear of knowing and an equal determination

that it couldn't be true made her turn toward the creek.

"Bring her to the water!" she called.

She kicked Sache to hurry on ahead so she could spread out the blanket tied in a roll behind her saddle and have it ready for Cotannah. That done, she ran to the creek and plunged the petticoat into the water.

She was kneeling on the bank when Tay rode up, out of the sun and into the shade of the huge, old tree.

"Is she . . . alive?" Emily cried. Her hands shook as much as her voice quavered.

"She's breathing," he said as he reined in, "but she's not sweating. We've got to get her cooled down before we make a run for the house."

He held Cotannah in one arm as he stepped down off the horse and then cradled her in both again as he strode across the bank and right on into the creek toward Emily.

"Oh, Tay," Emily gasped. "Oh, Tay, you *did* get her out!"

She reached for Cotannah, too, and helped him hold her full-length in the cool, shady water. His hard, callused hand brushed hers, its heat warming her blood.

"*We* got her out, Emily." He looked at her, his eyes bright as stars in his dark, dust-covered face, blazing at her. "We do make a pair, now, don't we?" he drawled.

Her heart went right out of her body. A pair. The two of them made a pair.

They stared at each other for a long, startled moment with their hands barely touching and Cotannah between them.

Chapter 11

Bathing her in the creek water cooled Cotannah for a little while, but even though they wrapped her in the wet petticoat and stopped twice to trickle water into her mouth and onto her face and throat, by the time they got her to La Casa, her skin was burning with fever. When they brought her into the house, she seemed to sense for the first time that she was safe: She roused from her stupor enough to say, "Tay? Tay, are you there?"

"I'm here," he said. "Don't worry, 'Tannah, I'm here."

His voice broke when he said it, just like Emily's heart. She stayed right behind him, with Maggie and Oleana and half the household following her, as he carried Cotannah up the stairs and into her room to lay her in her bed. Sinking down into the cool sheets caused her to rally again, enough to turn her head frantically from side to side and call out in a loud, panicked voice, "Mimi! Mimi! Help me! Help me!"

Emily grabbed her searing hot hand in both of hers and bent over to lay it against her check. "Here I am, 'Tannah, and I am helping you. You're safe. You're going to be all right—the bandits are gone now."

But so was Cotannah. Emily squeezed her hand and patted her.

"Look at me, 'Tannah! Look! I'm here and so is Tay—he's right there."

But Cotannah lay limp as a rag, vanished into her own inner world again.

Emily glanced up frantically, her heart racing with fear. "She has not opened her eyes at all, not once!"

Tay shook his head, looking down at Cotannah with worry etched in every line of his hard-set face. "Not a flicker of an eyelid."

"Don't worry, *Senor* Tay, it's the fever making her so sick. We will bring it down," Oleana said, pouring water from the pitcher into a bowl and bringing it to the bedside, edging him aside. "We will wash her and we will soon see what those devil bandits have done to our sweet *senorita*."

Tay took the hint. "I'll go and wash up myself."

"You, too, Mimi," Maggie ordered, when he had gone. "You're swaying on your feet, you're so hot and tired."

Emily didn't move. She couldn't because she couldn't stop looking at Cotannah's wounds, and the sight of them drained the very life from her body.

"There's a thorn in her thigh here; that's

what a lot of the bleeding was . . . Now it's
turning black. Maggie, she needs a doctor . . ."

"When we rode out to meet you all coming
into the yard, I sent Jorge for Dr. McPhee the
minute after I sent Balthazar to find Cade,"
Maggie said, bending over Cotannah. "If you
didn't hear me do that, it just shows what a
state you're in, Mimi. Go."

Emily had been in her room washing up and
changing her clothes no more than ten minutes
when Cotannah's screams of "Mimi! Mimi!"
and "Tay! Tay, where are you?" rang through
the house. She threw on a fresh dress and ran
back down the hall to Cotannah's room without even putting up her hair, her blood running
cold with fear. Tay was already there.

Their voices calmed Cotannah, but still she
never opened her eyes or gave any other indica-
tion that she was aware of anything. Tay stood
and looked out the window while Emily helped
Oleana and Maggie finish washing her and
putting on her nightgown.

"I will never be afraid of *los bandidos* again,"
Oleana said as they finished.

She met Maggie and Emily's shocked stares
with her eyes blazing and her round face full of
fury.

"I will attack them first," she declared, "for
what they have done to our *Senorita* Cotannah!"

"As far as we know, though, it could've been
a whole lot worse," Maggie said with a signifi-
cant glance at Emily. "Let's be thankful for
that, Oleana."

Emily pulled a chair up beside the bed and sank into it, fighting the sick feeling in the pit of her stomach. Thank God. If 'Tannah hadn't been raped, if they could get the thorn out and get her fever down, surely she'd get well. Surely she would.

Maggie and Oleana left to help Aunt Ancie make the medicine for the poultice to try to draw out the thorn and another to bring down the fever. Alone together, Tay pulled up a chair beside Emily's. He was so close, she could smell the soap on his skin.

His nearness gave her the strangest feeling. On the one hand, she wanted to turn to him, throw herself into his arms, and cry her eyes out over the terrible condition Cotannah was in . . . and let him kiss her tears away. On the other, she wanted to scream at him for ever coming here in the first place. 'Tannah would never have taken such a chance to pick the berries if he hadn't.

And she herself would never have known what it was like to kiss him, to be his partner and friend, to go through hell with him and come out on the other side to hear him say, *We do make a pair, now, don't we?* To wish with every bone of her being that they truly could be a pair forever.

"Tay," Cotannah murmured, tossing her head back and forth on the pillow, "Tay?"

"I'm here," he said, leaning forward to take her hand. "You're safe, 'Tannah. Honey, you're safe."

The endearment struck fire to Emily's belly.

"If you call her things like that later on when she can hear you, it'll just make it harder on her."

He cocked his head and glanced back at her, his sharp eyes boring into hers. "Are you admitting something to me?"

"N-no! I-I mean that she's half-d-dead and in this h-horrible shape because she thinks she's in love with you. Once she knows that you're the one who rescued her, you'll be d-double the hero you already are in her eyes, and that's nothing short of Sir Lancelot already."

Her breath ran out, so she had to stop talking, but more words, more *feelings*, pushed and crowded in her brain and formed a knot in her throat. She needed to say something more, something else, but she didn't know what.

He smiled. "And you think I can't live up to Sir Lancelot?"

He was teasing her, charming her, trying to make her admit there was something between them. Well, she couldn't, wouldn't, admit it, no matter how she had felt when he kissed her. When he first looked at her. When they had looked into each other's hearts out there in the hay. And when he had said that they made a pair.

No. If she ever said it in so many words, then all of their lives would be ruined.

"Sorry," she said, forcing a light tone into her shaky voice, "I didn't mean to imply such a thing." She made herself meet his eyes, made her lips curve into a smile.

He smiled back. "So. Let's go back to the beginning. Why is it that my using endearments with Cotannah will make things harder for her?"

She snapped her lips shut and glared at him defiantly.

He leaned back in his chair, crossed his arms, and let his shrewd gaze drift over her face. Her *blushing* face, judging by the heat rising in her cheeks.

"I-I have no idea *what* I meant. It was a silly thing to say. F-forget it."

"How can I when it was so intriguing? For just a moment there, I thought you were saying something about you and me."

She held his gaze. "No. I wasn't."

Tiny flames sprang to life in his eyes. "You might as well. Someday soon I'll drive you to it."

"I have no idea what you're talking about."

"Yes, you do. Just as you know full well that you don't love that coward you say you're going to marry."

She gaped at him, horrified. "I *love* Lee! How can you possibly say that I don't? And why do you call him a coward?"

"Because he harassed you after I challenged him in the canyon. Because instead of settling it with me, he took it out on you, a woman."

She set her mouth stubbornly. "Of *course* he questioned me about you! What man wouldn't have? You acted like a madman. He wasn't harassing me, he just wanted to know what was going on. I love him."

He let those last three words hang in the air between them. "Listen to yourself," he said. "Do you believe that?"

"*You* listen to *me*," she cried. "I'm going to marry him . . ."

"Marrying is one thing, passionate love is another thing entirely. I know passion when I see it, and I haven't seen it between you and Lee."

Panic flashed through her like lightning, whirling her mind like a tornado. Of course he saw it.

"Whatever's between you and Lee is nothing compared to this thing between you and me. Isn't that right, Emily?"

She couldn't move. His silver eyes held her still until Maggie called from the doorway.

"Mimi! Come get this basin, quick, before I drop it."

Seething with shame for forgetting about Cotannah, even for an instant, Emily jumped up and ran to help with all the sickroom paraphernalia Maggie held piled in her arms. Tay got up and came to help, too, and Emily flashed him an angry look.

He was waiting for it, looking straight at her, even as he reached to take some of Maggie's burden. There was *such* a look in his eyes that Emily's heart went still.

Through the long night that followed, she kept trying to fix her mind on Cotannah and on Lee, who was out supervising all the patrols so that Cade could be with his sister. However, she remained with Tay in the room. She tried not to look at him, she tried not to think about him, but she was always aware of him.

Cotannah continued to call only for Tay and for Mimi, and although Aunt Ancie, Uncle Jumper, Mama, Maggie, Cade, and Oleana all kept their vigils, Cotannah never knew they were there. Tay and Emily left her only for short periods of time.

There was no possible way the doctor could arrive before noon the next day, if Jorge had to go all the way to his home in Corpus to find him, so they poulticed the imbedded thorn with a paste made from jimsonweed seeds. They worked to keep the fever down by bathing Cotannah in cool water and trying to get her to drink a concoction made from pounded roots that Aunt Ancie said was first used by the Louisiana Choctaws. They succeeded in getting only trickles of it down her throat, and they piled the covers on her, hoping that a sweat would break the fever.

Finally, toward morning, while Cotannah lay quietly, Aunt Ancie went away to mix more medicine, leaving Tay and Emily on watch. Emily leaned her head against the tall back of the straight chair and sighed. Every muscle in her body ached from the long, hard ride to rescue Cotannah; every nerve still trembled from the harrowing day; every corner of her heart wept over Cotannah's condition.

There was nothing of her left to deal with Tay Nashoba and her feelings for him.

"Why don't you go on to bed?" she said. "I'll send for you if Cotannah calls you."

"I was just about to say the same."

She considered it: slipping into her loose cotton nightgown, turning back her coverlet and stretching out on the cool sheets in the dark, alone in her peaceful room where the cool night breeze could come in through the window and soothe her warm skin, knit her ragged self back together again. But then the midnight thoughts about Lee might come around.

And thoughts of Tay might seize her heart again.

"I have to stay," she murmured.

"You aren't accustomed to such a harrowing ride as you had today, and you have to be exhausted."

Emily rubbed the back of her neck. "What about you?" she challenged. "According to what I've heard, you're more accustomed to making speeches and asking for votes than riding into a nest of bandits with guns blazing."

She let herself have just a glance at him. He had stopped pacing, finally, and was standing at the window in a wash of light from the low-riding moon, feet set apart, hands loosely at his sides. He looked big as a mountain, solid as the earth.

He chuckled. "A man has to be tough to survive in Choctaw politics."

"Do you think you'll become Principal Chief?"

"I'd better," he said darkly. "If Burton wins, the whites will cheat him out of all our coal, rock, and timber, and the intruders will flow in worse than ever. The Nation won't survive."

Something else lurked deep in his tone, something he wasn't saying. She guessed at it.

"But do you *want* to be Chief?"

He waited a long moment before answering. "Yes and no," he said slowly, as if deciding what he wanted at that very moment. "I'm weary of conflicts and of responsibility for other people—I've had nothing but that ever since before the War. Sometimes I think it'd be heaven to do nothing but farm and breed good horses and sit on the porch and read."

"Then why are you running?"

"It's my duty. I'm the only one who's savvy enough and diplomatic enough to pull the Nation together and save it. I won't take bribes."

"Have you always felt such a duty?"

He turned around and stared out the window. "Ever since I lost those boys."

Emily's heart broke for him. She ached to comfort him, but she had no idea what to say. Finally she said, "Do you think you'll win?"

"It's going to be close. Choctaw politics are hard-fought and wild, sometimes violent, always *passionate*."

That word again.

"So everybody gets involved."

"Yes. The People love gathering in large groups for speeches and arguing, dances and games. Politics is a great excuse."

"Do you love all that, too?"

"Yes," he said solemnly. "I love it all." He hit his fist on the window facing and added, "I love it and I won't let it be killed."

He kept staring out the window. It was a north window, she realized: He was looking toward his beloved Nation—his duty.

Just as Lee and Katie were her duty. Why, no telling what would happen to those two without her—they both loved her so much, and they needed her to make a real home for them. That, along with her teaching, and Mama, and Maggie and her family, would make her life complete. And safe.

Tay cocked his head to one side, listening. Soon a shout came from the lookout tower.

"Buggy wheels," he said, "and there's an outrider. I think the doctor's here."

Relief, a relief so deep that it took her heart away, held Emily helpless in her chair. The doctor. Thank God. Now he would bring poor Cotannah back to herself.

"It's nearly dawn," Tay said. "The time when this world and the unseen one are closest together. Maybe it's the time for Cotannah to come back to us."

He came to the bed and touched Cotannah's hand, crossing the floor as silently as the moonlight had been doing all night long. It was fading fast now; the moon was setting on the other side of the house. A new day was coming.

Emily got up impatiently and went to take Cotannah's other hand. "Oh, I think she's cooler," she cried, "and the doctor will be able to break the fever all the way. She'll start getting better as soon as he sees her, I know that she will!"

Soon there was a stir outside, and then downstairs, voices sounded, including Cade's and Maggie's. Emily bent over Cotannah's still form.

"The doctor's here, 'Tannah," she said softly, "and he's going to make you well!" She glanced up at Tay. " 'Tannah's skin feels cooler on her forehead, too," she said, brushing back Cotannah's hair.

The room soon filled with people: Aunt Ancie and Uncle Jumper, Maggie and Cade, and Dr. McPhee whom Jorge had luckily found at another patient's place several long miles this side of Corpus Christi.

"Light some more lamps if you would, Mrs. Chisk-Ko," the doctor said, bustling happily about as if he'd had a full night's rest and a good breakfast to boot.

Emily helped light the lamps while the men stepped out into the hallway for the doctor to examine Cotannah.

"Mmm, well," he muttered, almost to himself, "they slapped her around some, but she's got no broken bones." He went around to the other side of the bed and pulled loose the poultice. "Probably got the thorn when they took her. She was fighting to get away, no doubt, and ran or fell into the huisache, most likely."

He looked Cotannah over carefully. "She's

got scratches from a lot of thorns, but only this one got imbedded, it seems."

All the women looked silently at one another, imagining Cotannah's horror and panic as she struggled fruitlessly to escape from the bandits. The doctor put the poultice back in place and then stood still, staring down at Cotannah, frowning, feeling the pulse in her wrist.

"This fever's a bad one, though," he said, shaking his head. "I don't know. I can't tell about it."

Emily's heart froze. "She's lots cooler than she was at first," she said eagerly. "I *know* the fever has gone down."

"That doesn't mean much, it'll come up again," he said, turning to open his bag. He set it on the chair where Emily had sat and began taking bottles and tools out of it. "It's partly from the thorn but . . ." The doctor looked up and glanced from one worried face to the next. "You say she hasn't been conscious since the rescue?"

"No," Maggie said, "not even right before it, isn't that right, Mimi?"

Everyone looked at Emily.

"Yes, she hasn't opened her eyes or seemed to know anything at all," she admitted. "But she *does* sense when Tay and I are near her."

"It may be her mind," the doctor said, frowning even more fiercely. "She may have locked everything out of it to escape her captors."

Emily's throat filled with tears. "Wh-wh-when we f-f-first saw her from the h-hill," she said, "sh-she was slumped in the saddle with her head hanging down as if her s-spirit was g-gone."

Her voice slid up and broke on the last word and she buried her face in her hands, trying to hold back the tears. She bit them back, then looked up at the doctor again. "Th-that's not like Cotannah."

"No, as I recall, she's a very spirited girl," he replied with pity in his voice.

"Doctor, what can we do?" Maggie demanded.

"Wait. Treat the fever and the thorn's poison, and wait."

Horrified, Emily stared at him as her cold heart turned over. What if Cotannah never got any better? Oh, dear Lord, what if she died?

"But she will get well, won't she?" Maggie cried.

"We hope so," Dr. McPhee said, turning to his concoctions again. "We do hope so, Mrs. Chisk-Ko." He raised his voice so that it would carry out through the open door. "Mr. Chisk-Ko, would you please come back in?"

Emily turned and ran. She couldn't hear him pronounce his doubtful proclamation again. She *wouldn't* hear it.

Cade and Uncle Jumper stepped into the room just as she slipped through the doorway into the wide hall. Right into Tay.

"Oh, Tay!" The instant she said his name, the tears burst through her defenses and started flowing. "Tay, did you hear him? I'm afraid she'll die, or if she lives, that her mind will never be right!"

Tay wrapped her in his arms and cradled her head against his chest.

Chapter 12

"Shh, sh-sh, shh, sh-sh," Tay murmured in a rising, falling rhythm. "Hush, now, hush."

Vaguely Emily was aware that he was pulling her away from the open doorway, taking her across the wide hall into her own room.

"Let's not alarm everyone," he said softly. "Cade needs to talk to the doctor. Come on, Emily, honey, hush, now, hush. We don't *know* yet, we just don't know."

Her sobs came harder as she choked out, "We need to do something. The doctor said only to wait . . ."

"No, no crying now, my little *yaiya*, shh, sh-sh, shh, sh-sh."

He rocked her back and forth in his arms, holding her head tight against his hard, warm chest. She clung to him as if she were drowning.

"Shh, sh-sh, shh, sh-sh."

Her sobs finally lessened while he stroked her hair.

"Better," he whispered, stroking her hair,

then her shoulders and her back. "Better, that's better now, isn't it?"

She couldn't respond. She couldn't move— she would never move again. She'd stay inside this safe circle made of his iron-muscled arms and not think about anything, nothing at all.

He rested his chin on the top of her head and held her even closer for a moment while the sweet dawn air rose and stirred, caught them in a cross-breeze between the windows and the door. Then he leaned back, tilted her face up, and looked down at her with his melting silver eyes.

"You have so much heart," he said, shaking his head in wonder. "Mimi, darlin', you've nearly used yourself up."

The endearment struck her ears like a melody. All the strength, every bit of it, went out of her legs and she sagged against him.

He picked her up and carried her toward the bed. "You're about to faint," he said. "If you had gone to lie down when I told you to . . ."

She threw her arms around his neck and held on tight. "So have you," she murmured. "You have nearly used yourself up, too."

He chuckled. "No, I've got a lot left yet. You get some rest now."

His hair was tied back with a thong of leather, as it had been on that evening when he arrived at Las Manzanitas, and the shirt he'd changed into when they'd brought Cotannah home was a collarless one of thin, white cotton. It made a fascinating line against the dark copper color of his skin.

Suddenly it was all she could do not to bury her face against his neck, right there, at the very edge of the shirt where his skin looked smooth as silk. Her lips ached to touch it, to kiss the sure, steady rise and fall of his pulse she could see beating.

"You smell like the fresh air of the early morning," she murmured, "and you haven't even been outside yet."

"You smell like roses," he said, "and so does your room."

"Or my room does and so do I."

He smiled and shook his head again. "See how silly you are? You're on the ragged edge of exhaustion, Mimi . . ."

She couldn't resist it for another minute, she pressed her mouth to that sweet spot on his neck. And she was caught, caught as surely as a magnet would catch metal, but this was her flesh melded to his.

This was the way she had felt when he'd kissed her on the caprock: as if they would never part because they physically couldn't. He felt it, too. He stopped still and sucked in a deep breath; he didn't move until his blood pulsed beneath her lips.

Then he turned his head and laid his cheek against hers, only for an instant. "Emily . . ."

The sound of her name was a plea, a prayer. Then, in the next instant, he was no longer the supplicant, he became the all-powerful Chief and she the one incoherently begging for mercy because he took her mouth and began kissing her senseless. He took two long strides and laid

her down on her bed, never letting a hairs-
breadth of space come between them.

If he had, she would have closed the gap in
an instant, for the only thing wrong at that
moment in time was that they couldn't get
close enough. She took his hard-angled face in
both her hands and he kissed her and she
kissed him back until neither of them could
ever hope to breathe again.

When they broke apart at last, they were
gasping for the fresh, raw air from the window.

"Tay . . ." she whispered, "Tay . . ."

He smiled, but neither of them could say any
more; they had no will for words. She smiled
back at him and ran her palms over the bulging
muscles of his back, feeling the power and the
contour of every iron-bound one. Iron beneath
the thin cotton of his shirt and the warm satin
of his skin.

She pulled his shirt out of his pants and
slipped her hand up beneath it, found the
cunning tunnel of his spine and followed it
with the tip of one finger. The corners of his
sensual mouth lifted, but his eyes didn't smile.

"*Em*-i-ly," he said.

Shock came over her for this new, incredibly
intimate thing she had done. He saw it, it made
him laugh against her lips as his mouth came
down on hers again.

She whimpered, deep in her throat, and ran
her hands hungrily over his shoulders, down
his massive arms. He was making the kiss slow
and sweet this time, so achingly sensual that it
roused a whole new desire deep within her, a

wanting, a terrible longing that she had never known. A longing for what, exactly, she did not know, either. The tip of his tongue trailed along hers and sent a shooting ache through her loins.

When his lips left hers at last, she gave a broken cry of protest and turned her head with a wild, abandoned movement that brought his lips brushing against her throat. He kissed her there.

Then he began to place a slow row of deliberate, deliciously hot kisses straight down to the neck of her dress. But when his hand found her breast and closed around it, she lost track of his mouth. He rubbed his thumb across the aching tip, and the sharpest desire she had ever known shot through her.

Only this exultant thrill was real now, this sparkling excitement in her blood that danced into every single vein in her body while he opened all the buttons of her dress, fast and smooth. His mouth followed his fingers to blaze a burning trail on her skin between her throbbing breasts. Her hands plunged into his heavy hair, tore it loose from its rawhide thong, and cupped his head while he lifted it and took her breast into his mouth. His tongue was searing and wet and it held a magical power. The excitement he sent plunging through her made her afraid of herself. Never, ever had she known she had so much desire deep inside her.

Her fingers froze in his hair when the sounds from outside burst into her ears: horses' hooves, lots of them, pounding into the yard, men's shouts and then Lee's voice, loud and light with excitement.

"Watch your prisoners close, boys. Keep 'em on their horses till I find out what the boss wants done with 'em."

Tay lifted his head and looked at her.

Saddles squeaked, bits jingled, and horses stomped.

Solemnly they looked at each other for a long time, searching each other's eyes, letting the early morning sweep in and swirl around them, devouring each other's faces in the growing pale pink light. Then she stroked his face, ran her fingertip over the sharp rise of his cheekbone.

"Lee is back," she said.

"So I hear."

A wry smile tugged at the corners of his mouth. His mouth. His mouth had become her whole world. It held her motionless now, held her breathless and helpless and silently begging for it to kiss her again.

He knew that, too. He lay above her, his length warm and pulsating and possessive of hers all the way down her body. He kissed her once, hard and quick, then let her go and sat up.

Dazed, her movements heavy and slow, she sat up, too, and began to button her dress. For a little while there, until she had heard the sound of his voice, she had forgotten that Lee existed. *Lee!*

She closed her eyes as recognition screeched through her, as it flew like a cold bullet through the slow, hot, heavy pounding of her senses to hit her dormant brain. How could she be so faithless?

She had forgotten not only him, but her promises. She had promised to marry him and to love him, and just look what she'd been doing—why, she had no honor, she was as bad as her father!

"Oh, dear goodness," she muttered, barely choking out the words.

The sound of bootheels struck the porch.

"Hello the house," Lee shouted, and she heard the squeak of the door opening. "Oleana! Is anybody here?"

She looked up at Tay. "You sh-should g-go," she whispered dully.

"Should I?"

She flashed another look at him. His touch was still warm on her skin; she was still filled with the languor created by his mouth on her breast.

No! No! Don't go. I never want you to leave me, ever again!

But there was Cotannah, too! God forgive her, she had forgotten about Cotannah as well as Lee!

"Yes," she cried, leaping to her feet. "Go across the hall. Lee's coming up here because Oleana's out at her own house and no one's downstairs."

"Let him come."

"Tay! Have you no sense of honor or decency? I'm *betrothed!*"

"*I'm* not."

"Oh? Are you saying that this . . . shameful little . . . e-episode is all my doing?"

"No. I'm saying that I am perfectly free to kiss anyone I please, and you could be, too."

"Kissing would be bad enough. But this . . . th-this was a bit more than k-kissing, I'd say!" she said indignantly.

"So would I."

She jerked her head up to look at him. "Well, then!"

"But I wouldn't call it shameful."

"You wouldn't?" she demanded. She steadied her hands by sheer force of will and succeeded in buttoning the last button. Now she was decently covered all the way up to her neck.

"Because there's a lot of caring between us and we've been through a great deal together lately."

"Think about Cotannah!" she said urgently, grabbing his arm.

He stood up.

"Think about it, Tay—she's so sick and she's been through so much and she's so in love with you. Please go so that Lee won't make a scene that she'll hear about when she wakes up!"

He let her pull him toward the door.

"How embarrassing would it be for *me*, anyway, if *any* of the family . . . Oh, Tay . . ."

They were standing in the doorway with her

hand on his arm when Lee reached the top of the stairs and turned in their direction. The sight of them checked him in midstep, but only for a moment, then he strode toward them faster.

"What's going on here?" he demanded.

Emily dropped her hand to her side.

It felt empty, she felt terribly separate, alone, bereft, not to be touching Tay. And she felt highly ashamed, humiliated, to have been touching him in the first place. She felt as guilty now as she had in the canyon when it was Lee she'd been touching.

Her head went dizzy. This was like being caught in the confluence of two rivers with their currents running swift and strong in opposite directions. They were about to break her apart into little pieces.

She didn't trust her voice to speak, but Tay said nothing, and someone had to answer Lee.

"We're discussing the doctor's opinion about Cotannah," she said as he walked up to them.

There. She hadn't exactly told a lie. No need to add that to the list of her dishonorable actions this morning.

"Cade's with her?" Lee said, more as a statement than a question because they could hear Cade's voice and the doctor's coming from Cotannah's room.

Then, either because he realized that he had once more put his work first, or because he was jealous of Tay standing so close to her, he reached out and touched Emily's cheek. His hand felt like a stranger's.

"How's she doing?" he asked gently.

Tears flooded Emily's eyes, and to her mortification, not all of them were for Cotannah. "She's bad, Lee," she whispered, surprised she could even talk with her lips so stiff. "Dr. McPhee says all we can do is treat the fever and wait."

Lee glanced at Tay and slapped his hat against his leg as if to shoo him away. "She'll pull through and she'll be fine," he said, speaking directly to him as if Tay were the one most in need of comfort. "From what I've seen of Cotannah, she's a fighter."

"I agree," Tay said.

Lee stepped to Emily's other side and slipped his arm around her shoulders.

"We brought in six of th' *bandido* devils," he said, obviously bursting with pride. "Come with me to check on 'em while we wait for Cade to get done talking with the doctor." He turned and looked directly at Tay. "Will you please tell Cade that I'm outside and that I need to see him?"

"Emily is exhausted," Tay said. "I brought her to her room to encourage her to rest—she sat up with Cotannah all night and she really needs to lie down."

Lee stiffened. "I reckon *Emily's* the one to say when she needs rest."

"I agree," Tay said with maddening smoothness.

They both looked at her, waiting for her decision.

All her roiling feelings coalesced into flaring

anger. What was Tay *doing*, trying to make her choose between him and Lee? Dear Lord, she had to get out of here!

"You're both exactly right," she cried, and bolted from beneath Lee's arm to stride down the hall toward the stairs.

Lee caught up with her as she started down. "I knew you'd want to see the ones we caught," he said. "You can tell me if any of them are the ones that had Cotannah."

Her empty stomach churned. "I don't know if I can say that for sure," she said. "Lee, I really *don't* want to see them."

He seemed not to hear her. "They put up a pretty good scrap when we rode up on them," he said. "But it didn't take us long to shut 'em down. Used some of the old Ranger tactics."

Lee didn't care whether she could identify any of the thieves or not, she realized suddenly, he only wanted her to see the prizes he'd brought home and praise him for his success. And well she should—he had risked his life to make the *rancho* safer for them all, hadn't he?

She was his betrothed, wasn't she? That was part of her duty, and it would be when she was his wife, wouldn't it? To brag on his accomplishments and encourage him in all his endeavors. From what she had seen of other marriages, all wives were expected to do that.

Yes. She was his betrothed. But the thought closed off her breathing passages somehow and she ran the rest of the way down the stairs and burst out the front door in a frantic rush for fresh air.

To her complete shock, Oleana's three little girls and Katie were gathered on the front porch, hastily dressed and with their hair barely combed, clinging to the balustrade and staring at the bound prisoners who sat their horses out in the yard. They all ran to Emily, to cling to her skirts instead.

She reached to put her arms around them as she gulped a mouthful of the morning wind. This, obviously, was as far as she could run—they weighted her down like four little flesh-and-blood anchors, sweet-smelling and still warm from their beds.

"Girls! What are you all doing out here so early?"

"We came to see *los bandidos*, Miss Emily," Luisa said. "In school I will write you a story about them, the bad men."

Katie clasped one of Emily's hands in both of hers. "My papa caught them and took the Running M horses and cows away from them," she announced. "They were stealing them to Mexico, but they couldn't get away from my papa, 'cause he used to be a Texas Ranger once."

"We recovered ten head of the good horses," Lee said from behind them, "and more than a hundred head of cows."

He spoke offhandedly, but Emily could hear the undertone of satisfaction. And the hint for praise.

"I-I-I'm very proud of you, Lee," she said.

And she was. He was a good man and he loved her and he would keep her right here in the middle of her family surrounded by these children she loved.

He put his hand on her shoulder in answer, and she made herself feel its warmth, made her ears listen to the excited chatter of the little girls, happy now that she was there to make them feel secure in the face of such dangerous men. This was reality, her real life. Up there in her room with Tay, that was pure fantasy, an illusion, a fairy tale and nothing more. Neither of them would ever have behaved in such a fashion if they hadn't been exhausted and worried beyond measure about Cotannah.

Never again. The thought sank down through her body like a rock falling, but she held on to it and made it into a promise, a *vow* to herself. Never again would she be alone with Tay Nashoba, nor would she touch him. Nothing could ever come of it, and it would only feed this wanting still pulsing inside her that made her think she was going to die of it.

Tay was bathing her in cool water, dipping a cloth into the creek with a lovely, lazy, slowly delicious motion of his hand, laving it over her and letting it run over her bare, hot skin. His big hand was stroking her, caressing her naked body all the way down her side and over her hip, along the back of her thigh to her knee, to her ankle, to her curling toes. Then it came back up to the side of her neck and started doing it all over again.

The water cooled her, but his hand made her feel hot, so hot.

This time he did something different. He trailed his callused fingertips along her neck and sent thrills all through her, then he caressed her breast. Her breath stopped. She waited.

She fitted exactly into the palm of his big hand. He ran his thumb back and forth, back and forth, over her straining, throbbing nipple. It felt so magically wonderful, it made her turn and twist on their grassy bed and it made her cry out.

Suddenly she was awake.

Emily wasn't naked at all, she realized. She was fully dressed as she always was when she napped in the sickroom. And Tay wasn't there, she was alone on the cot.

There were mutterings from inside the room and peaceful singing from outside, but none of the voices belonged to Tay. The singing was soothing, serene and melodic, floating in through the open window on the cool breeze of fresh air. But it wasn't Tay singing.

She squeezed her eyes closed and tried to make it be Tay's deep voice, but it was Uncle Jumper's. He sang and smoked the house with cedar at dawn and dusk every day of Cotannah's illness. Tay was not here.

Bitter disappointment stabbed through her before she could completely lose the dream. Fighting it off, trying to put her conscious mind in control, she sat up and opened her eyes to the sky blazing bright pink through the window.

She had better be *glad* it was only a dream,

because Emily had sworn it would never be real again. If she ever broke that vow, she couldn't survive, for the memory of those few, brief minutes with him on her bed was haunting her night and day.

An unutterable weariness washed over her. Here was another whole, horrible day to get through—avoiding Tay at every turn and trying to push even the thoughts of him away, yet being forced to see him and talk to him while they kept watch over Cotannah.

Then it hit her and her whole body went cold. Dawn. This was dawn of the fourth day. Aunt Ancie still swore that Cotannah's condition would turn one way or the other on the fourth day.

"Mimi, oh, Mimi, you're awake," Maggie cried.

Emily jumped up and ran to Cotannah's bedside where Maggie, Aunt Ancie, and Mama were all gathered, smiling joyously. Maggie snatched up Emily's hand and placed it on Cotannah's forehead.

"She's cool," Emily cried. "Completely cool to the touch!"

Cotannah's face was serene. Her breathing was easy, calm, her whole body was relaxed. She wasn't unconscious—she was truly sleeping. Emily's heart beat such a tattoo of joy that it nearly felled her.

"Sh-sh-she's going to b-be all right? Sh-she'll *live?*"

Maggie's blue eyes blazed pure joy. "Yes! She had a terrible chill and then sweated the sheets soaking wet about thirty minutes ago, and she came to and talked to us. Her mind is all right, too, Mimi!"

Emily grabbed Cotannah's hand and squeezed it, tears of joy running down her cheeks. "Oh, 'Tannah, I'm so happy. I'm so happy that you'll get well!"

Gently Mama pulled her back. "She's completely exhausted, sugar. This is the first real sleep she's had all this time—she may sleep all day."

"But she should eat!" Emily said.

Suddenly she needed desperately to look into Cotannah's eyes, she needed to speak to her, needed to hear her voice.

"She took a few swallows of broth after her fever broke," Ancie said, "and some water. She needs rest more than anything now."

Emily stood there and looked down at her dearest friend. Cotannah had been through hell on earth. Now she deserved heaven, and Emily would help her find it. Even if heaven, to Cotannah, meant Tay Nashoba.

Yes. That would be best for all of them.

Chapter 13

Tay leaned his chair back against the balustrade of La Casa's front porch and let the conversation roll on without him while he watched Emily for a moment. She was rocking back and forth, slowly, in one of the high-backed woven-leather rocking chairs, her chin resting lightly on the head of the tired child in her lap, Lee's daughter, Katie.

A sharp stab of jealousy struck him in the heart. She looked like a Madonna in a painting with her hair glowing gold in the light of the setting sun—this was the way she would look when she was married to Lee, when she was holding a child they made.

Lee, who didn't know how to really love her, Lee, whom she didn't really love. Lee, who was sitting on the top step, leaning back against the post, almost at her feet. He was close enough to touch her, close enough to lift his hand and brush hers every time she rocked forward, but in the hour they'd all been gathered here, he never had. The man was forty kinds of a fool.

But a person could certainly say the same

about him, he thought savagely. Emily had made it perfectly plain more than once in the past week that she was not about to change any of her plans, that she knew where her duty lay and she was going to do it—never mind the fact that she'd kissed him with a passion that had stopped his heart, and her body had melted into his as if they were meant for each other.

The minute Lee appeared she had dropped her hand from his arm, and their only contact since had been polite conversations beside Cotannah's bed. Away from the sickroom, she had avoided him like the plague: She stayed with someone constantly, never went out riding alone, never roamed around the house and yard alone, never even slept in her room alone. Every night she slept on the cot in Cotannah's room.

It was driving him crazy, making him wild, and all for no good reason. What was he going to do, take her away from Lee and marry her? That'd be a good way to lose the election after the whole Nation knew why he had come to Texas. And Uncle Kulli, who had done so much to help Tay all his life, would be devastated.

He narrowed his eyes and studied Emily's serene face. How could she *be* so calm? She didn't make a practice of going into a man's arms and kissing him, of melding herself to him and pulling him down with her onto her bed; he would stake his life on that. She had felt the same incredible desire that he had felt, the same inevitable *connection*. He had seen it in her eyes the moment Cade introduced them, lying with her in the hay, on the caprock when they'd kissed, at the creek when they'd rejoiced because they'd rescued Cotannah—dear God, he'd seen it in her face a hundred times.

He clenched his hand around his lemonade glass so hard he almost broke it. Damn it all to hell, why had he ever come here in the first place? Why hadn't he had sense enough to stay home?

He set his chair down with a thump. "Hey, Kincaid," he said. "We've been sitting around here way too long. How about a little wrestling match to get the kinks out?"

It might be childish, he thought, looking at Lee Kincaid's startled face, letting his lips curl into a challenging smirk. But he had to do something to relieve all the fury and frustration piling up in him, knotting his nerves and crowding into his muscles, pushing him to the brink of even more foolish behavior than this—like throwing Emily over his saddle and riding away with her to a place where no one could ever find them.

All conversation died.

Lee stared at him. "Why, uh . . ."

"You're not scared to take me on, are you? An old Texas Ranger like you?"

The taunt did the trick. They got up at the same time, stood for a moment with all eyes fixed on them, looking each other up and down to take measure.

"I wouldn't be scared of you if you was ten

feet tall and bulletproof," Lee said. He hitched up his belt.

"Come on, then," Tay said. "Right over there looks like a nice, soft patch of grass."

He set his glass on the balustrade and strode down the steps behind Lee while the family got up and began to gather at the edge of the porch, calling out in surprise. From the corner of his eye he saw one of Oleana's small boys running toward the stable, calling to others to come see the fight.

Kincaid turned and dived at his legs then, and he hit the ground with a thud that threatened to knock some sense into him. The smaller man was all over him like a hive of bees, and Tay gave a grunt of pure satisfaction: This would keep him busy, all right, this'd take his mind off everything else.

He got a grip on Lee's wrists then and overpowered him with pure strength, pulling him off him and flinging him onto his back on the ground. Dimly he heard the shouts of excitement and encouragement from the boys and vaqueros gathering around out of nowhere, but he didn't even care who would come out on top when it was over, all he wanted was some ease from the tension roiling through him.

He landed on Kincaid with a thump and got one arm twisted behind him, then lost it again just as fast. He laughed at the challenge and butted his head into Lee's chest, bucked and rolled over when Lee tried to lock Tay's neck into the crook of his arm.

Kincaid was a whole lot faster than Tay had expected, and twice as strong as he looked, to boot. He countered every move that Tay made and used some good ones of his own. He wrestled him all over the grass, across the hard, flat stones of the walk, and into the snowball bushes and out again. They wrestled until Tay's blood was pumping fast and hot and his muscles were moving easy and quick. Then they wrestled some more until they were out of breath and panting, holding each other still while their lungs screamed for air.

"Draw?" Tay could barely say the word he was so spent.

"Draw." Lee couldn't even whisper; Tay read his lips.

They helped each other up then, but they didn't touch each other again when they had struggled to their feet except to shake hands.

"All bets are off," one of the white vaqueros shouted. "It's a draw, boys!"

The men and boys groaned and began to disperse. Tay and Lee went to the pump at the side of the house and held their heads under the cool water, took off their shirts and wrung them out, then put them back on.

Cade and Uncle Jumper and Jorge slapped them on the back when they rejoined the group, and Maggie sent for more lemonade.

"That was quite an entertainment," she said.

"Good wrestling!" Uncle Jumper said.

Lots of voices spoke to him and to Lee, but Emily said nothing. Dusk had fallen in earnest and her face was in shadow, although Tay kept trying to see it as he leaned against a post of the porch and drank from his refilled glass.

And just what did he expect from her? he asked himself as he paced to the end of the porch and back. Did he expect her to be impressed with him now? Did he expect her to finally admit to this feeling between them?

If only he *could* accomplish that with the strength of his muscles and the force of his will!

At least the cool water and his wet shirt had cooled him off, and the physical activity had relaxed him a little bit. Not enough to sit quietly, but enough so that he didn't feel his whole body would burst with frustration. He paced the porch again while Maggie and Cade resumed their bantering back and forth.

"You're right, darling," Maggie was saying, "Randy and Cole are more like you than me because they do everything on Indian Time. Whenever I try to get them to sleep, they refuse to go until the Spirit moves them . . . and the moon and the stars are lined up just right . . . and the wind blows from exactly the right direction . . ."

Cade's disdainful snort made everyone laugh. "Then you must be a full-blood yourself, Mrs. Chisk-Ko. You do things on *your* own good time—like looking over the neighbors' new thoroughbreds until it's so late, we have to stay there all night."

That brought great whoops of laughter from the whole company and even coaxed a low chuckle from Cotannah. Tay turned on his heel to watch her smile in the new moonlight—ever since she regained consciousness, she always seemed so filled with sadness.

She was gorgeous, nothing short of gorgeous. She sat beside Emily looking around at her family with her lush mouth smiling faintly at each of them, yet her eyes held a dark moodiness. She was more beautiful than ever, now that she was recovering from her ordeal, and her new, quiet hesitancy tugged at his heart. She constantly wanted him near her, she needed him terribly. His mouth twisted in a wry grin: That was always a quality hard for him to resist—others' need for him.

Whereas Emily didn't seem to need him at all.

Cotannah felt his eyes on her and looked at him. Her smile was the least bit tremulous now, instead of proud.

He smiled back at her and went to her, bending to whisper in her ear. "You'll recover and eventually you'll forget to be afraid. Everything will be all right someday."

"Tay?" She said his name softly, looking up at him, meaning to speak for his ears alone, but all other conversation ceased. Cotannah didn't talk nearly so much as she had before she was kidnapped, and when she did, everyone stopped to listen, her every word was the family's command.

He stepped around his chair, which she had made sure was near hers, sat down, and leaned toward her. Poor darling. Proud, beautiful Cotannah, surrounded by her whole family,

guarded by an army of vaqueros, was afraid.
Her eyes no longer flashed challenge.

"Yes, 'Tannah?"

"I don't mean to be inhospitable," she said,
"but when are you planning to leave for
home?"

The thought hit him like a tree falling. That
was what he should do. He should ride out
tomorrow and leave this whole, insane situation behind, leave Emily to Lee and forget her.

Mama and Maggie gasped, and Aunt Ancie
dropped her beadwork into her lap.

"Why, 'Tannah, don't you be rude, girl . . ."
Uncle Jumper said.

Cotannah held up her hand. It was trembling. "I'm not trying to run Tay off," she said,
"I'm wanting to ask if we can all go with him."

Emily rocked forward with Katie and
stopped with her beautiful face fully in the
moonlight. Tay could feel her gaze fixed on
him, but suddenly he didn't dare look at her.

Tay had never looked more handsome than
he did at that moment in the moonlight, Emily
thought, with his hair and his shirt wet and
clinging to his finely shaped head and his
magnificent body. He couldn't be leaving.

Tay, *leaving*? Tay, going hundreds and hundreds of miles away? Pictures, memories, of the
long, hard miles of traveling that same dangerous trail rolled through her mind—now it
seemed that Van Buren, and the Choctaw Nation, must be as far away as the moon. Her
heart began beating fast and hard as stunned
silence swept across the porch.

Cade broke it. "I don't see why not," he drawled. "It's about time the twins learned to be real Choctaws."

"But what about the bandits?" Maggie said.

"What about waiting to be invited?" Aunt Ancie said.

"What about letting *Tay* answer?" Uncle Jumper said with a stern sideways look at Cade.

"I mean you, Mimi, and Mama Harrington, too," Cotannah said. "All of us. I wish Oleana could go."

"What?" Emily gasped.

Tay turned and looked at her with his eyes bright as flames. They burned her, but she couldn't look away, even when Katie stiffened in her lap, grabbed her hands and held on tight, shaking her head, no, no.

Not even when Lee stood up and leaned against the post by the steps and muttered, "Mimi stays here."

Cotannah cried, "Mimi has to come with me because it's not safe here. This is Texas, this is the border, and there'll always be raiders."

Emily broke away from the spell of Tay's eyes and freed one hand so she could reach out and pat Cotannah. "But, 'Tannah," she cried, "as long as you don't go off by yourself, you're perfectly safe."

"I want to go home. I want to go back to the Nation."

"You're not able to travel," Emily and Maggie said in unison.

"Staying here is going to completely wear me down."

She sounded so bleak, Emily couldn't bear it. "Oh, 'Tannah—"

"I don't like living here anymore," Cotannah interrupted, "at least, not right now. I hate to admit it, but I'm afraid. All the time, I'm afraid."

"Our patrols are everywhere," Cade said. "As long as you aren't running around by yourself in the dark—"

A strangled sound from Cotannah stopped him in midsentence. "I'm sorry," she said tearfully. "I can't help being afraid and I can't help crying."

"I'm sorry I said that, honey," Cade said quickly. "Don't cry, please don't."

Emily put her arm around Cotannah's shaking shoulders.

"You *can't* go away, Miss Emily," Katie cried. "Can she, Papa?"

"No," Lee growled beneath the excited buzzing of all their voices. "Your place is here, Emily."

Emily kept her head turned away and didn't answer. When he used that tone with her it made her angry enough to spit.

"*Emily*, did you hear me?"

"I won't be gone long," she said without turning to look at him. "Cotannah needs me, Lee."

"So do I. So does Katie."

"Please don't go, Miss Emily," Katie whispered.

Guilt grabbed her stomach and squeezed it. How could she do this? Go away and leave this sweet child? And Lee? How could she do such a thing?

Cade's deep voice cut through the general chatter. "It's about time we get the word from our host," he said. "Tay, what do you think?"

"Come on," Tay said heartily. "We can teach Mrs. Harrington and Emily to do the Jump Dance. And all of us together can completely confound the Burton faction."

"I hate to throw cold water on this election campaign," Maggie drawled, "but are you planning to just *give* the Running M to Cortina, or what?"

Lee stood up very straight and looked at Cade through the dusky light. "I was just about to ask the same question, Miss Maggie, and to add that Emily's place is here. She's betrothed to me and she has a wedding to prepare for."

Fury flared to life all over Emily's body. "It wouldn't be proper for me to stay with all the family gone," she said.

"Miss Emily, are you going away?" Katie asked.

"No, she isn't," Lee said sharply.

"I might," Emily said firmly, looking at Lee, "but I won't be gone long."

"What about your school?" Lee demanded. "You need to get your lessons ready for school."

"You've never worried about my school before. I'll be ready when it takes up."

"You have no business—"

Cade interrupted Lee. "Why don't you come, too, Lee? You could stay a couple of weeks and then come back with me for fall roundup."

Lee snapped his mouth shut and stared at him, then he came to his regular senses. Emily could all but see him thinking that this was his big chance and he'd almost thrown it away.

"No, thanks, Mr. Chisk-Ko," he said in the respectful tone he habitually used with Cade. "One of us—you or me—has to be here."

Well, that was quick enough, Emily thought. Now that he's indispensable to Cade, it's all right for me to go.

"Thanks," Cade said, "I won't even think about the horse thieves, knowing you're in charge. Call in some of your ex-Ranger buddies if you want to beef up the patrols some more."

"I'll do that," Lee said. "And don't worry. I'll hold the fort."

Katie twisted around in Emily's lap and threw her arms around her neck. "Don't go, Miss Emily. Please! Please don't leave me," she begged, beginning to sob. "You might get hurt on the trail. The bandits might get you."

Emily squeezed her tight and tucked Katie's tousled little head into the curve of her shoulder. Her heart broke for the poor baby who, after all, had already lost her mother once. A horrible guilt came over her. Why was she putting the child through this? She should go ahead and marry Lee and stay here and do her duty by him and Katie. That was what she ought to do.

But Cotannah needed her more. Cotannah

was recovering physically, but she was not her old self again by any means. She needed this change of scenery and she needed Emily's support to help her be happy and confident again. And Tay. Cotannah needed Tay. Maybe Emily could help bring them together—hadn't she vowed that she would?

"I'll be back, darling," she promised, hugging Katie fiercely. "I'll be back before you know it."

She looked up and her eyes met Tay's. For an instant, for the space of one heartbeat, they looked at each other and she wondered what she had done.

Four frantically busy days later, they were all packed and ready to go. Lee was working overtime, even for him, but he still managed to spend some time with Emily every day, and Katie would hardly leave her side. She felt so bad that on her last evening at Las Manzanitas she suggested cooking a private dinner for three at Lee's house.

It was the best way she knew to comfort them, and it turned out to be very good for her, too, because it helped assuage her guilt at leaving them. The novelty of the situation distracted Katie from thoughts of parting with Emily, and it pleased Lee so much that he actually came home before dark.

"I like this," Katie said as she helped Emily serve the lemon pie she'd made for dessert. "After you are my mama, we'll eat at home all the time. We'll have our own family."

The eagerness in her voice made Emily's eyes fill. She loved Katie so much, she thought, more than she had even realized.

"Yes, we will," she murmured around the lump in her throat. "Yes, Katie, we will."

After she had finished in the kitchen and she and Lee had put Katie to bed, after she'd assured the child a hundred times that she would come back from the Choctaw Nation before time to take up school in the fall and they'd sat with her until she fell asleep, a great restlessness seized her. She went out with Lee to enjoy the evening breeze on his porch, but she couldn't bring herself to sit down.

"Thank you for a great meal and a good time for Katie," he said, coming up to stand beside her at the corner post where she was staring out into the darkness. "You're a wonderful woman, Emily."

How was it that only four or five weeks ago she had longed for one loving, approving word from him? Now she just wanted him to leave her to her thoughts. She was losing her mind. She was an ungrateful, unfaithful woman who had better get control of herself.

He put his arm around her waist. "I'm thinking I'm getting mighty anxious to have you here in this house with me all the time," he murmured, pulling her closer.

But he hadn't asked her again to marry him early, which she'd thought he would do when he was telling her she couldn't go to the Nation. Later she'd realized that on that occasion he didn't want to risk a public rejection.

"This will be a great opportunity for you," she said, "running Las Manzanitas while Cade and Maggie are gone."

"Yeah," he said proudly.

Then, suddenly, his hand tightened at her waist and he blurted, "I know you think I don't pay you and Katie enough mind sometimes, but I'm working for *us*, Emily. If Cade'll give me enough calves as bonuses, we'll have our own herd built up before you know it."

His vulnerability touched her.

"I know," she said, leaning back against him, "and I appreciate all your hard work, really, Lee, I do."

"I know you do."

His voice held real understanding. He had actually put some thought into her feelings, and that touched her.

She turned her head and smiled up at him. "Are you going to miss me?"

"Like crazy."

The rough, husky tone of his voice was so unusual that it moved her. He really meant it.

"If you'll come over here and sit with me just a minute, I'll show you how much I'll miss you," he said, leading her to the porch swing and seating her in it. "Don't move. I'll be right back."

Mystified, she did as he asked. Had he bought her a going-away gift? Surely not. It simply wasn't like him to spend money on such a thing.

He came back out of the house and sat down beside her. By the light spilling through the window from the parlor lamp, she saw that he held a small box. He opened it and revealed a ring.

"I want you to wear this so all those Choctaws will know that you belong to me," he said.

"But I can't wear my wedding ring until we're married!"

He held the box closer and the lamplight caught a shining stone. Her breath caught. It certainly wasn't the plain, wide gold band she'd expected—it was a narrow gold circle set with a gleaming opal.

"This isn't your wedding ring. It's your betrothal ring."

"Oh, Lee . . ."

It was beautiful. But just looking at it gave her a terrible feeling, a hollow, trapped, hopeless feeling.

It was beautiful. But she didn't want him to put it on her, she didn't want it surrounding her finger.

For a moment she couldn't speak.

"It's something to make you think of me while you're gone," he said gruffly, and she suddenly felt like crying.

"Oh, Lee, it's beautiful! But it's so valuable . . . and we might get robbed on the trail . . ."

"It was my mother's," he said. "I was saving it for Katie, but now I know I want you to have it. Emily, I love you more than I can ever tell you."

He had never spoken with such deep emotion, such heartfelt truthfulness. It warmed her through and through. He was sweet, truly he was, and he did love her. She loved him, too.

But when he reached over and took her left hand in his, she had the sudden, insane urge to snatch it free. She fought the feeling down.

"Think about me every time you look at this ring shining on your hand," he said solemnly, as if making a vow.

She thought she would suffocate; it was as if all the air in the whole yard, all the air on the whole ranch, were suddenly used up. Why in the world was she having this panicky feeling? After all, she *did* want to marry him.

Maybe she didn't feel the same trembling, hot excitement when she was in his arms as she felt within Tay's, but she felt truly safe with Lee. Lee wanted exactly what she wanted: a secure home with Katie and several more children right here on Las Manzanitas—in the bosom of her family.

"Wear it in good health, sweet Emily, and travel safe."

He slipped the ring onto her finger. Then she let him pull her close to him and kiss her.

She didn't feel what she'd felt with Tay, no, but then that was by far for the best. If she tried to live every day with that raging desire, it would kill her.

No, she thought, as she wrapped her arms around Lee and made herself kiss him back. No, she was not to be Tay's lover, not ever. Tay belonged to Cotannah, and that was the way things were meant to be.

Chapter 14

The next morning, Tay woke before anyone else, and by the time the house was stirring, he was dressed and packed. He avoided the dining room where Oleana was serving a quick breakfast—strong coffee, fried ham, and biscuits, judging from the aromas he smelled as he passed down the hall—and headed out for the stable so he'd have time to warm Eagle up a little before he saddled him.

And so he'd have a few minutes alone there to remember another early morning, the first morning he'd been here on the ranch. The morning after he'd met Emily.

The morning he'd held her in his arms for the first time.

A surge of hope rose in his blood as he swung his bag onto his shoulder and pushed open the back door. He was taking Emily home with him, after all. Maybe there were more magic early mornings still to come.

He wouldn't let himself think any further than that, not to what the People might think about him and Emily together, not to what might happen in the election. All he would think was that Emily was going to the Nation, and she had decided to go despite Lee Kincaid standing by her side, telling her no.

Whistling a scrap of a melody, he strode across the yard and around the round pen, looking up again and again to take in the red-streaked beauty of the early morning sky, crossed to the stable doors, and stepped inside. There was plenty of light to see by, streaming in through the high windows that faced the east.

He could see the horses clearly, standing in their stalls, and the stacked hay and the cross ties and the work saddles in the aisleway on their racks. He couldn't see Emily, though, but he knew she was there.

The minute he stepped inside the barn, he could feel her presence. He stopped and waited.

In a few moments he heard her voice coming from the back, from Sache's stall, no doubt.

"You'll have to be tied to the back of the coach sometimes," she was saying, "but I promise to ride you as much as I can."

He started walking toward her. "Maybe she'd be glad of a rest," he called. "Have you thought of that?"

"Tay!"

She sounded glad to see him. And when he came within sight, she looked it, too.

"Are you so journey-proud that you're skipping breakfast?" he asked.

She smiled. "Are you?"

He laughed. "How is it that every time we find ourselves alone in this stable at dawn, we waste our breath demanding reasons why we're here?" He walked up to the side of the stall and dropped his bag to the floor. "From what I overheard you telling your filly, I take it that you're riding in the coach today."

She ducked beneath Sache's neck and came to the near side of her to continue brushing her down. "Yes. I'll ride with Cotannah as long as she's in the coach. I think when we get two or three days away from the border, she'll want to ride horseback instead."

"Probably."

He watched her graceful movements, her slender fingers holding the handle of the brush as she tended the filly.

"Who all will be in the coach?"

"We're taking two because we'll have Aunt Ancie, Uncle Jumper, Maggie, Mama, the twins, Cotannah, and me. Then you and Cade and the outriders on horseback."

"Quite a caravan, I'd say."

"Yep," she said, bending to brush the filly's legs, "practically an *entrada*."

"What's that?"

"It's when a whole lot of people all move somewhere together in a great procession—my grandpa brought a whole village here from Mexico to work on the ranch. He thought of it when he saw he'd bought up all their cattle and they didn't have anything to do nor anything to eat."

She straightened up and reached with her

other hand, her left hand, to hold Sache's mane while she brushed it. And he saw the ring.

He froze in position, staring at it. The bitter betrayal he'd felt that day in the canyon came flooding back through him, only a thousand-fold stronger. The urge, the *need*, to hit something, to drive his fist through the wall, almost lifted his heels off the floor. Yet he couldn't move. He was silent so long, she turned and glanced up at him.

"Where'd you get the ring?"

Her delicate skin turned crimson. "Lee . . . g-gave it to me."

"To brand you as his."

Quick anger flashed through her embarrassment. "We are betrothed. You know that."

"Yet you're going home with me." His flat, accusing tone echoed off the walls.

She whirled to face him fully, raising the brush in her hand as if she would throw it. "I'm going with *Cotannah*. To help her *recover*."

"*Yeah, sure.*"

Then he turned on his heel, picked up his bag, and walked out.

Lee stood in the yard beneath the live oak tree feeling as if he had turned to wood. He hoped he had. How else could he stand to kiss her good-bye and watch her coach roll off down the driveway?

Thank goodness Katie was still asleep. She'd be out here bawling and squalling and clinging to Emily, and in general behaving the way he himself would like to.

He saw Emily then, coming out of the stable

leading that aggravating Sache filly, walking toward him and the coaches there. He tried to swallow the knot in his throat. How the *hell* was he supposed to just stand here and let her go?

He had to, though, he knew that. When she took the bit in her teeth and announced her decision in that soft, firm voice she'd used that night on the porch, he knew that she wouldn't budge, come hell or high water. And it was just like Emily not to budge from helping out when some sick person needed her. If Cotannah hadn't been sick and begging her to go with her all the way up there to the damn Choctaw Nation, Emily never would leave him.

She was trying to smile when she walked up to him, but she was doing a pretty poor job of it. That made him feel better. She was hating to leave him just as much as he was hating for her to go.

He went to take the filly's lead rope. "You oughta leave her here and let me take some of the sass out of her while you're gone," he said. And then he had to swallow hard again.

"Oh, Lee, you know I can't be without her. And if I wasn't here, she'd probably turn all wild again."

"Be a good thing if she did," he muttered. "Keep foolin' with her and she'll toss you over the moon someday."

Be damned if his hands weren't shaking till he could hardly make a knot. He did it, though, and got the filly tethered to the back of the coach just as Maggie and Cade came out of the house, each one carrying a sleeping baby.

Lee took Emily by the arm and walked farther back under the tree with her, back into the early-morning shadows.

"Don't forget me," he said.

"Oh, Lee! How could I?"

She sounded pitiful then, and that made him feel better, too.

"I'll think about you every day," he said, "and so will Katie."

"Don't mention me to her all the time, though. Time stretches way too long for children. Let her forget me if she can."

He reached for her hand, the one with his ring on it, lifted it to his lips, and kissed her palm. Then he pressed it to his cheek. "You look at that ring every minute," he said, and then he had to clear his throat before he could go on. "And it'll tell you how much I love you."

"I-I w-will."

The others all came around then, readying things to go, and the drivers climbed up and gathered the lines. Cade came to him with some last-minute instructions, so he went ahead and helped Emily up into the coach.

"I'll be back in a minute," he said, "to kiss you good-bye."

She was crying, and that made him feel better, too, because he knew she would miss him.

But all the time he was talking to Cade, all the time the outriders were riding up and surrounding them, even when she leaned out of the coach window and kissed him, he had to fight an awful foreboding. He would never say it out loud for fear it would come true, but all that time and while he watched the whole caravan roll down the driveway and create a cloud of dust up on the road, he felt like he might never see Emily again.

Emily settled into the seat beside Cotannah and held a handkerchief against her face to try to stanch her tears. "Thank goodness that's over. I tell you, partings nearly tear me apart. I-I hate to say g-good-bye."

"You won't be gone from him very long when you consider the whole rest of your lives," Cotannah said, patting her hand, "and it's so romantic that he gave you the ring because you're leaving."

Emily felt the ring like a weight on her finger. "W-w-well . . ." she said, "that's tr-true, 'Tannah. We won't be gone all that long."

"I may," Cotannah said sadly. "I may not *ever* come back."

Her tone of voice struck fear to Emily's heart. "Oh, but you have to! You promised that we'd see each other at least twice a year, remember?"

"You'll have to come to the Nation."

You'll have to come here, too.

But Emily didn't say it. Cotannah sounded too forlorn, too exhausted and pathetic, to argue with her.

Emily reached over and took her gloved hand and held it, trying to squeeze some of her own strength into her friend.

"I've never been safe anywhere but in the Nation," Cotannah whispered brokenly.

"Dear goodness, 'Tannah, this isn't like you," Emily cried. "Where's the old Cotannah who would spit in the eye of danger?" Emily wiped her eyes again, then resolutely put the wet handkerchief away. How could she cheer Cotannah when she was crying her eyes out?

"Lost, I guess."

Emily's heart filled with pity. "Well, we're going to find her again! I promise you that."

Emily waited, but Cotannah didn't answer. And she made no reference to marrying Tay or to Tay's protecting her or to becoming the wife of the Principal Chief.

A terrible thought came into Emily's head and guilt slashed through her, right to the bone. Did Cotannah know, somehow, that she had kissed Tay . . . twice? And done more than that? Had someone seen them that day on her bed and told Cotannah?

Had *Tay* told her? Maybe he'd felt guilty, too . . . Or maybe he had decided definitely not to marry Cotannah and he wanted to stop her expectations . . .

No. No. Dear Lord, she was losing her mind. She had to get a grip on herself. There was no reason to feel guilty, because she would never touch Tay Nashoba again.

She let her head drop back against the seat and took in a long, tremulous breath. Cotannah would be better soon—right now she was still very weak from being so sick. Once she was well, she'd be all set to get Tay's attention again, and Emily would help her every way she could.

But oh, how could she do such a thing? *Her* body was the one that had melded to Tay's as if made for that purpose, her own mouth had known his from some other time, her tongue had held the taste of his kiss since that first day on the caprock.

Her heart was the one broken by the look on his face when he saw Lee's ring on her finger. God help them all!

Without even realizing what she was doing, she let go of Cotannah's hand and wrung her own together. The opal ring was a tiny weight dragging her down. How could she bear this? How in the world could she bear it?

"I'm glad Cade said the railroad's too far out of our way," she said suddenly. "I'd hate for all of us to be cooped up together in one of those narrow little railroad cars."

This was better. This was much better to have Tay horseback with Cade and the outriding guards. She could probably make this whole trip without ever really being near him or alone with him. Even when she got out of the coach to ride Sache, she could ride on the other side of the road from him.

That comforting thought lasted only until the midmorning rest stop. While they ate the biscuits and fried quail that Oleana had prepared and two of the vaqueros scouted ahead, Emily walked alone to the edge of the little roadside grove of live oaks. She took off her hat and leaned back against the trunk of the largest one, listening to Cole and Miranda calling to each other as they played, hoping they wouldn't see her for a moment so she could try to get her feelings under some kind of control.

"Aren't you afraid you'll lose your new piece of jewelry to a bandit?"

It was Tay, speaking very quietly, as if they were in a conspiracy together. "Didn't Lee think of that?"

Her heart leapt and started beating in a wild, fast rhythm. He was standing right at her shoulder, and she didn't dare turn to look at him.

"*I* thought of that. I would so hate to lose it because it was his mother's," she said, barely breathing out the words.

She bit her lip. That was the wrong thing to say, but he always had that effect on her. He made her lay her whole self open, right to the heart. He could do it simply by looking at her.

"Oh? Do you not care for *your* sake if you lose it or not?"

She whirled on him. "I care," she cried. "I love Lee and Lee loves me very much, as if that's any of your concern!"

"I can make it my concern the minute you say the word."

His eyes glinted dangerously, two points of bright light in the darkness of his face, doubly shaded by the tree and his new Texas hat, which he reached up and pushed back onto his forehead. Then he reached for her and she felt her blood still in her veins.

He touched a long lock of hair that had come

loose from the chignon at the nape of her neck, brushed it back and forth with his fingertips against her cheek. She felt the light caress in every inch of her body.

"I'll make it my concern in a heartbeat. I want you, Emily."

The timbre of his voice was bewitching, dreamy and determined at once, vibrating with desire.

And I want you. Oh, Tay, how I want you!

She could not speak or she would say it. Yet she didn't need to say it—he saw it in her face.

He cocked his head and smiled to tell her so and held her gaze with his for a long, sultry time to say that he would wait until she told him so with words. Then he embraced all of her with his silvery gaze.

"You should never, ever, wear a hat," he said. "And it should be illegal for you to wind your hair and tie it into such a knot. Your hair needs its freedom." He let his eyes drift down to her lips and linger there. "All of you needs freedom."

For a long, breathless moment, she looked at him, tempted, tempted beyond what a human being could bear to simply tilt her mouth up to his. She could already taste his lips. And the light breeze stirring through the trees was bringing his scent to her nostrils: horse, leather, sweat, soap, and *Tay*, that woodsy smell that was his alone.

Desire, *aching* desire, already so familiar now, stirred deep inside her, the desire that had come to full life that early morning on her bed. That morning when his hand held her breast . . .

But where could such a liaison lead? Nowhere.

To tragedy. For them and for other people.

"Cotannah," she whispered, although she didn't think that her lips could move. "Cotannah needs to be your concern."

"If that's the way you feel." He spoke as quietly as he had in the beginning, but now there was a proud edge in his tone sharp enough to draw blood.

"She isn't well," she said quickly, trying to force the conversation from herself to her friend, "not as well as we've been thinking she is. We all need to try to cheer her, encourage her, try to make her happy again."

He stood silent for so long, looking at her, that she thought he hadn't heard.

"Emily," he said, "someday you'll wake up and realize that the only person you can make happy is yourself."

He stared down at her with his eyes like gray flint—flint arrowheads to cut up her heart. "You'd better pray that day doesn't come too late."

"Oh? And who are you to give such wise advice? You don't strike me as the happiest person in the world, Tay Nashoba!"

He raised one black eyebrow and his eyes changed from hard flint to soft clouds. Raging storm clouds. "Touché," he said, "Miss Emily."

He turned on his heel and walked away. She

reached for the tree and pressed her palm to its rough bark until it broke the skin.

For the rest of the long journey, Emily comforted herself with the thought that Tay had begun paying more attention to Cotannah. However, the reality was that he had not; she acknowledged that late at night when she was trying to fall asleep beneath the stars. He had remained as solicitous of Cotannah as he had been when she was so ill, but his was the same kind of attentiveness that they all gave her: She was their wounded darling, their innocent hurt without reason, and they all would do anything, give anything, for her to be her old self once more.

What truly had changed, she finally realized, was that Tay paid less attention to *her*, Emily, than he had since the day they met. That was good, that was fine, that was exactly what she wanted. Wasn't it?

But then the old midnight doubts about Lee would begin to nag at her and the new, wild woman who lived deep inside her would spring to life again, screaming that she wanted a life full of passion. That word brought the taste of Tay to her lips and his chiseled face to her mind every time; then she would have to work all the next day to not pay attention to him.

He didn't speak with her alone again until they had traveled for what seemed forever and had arrived deep in the Choctaw Nation. "One more day," the twins were chanting as the expedition made its way through the wild and beautiful Kiamichi Mountains early that last evening of the long journey. "One more day to Un-cle Kul-li Ho-te-ma's house." Emily was on horseback, with Cole in front of her in the saddle and Miranda behind, as the two coaches, the supply wagon, and the outriders all moved on, determined to make one more mile before dark, when Tay rode his horse up beside Sache.

"Have you all been listening?" he asked.

"Listening to what?" Miranda asked.

"Wagon wheels," Cole answered.

Tay chuckled. "Besides the wagon wheels, what else do you hear in the Choctaw Nation that you also hear when you're home on Las Manzanitas?"

They listened. The high, wavering animal call they had just heard came again.

"*El coy-ote!*" Cole cried.

Maggie came trotting up from the rear of the group where she'd been riding beside Cade.

"Once Cole decides to talk, he speaks two languages instead of just one," she said, laughing and holding out her arms to her son.

Immediately both he and Miranda wanted their mama instead of their Mimi, so both Maggie and Emily stopped their horses and made the transfer.

"We'll teach him to speak Choctaw while you all are here, and you can learn it, too," Tay teased Maggie.

He turned the full force of his smile onto

Emily, and she felt the power of it as much as that of the setting sun.

"Miss Emily, the teacher, may have to help me, though," he said. "I have no experience to draw on."

"You'll need a *lot* of help," Maggie said, laughing as she rode away with her children, "because it's really hard to keep our attention."

When they had gone on ahead, Tay continued to ride beside Emily at a slow trot.

"Did you know our Comanche brothers and other tribes out west call *el coyote* the song-dog?" He spoke in an easy, conversational tone that made it seem they had been talking together for hours.

"Yes," she said, "I had that very thought when I heard him."

"Perhaps he will come and sing for the dancing at Uncle Kulli's place."

The dancing. Oh, but that made her think of the fiesta and of the dance they had shared. She shot a quick look at him and his gray eyes caught hers.

He had intended to make her think of dancing in his arms, his glance told her. He wanted her to remember.

The coyote called again, a rising howl, wild and dark and elemental. It set an excitement stirring in her, something new that she could not name, a fire running high in her blood. A fire of desire for Tay.

She had to take her mind from it, had to talk about another subject. But the vision, the feeling, of herself in his arms had already taken hold.

"Wh-what other music will there be, in case *Senor* Coyote is busy that evening?" she murmured.

"Drums and claves, flutes, bells, and gourd rattles. And, of course, the *human* singers singing."

When they had danced, his shoulders had felt like steel beneath her hands, steel ropes covered with silken skin and cool cotton, and they had held her in an invincible circle of safety. Oh, dear Lord, how would she ever live for the rest of her life never going into his arms again?

She had to get away from him. She must put Sache into a long, fast trot and ride away from him.

Instead, she held her mare steady and stayed beside him. She swallowed hard. "What are claves?"

"Striking sticks." His gaze held on to hers again. "Sometimes they are the only rhythm makers there besides the bells and the gourd rattles the dancers wear." The flames deep in his eyes grew hotter. "Will you dance with me, Emily, even though you are a woman betrothed?"

There was an undertone of challenge to the question, a tension that danced along the hard edge of his tone. Oh, dear Lord, he hadn't quit on her after all!

The barefaced boldness of his look set her nerves screaming to touch him, made her lips throb and ache for his kiss. She actually stood, for an instant, in the stirrup nearest him, as if to lean across the narrow space between them.

This insanity had to stop and stop now.

"Dance with Cotannah," she said, almost choking on the words, as she put her heels to Sache and started on ahead. "She's the one you need and she needs you, Tay."

Chapter 15

The next afternoon Emily found out how frighteningly true those words of hers were. She was pacing the room she and Cotannah shared in Uncle Kulli Hotema's house, alternately dressing her hair for the welcome celebration and looking out the window, watching the early arrivals who were already getting things under way out in the yard. A cold knot lay in the pit of her stomach and a new, hot rage was building in her blood against Cortina's *bandidos*—because Cotannah was worse, not better.

That truth had occurred to her the moment after Cotannah left the room a half hour ago. It seemed inconceivable, incomprehensible even, but the closer they had come to the seat of the Nation and Cotannah's extended family and old home, the farther they had traveled from the Nueces Strip and the bandits who had brutalized her, the more fragile Cotannah's spirits became. Her body was healing more every day, yes, but her mind and her soul seemed even more wounded.

Emily dropped down into the window seat of the bay window looking out to the south and stared down at Uncle Kulli's servants setting up a speaker's podium on the lawn. All the candidates for tribal office would speak, Uncle Kulli had informed Tay happily when they'd arrived yesterday. But right now she was worrying about Cotannah.

There was a selfish reason, too, for her to try to do something to cheer her friend. Her ragged nerves, her torn heart, simply did not have the strength to deal with her feelings for Tay and be in this state of panic and consternation about Cotannah all at the same time.

That thought made her legs turn to mush and she leaned back against the window facing to watch the door as she heard Cotannah's voice in the hall, chatting with Pansy, the maid. It would be a wonderful relief if *she* could talk to *her* best friend about *her* troubles, too. If Cotannah weren't so lost in her own dark thoughts, she would've demanded to know what Emily was hiding long before now.

Pansy came in with Cotannah and began laying out her clothes while Cotannah went to the dressing table and began combing her long, wet hair. Emily drew up her knees, folded her arms around them, and tried to think exactly how she should begin after Pansy left them. She had to force 'Tannah's low spirits out into the light of day without making them worse.

"Oh, Mimi, it's so exciting," Cotannah said, meeting her eyes in the mirror. "People have been coming in from the mountains all night, and they're setting up camp in Uncle Kulli's meadow and all along the edge of the woods. Dozens of families—maybe hundreds, even!"

Anybody else, any stranger or slight acquaintance, would think Cotannah was happy and looking forward to all the excitement to come. But her tone was so false that her voice nearly broke.

"Anything else right now, Miss 'Tannah? Want I should he'p you dress your hair?"

"It'll be best to wait till it dries, Pansy," Cotannah said. "Why don't you leave us for a while? I'll call you when I want my dress."

Cotannah kept her back to Emily as the maid went out the door and closed it; she continued combing the tangles from her long hair with her hand trembling so that she created more.

"You might as well talk to me, 'Tannah," Emily said. "Something is eating away at you inside . . ."

She stopped. The awful thought that had tormented her before struck her again. What if Cotannah had sensed Emily's feelings for Tay? Worse, what if she'd seen Tay's interest in her?

Cotannah whirled around on the vanity stool so she could face her. "Something must be wrong with me," she blurted, shaking the silver-trimmed comb for emphasis. "I know there is, Mimi, and I don't know what to do about it. Maybe there's nothing I *can* do."

The anguish that cracked her voice tore Emily's heart right in two.

"Nothing's wrong with *you*," she cried,

wanting to jump up and run to Cotannah, but staying still, working at keeping her voice calm and empty of pity. "It's the bandits that have something wrong with them; oh, honey, it's not *you*!"

Cotannah's manner, the way she held herself, so unlike her usual proud posture, was the embodiment of despair, and she dropped her comb in her lap in a gesture that was entirely hopeless.

"It has to be me," she said. "What other girl or woman do you know who has been mishandled and insulted as I've been, and by different men at different *times*?"

Tears sprang into Emily's eyes, but she blinked them away. Even in this weak state, Cotannah would storm out of the room in a fit if she sensed that Emily pitied her.

"That was only a coincidence," Emily said fiercely, "a stupid, rotten, *horrible* coincidence."

"Do you really believe that?" Cotannah asked quietly.

"Yes! Of course I do! I wouldn't say it if I didn't!"

"Then why does Tay refuse to court me?"

She stared at Emily, who stared back at her, speechless.

"Because he thinks something is wrong with me," Cotannah said triumphantly. "He knows other men have torn at my clothes and looked at me and had their hands on me, and he thinks I've done something to cause them to do it."

"No! No, 'Tannah, that's not true. Tay would

never think that!" She jumped up and ran to Cotannah.

"Tell me the truth," Cotannah said, regaining enough of her pride to lift her chin and stare defiantly into Emily's eyes. "Don't try to spare my feelings, Mimi. I need to know the truth. Tay is your friend, I know that—has he talked to you about me?"

Cotannah was trembling all over, violently, as they fell into each other's embrace, and Emily clamped her arms around her hard, as if she could stop the shivering with the warmth of her own body.

"He saw the bandits touch me, Mimi, he saw them! Now he doesn't want me, he'll never ask me to marry him, and it's all my own stupid fault!"

She held Emily so hard, she thought she would never breathe again, then suddenly Cotannah jerked free and whirled around, grabbed up the hairbrush from the dressing table, and whacked herself across the thigh with it.

"I could just kill myself!" she cried. "I'll never forgive myself. Tay doesn't want me anymore, and it's all my own stupid fault!"

Emily took her by the elbows and turned her to face her. "It was your decision to go out alone that morning," she said, speaking firmly and patiently as she would to one of the children in her class, "but it was the decision of Cortina and his bad men to attack you. *That* was not your fault."

Cotannah completely broke down. She

dropped her head onto Emily's shoulder and began crying great, deep, racking sobs.

"It was not your fault," Emily said, over and over again like a litany. "What the bandits did to you was not your fault."

She patted Cotannah's shoulder and hugged her around the shoulders until she finally calmed down. She left her to get a handkerchief from the chifforobe drawer.

"You're not guilty, 'Tannah," she said as she stood in front of her and put the scrap of cloth into her hands. "I used to think all the misery was my fault when my father would yell at my mother about something I'd done, but I've come to realize the fault was his."

Cotannah wiped her eyes and then looked up. "Maybe you're right," she said, "but the fact remains that I've got to do something to find out if Tay is ever going to court me or not. I've got to do *something*." She blew her nose fiercely and stood up to look at Emily eye to eye.

"You have been really, really sick, Cotannah! How could he court you?"

Cotannah stared at her. Emily watched the slimmest glimmer of hope come into her eyes.

"You're his friend, Mimi," she said. "He'll listen to you. Will you ask him for me? Ask him if he's going to court me now that I'm well?"

Dumbfounded, Emily stared at her in silence.

"I love him so much, Mimi," Cotannah said with a trickle of her old pride and spirit flowing back into her voice. "I love him so much that I can't stand it, and I have to know if he thinks he can ever love me or I'll go crazy. Will you find out for me, please?"

Emily turned away and looked blindly out of the window, her heart beating like a tolling bell. She had made that vow at the foot of Cotannah's sickbed on Las Manzanitas to help her win Tay Nashoba. Now was the time.

"Please, Mimi," Cotannah said. "Promise on your word of honor that you'll talk to Tay about me. I know it won't be easy to tell him how I feel and all, but think how hard it would be for me to tell him myself!"

The old zest for life, the old strength and determination, were all back in Cotannah's voice.

"Yes," Emily said, and clamped down hard on the protests of every instinct in her body while she looked at the new hope in Cotannah's brown eyes. "I promise. On my word of honor."

Tay arrived at Kulli Hotema's place for the Chisk-Kos' welcome celebration (which would include the first round of election speeches) wishing with all his heart that he were a Shape-Changer. He would change into a deer, he fantasized, so he could run into the woods and find a secret place, a quiet, cool cove of a place in among the low-hanging leaves where no one would notice him.

Thank God the animals couldn't talk or his horse would have been yammering at him the whole five miles over here from his farm. Ever since he'd been back home at Tall Pine, which was precious few hours, there had been somebody at his door, or at his table, wanting something from him as a member of the Board of Governors of the Choctaw or as prospective Principal Chief. Or his foremen telling him something about his farm and ranch business—somebody talking, talking, talking at him constantly when he needed to think. And now, in a little while, he had to climb up onto a platform and talk some more to a whole sea of upturned, expectant faces.

He set his jaw so hard, it made his teeth hurt. He was sick to death of trying to fulfill other people's expectations. *And* he was sick to death of trying to know what his own expectations were. How could he wish to marry a woman he loved when he knew the People wouldn't want her as wife of the Principal Chief? Why couldn't he ride over here to Uncle Kulli's each evening and begin a courtship of Cotannah and marry her, as the whole Nation expected him to do?

Why did he have his mind and his heart filled up with Emily all the time when she already belonged to another man? Of her own free will she belonged to Lee Kincaid and wore his ring to remind everyone of that fact—*after* she had lain on her bed with him, Tay Nashoba, and kissed him and reveled in his touch as if there would be no tomorrow.

After she had told him with her lips and her hands and the helpless sounds of pleasure from deep in her throat that he, Tay Nashoba, was the only man she wanted. How could she have done that? Emily, like himself, did not indulge in such behavior lightly.

He exhaled in a deep, long breath, trying to blow the thought and her image away, and then laid the rein against his horse's neck to turn off the road and in to the sun-drenched gravel drive that led to Uncle Kulli Hotema's house. As soon as he raised his eyes and looked at it, the muscles across his shoulders tightened into a knot.

They were already gathering, the People, and they would be here until the election was held. East of Uncle Kulli's house, in the hay meadow, stood many tents and small camps. His pens and corrals were filled with horses, parked buggies covered the barn lot, and the two acres of the east side yard held a swarming crowd. Half the Nation or more would be coming in from the mountains to hear and talk to the candidates and to vote.

They were *his* people. He had a great duty to them and to the Choctaw who had gone before them, to the ones who had survived the Trail of Tears and brought them to this western country. It would be an insult to the sacrifices they had all made if he let the Burtons and their ilk take over and fritter away the coal and timber rights and then, finally, the land itself. He couldn't quit now.

Leaning on his cane, Kulli rose from his seat on the porch as Tay rode in and thumped down the steps to meet him.

"That horse thief Joe Burton has been sneaking around through the crowd haranguing people all morning," he said. "I'm glad you're here to show him up for the no-good liar that he is."

The old man's passionate partisanship made Tay grin in spite of his dark mood. He dismounted and threw his reins to the little boys who ran up to take them.

"I thought about just riding right on by, Uncle Kulli," he said as he walked over to shake hands. "I'm about done with making speeches."

The old man grabbed his arm and gripped it affectionately. "You better not be," he said. "You better use that silver tongue of yours to save this Nation. Them crooked renegades of Burton's will sell us down the river—why, they'll give the coal and timber rights to the White-eyes with both hands if the bribes're big enough."

Uncle Kulli turned Tay around and began leading him away from the house and toward the podium he had had set up on a platform in the side yard. "This here election's going to be a close one," he said, shooting Tay a sharp sidelong glance. After a heartbeat he added, "I'm thinking my Cotannah has about come back to her full health."

Cool panic curled through Tay's gut. "It seems so," he said.

He would have to make a decision soon. Even though he and Cotannah hadn't had a chance to really get acquainted, he needed to court her and ask for her hand if he was ever going to, for the sake of the Nation. They should announce the alliance of their two old families in the next day or two so the celebration could become a part of the festivities, and traditions and Choctaw history would come back to mind.

But even as he had the thought, his eyes were searching the crowd near the platform and then the people gathering around the tables laden with food, looking for Emily. Looking for her hair, glinting golden in the sun, looking to see her sweet face.

As soon as he realized what he was doing, he was furious with himself. Emily was his *friend*, and nothing more, for God's sake! Emily had nothing whatsoever to do with whether or not he asked Cotannah to marry him. It didn't matter whether he would ever love her.

He turned his attention to what Uncle Kulli was saying about the Burton faction. He moved with the old man through the crowd, shaking hands and greeting people. And then, somehow, without ever glimpsing Emily anywhere, he found himself standing on the stage at the podium, about to speak to the People. But even looking down into their upturned faces didn't bring the devotion to duty that he usually felt at such times.

As he began speaking, though, his passions for the Nation took over and he spoke bluntly and honestly of his own record of service, comparing it to the checkered reputations of Joe Burton and his other, weaker opponent, Peter Tuska. Nothing he said was new to his audience, and most of them took it lightly, since they were accustomed to bribery and other corruption in their government and, as a matter of course, they expected each of the candidates to bring such charges against the others. But this time some of Joe Burton's relatives cried foul, and several other people, some of whom had just pledged Tay their support as he came into the crowd, joined in. Finally, sick at heart, he stopped his speech.

"It's up to you!" he shouted. "Vote as you wish! But remember that if Burton wins, the Nation is lost. If Tuska wins, it may take longer, but the results will be the same—the coal and timber rights will be gone, the Nation will be overrun with white intruders hungry for land, and the unity and spirit of the People will be torn to shreds!"

He leapt from the platform and pushed his way through the milling throng toward the peaceful green line of trees growing along the creek that ran through the meadow. He waved off Uncle Kulli and others who tried to approach him, but somehow, even in the press of milling bodies, the old man caught up to him.

"There'll be double this number of people here by daylight tomorrow," he said, gripping Tay's arm with fingers so strong and thin that they felt like claws. "And by then most of these fickle fools will decide that you're the best man for the job. Why, most of 'em think that right now. They just like to stir up a fuss and see a fight if they can cause one, *you* know that."

"I need some time to myself," Tay muttered.

"Go," Kulli said, "go to the running water. But don't be discouraged. You'll win, Tay Nash-oba, you'll win!"

Tay didn't speak to anyone else, didn't look to either side as he pushed on, and soon he was free. He strode into the blessed shadows of the moving leaves and made his way blindly toward the sound of the stream. If he lost his love for his People, for his duty, then what would he have left? If he no longer cared whether he fulfilled other people's expectations, what would he care about? Other people's expectations were all he had left in his life.

Emily dipped another piece of fry bread in honey, cupped her palm beneath it to catch the drips, and held it to Randy's rosy lips. But she fixed her eyes on the spot where Tay's broad shoulders, clad in a deep blue shirt, had disappeared into the trees.

She had to go to him. The anguish in his voice still echoed in her ears, and it was tearing her soul apart.

Miranda took a bite, then grabbed the whole piece of honey-laden bread in both hands to offer it to Cole. Emily reached across the picnic blanket for the wet cloth that Maggie held ready to wash her children's faces.

"I-I n-need to go . . ." she said, getting to her feet and wiping her hands quickly. She met Maggie's sharp blue gaze as she returned the washcloth. "I-I'll be back soon," she said as she turned away. "When Cotannah gets back tell her not to look for me—that I've gone to do what she asked."

She left them at a run almost, unable to bear the thought of answering Maggie's questions, but even more desperate to comfort Tay. Never, ever, in the weeks she had known him, not even when they watched the bandits mistreating Cotannah, had she seen him lose that smooth, cool composure of his. That scene a few minutes ago had been like seeing him tortured.

Most of the people in the crowd were moving away from the podium now, drifting toward the tables full of food or, in the case of most of the young adults and children, going to the games of bow shooting, jumping, and wrestling, so there weren't very many in her way. She ran toward the hackberry tree with the low-hanging branches that marked the way Tay had gone. It wasn't just that she was going to comfort him, she told herself, but she would also talk to him about Cotannah as she had promised. That would take his mind off his political troubles, at least, *or* it would give him hope that Cotannah could help him save the People.

She reached the edge of the narrow strip of woods and plunged in. The sound of water running rapidly over rocks hit her ears, immediately drowning most of the sounds from the gathering in the meadow behind her. Good. It would calm Tay and comfort him just to be near the creek.

Once she reached the bank, she stopped to look upstream and down. She saw no sign of Tay, not even a moving tree limb, so finally she chose downstream and began following the creek. After two steps she knew this was the right way, that she was coming closer to Tay.

Finally she pushed through a stand of thick cedars and found him in a secluded curve of the bank, surrounded on three sides by the woods and one by the water. He stood on the edge of the bank, which was cut deep in this bend, and stared at the tangled grove of young elm trees that grew across the stream.

She reached up and held on to a handful of prickly cedar branches to steady herself. His whole stance screamed despondency, although he held his back straight as ever and his broad shoulders squared. Anger did that, she thought—his hands were clenched and so was his jaw. He whirled to face her and she saw that his eyes blazed with it.

But they changed some as he looked at her.

"I didn't know you heard me," she said.

The corners of his mouth twitched. "I would've had to have my fingers in my ears not to hear you," he said. "You made more noise than a herd of buffalo."

"How flattering. You really know how to please a lady, Tay Nashoba."

He acknowledged that sally with the lift of one brow. "Just as I know how to please a crowd at a speech-making."

His tone was carefully light, but his pain cut through it underneath. It flashed in his eyes, too, although only for an instant, and ripped at her heart.

"Vacuous imbeciles," she said hotly. "Foolish simpletons. I could have waded into the lot of them with a hickory club if I could've got my hands on one."

He did smile that time. "Politics in the Nation has brought out the savage in you. Is that why you came after me? To tell me that?"

"Partly."

Neither of them moved, but suddenly it seemed to Emily that they stood closer together.

"What other reason?"

For a moment she couldn't remember. "To talk to you about Cotannah."

"What about her?"

"Sh-she's afraid that the reason you haven't come calling on her now that she's recovered is that you think it's somehow her fault she has been mishandled two different times in her life."

"Ah, no," he said, breathing it out as if he'd been punched in the stomach, shaking his head pityingly. Then the lines at the corners of his mouth deepened. "Damnit, what next? I never even thought of that."

This wasn't distracting him from his troubles, it was making them worse, but now that she'd started, she had to finish. She'd promised Cotannah.

"Or—or she thinks that you no longer want her because you saw the *bandidos* touch her and look at her . . . undressed. If either of those ideas is true, she wants to know it so she won't go on expecting you to court her anymore."

"I'll talk to her." He flattened his full lips into a hard line. "I am truly sick of trying to fulfill the expectations of other people," he blurted.

Startled, she looked up. "So am I."

The sapphire color of his shirt reflected in his eyes and made them burn with twin blue flames.

"I . . . I just don't understand why you aren't courting Cotannah," she said, not even knowing *why* she said it.

Maybe to fulfill her vow to make heaven for Cotannah.

Maybe to save herself.

Maybe to keep her brain and her tongue functioning beneath the onslaught of heated yearning that was making her legs go weak.

He held out his hand to her, his hard brown hand with its long, callused fingers.

"Come here and I'll show you."

Chapter 16

❧ ⟋⟍⟋⟍ ❧

In that instant she knew that she loved him. It came over her like the cry of the song-dog, in a rising howl from the wild woman within her soul.

I love you, Tay Nashoba.

The truth of it was as elemental as the excitement the dusky sound the coyote had stirred in her blood. This, then, was the name of that fire: love.

She took a step toward him. The wild woman had known this for a long time, since the dawn of that faraway morning when they'd lain on her bed.

He moved to meet her and then they were rushing together, desperate for each other's touch, starving for each other's taste. They melted together in a hard embrace. Tay ran his rough palms up and down her back, her sides, her upper arms, while she, on tiptoe, pressed her cheek against the jutting bone of his to imprint the rugged shape of his dear face into her skin.

His nearness, the scent of him, the feel, the taste, the sound of his voice moaning deep in his throat, filled all her senses. Then he was kissing her closed eyelids and she had to have that sweet and tender turbulence, that exuberant, *ripening* feeling that his lips were infusing into her blood and her skin.

His mouth moved, searching for hers, hers moved to meet his, and they kissed, hard and hungry with teeth and tongues, yet with lush, long, desultory tastings of lips. Finally, when they could not find one more wisp of air to breathe, they broke apart.

"Emily, Mimi, *ammi ohoyo pisa aiukli*," he murmured, caressing her hair with one hand as he pulled her farther into the shade of the trees with the other. "Come, come here to me."

"What did you call me?"

He drew her down gently to the sweet-smelling summer earth. "My fair woman."

His. His fair woman.

He let her go then, and she lifted her languid arm to bring him back to her, but he was ripping his shirt from his breeches and off over his head to spread it on the thick grass like a great, bright blue bird swooped down in flight to carry them off into a dream. This was a dream.

Tay reached for her, took her face in both his strong hands, looked deep into her eyes. Her whole being floated in air on the feeling he gave her.

"Oh," she said, through lips already swollen from his kiss, "oh, Tay."

He groaned, deep in his throat, and drove her down onto the bed he'd made, thrust his hands into her hair and tore it loose to come tumbling around her shoulders. It swirled down across her chest above the neckline of her dress, alive and hot from his touch. As she was.

Tay pulled her closer and threw one long leg over her thighs. "Stop me now if you want stopping," he murmured hoarsely against her lips. "Stop me now."

"I . . . couldn't . . ."

She couldn't talk anymore, either. She couldn't talk or think or move or do anything but look at Tay, at his eyes, dark gray with hunger as they roamed over her face and down her body.

"You're a golden fire in these mountains," he said, his voice rough and accusing, so hard that it made her even weaker. "A forest fire leaping from treetop to treetop, from peak to peak of the hills, dancing everywhere I turn, burning all the ground around me."

She threw both arms around his neck and pulled him to her. They kissed to distraction while they helped each other fight their way out of their clothes, kissed without stopping until they tangled tightly together with their silky skin caressing, hotter than if they lay in the sun.

He broke the kiss at last so they both could steal a breath; he rolled back to lean on one elbow and looked down into her eyes.

"Now that you're going to belong to me, you must take off that ring." His sensuous lips curved in a wondering smile. "Now that you are going to belong to me."

His smile washed her skin with warmth and her soul with light; it filled all her senses so that she didn't even feel the smooth stone and metal beneath her fingertips as she took off the ring. She fumbled in the folds of her dress, thrust the ring deep into its pocket without ever taking her eyes from his.

That done, she smiled back at him.

"Yes," he said. "Yes."

He cupped her breast in his hand, and then, with one last burning glance that set her completely on fire, he bent his head and took its aching tip into his mouth, fast, desperately suckling it with his rasping tongue and greedy lips until she arched her back and drove her fingers deep into his hair. She held his head cupped in her hands, uncertain whether to hold him there for more ecstasy or to pull him away because the pleasure had become too much to bear. After an agony of it, he decided for her. He moved to her other breast.

And his hands, his magic hands, were everywhere, exploring all of her, rousing her passions ever higher and higher until she arched up off the ground, almost sobbing, chanting a plea that was his name. He stroked her back, the insides of her thighs, then parted them, knelt between them, and bent his shining dark head to drop a kiss, a kiss light as the brushing of a bird's wing, on her belly.

When he looked up, she smiled into his silver

eyes and held out her arms. She pressed his face against hers and he held her, gently, as if she were a precious treasure, when he entered her. He lifted his head so he could see her face, his eyes darkening when the first, sharp pain made her gasp, and then once more they were smiling into each other's eyes as they began to move in the ancient rhythm of woman and man.

Oh, Tay! She tried to speak, she could only mouth the words.

He smiled again, a slow, seductive caress of a smile, a beguiling smile that narrowed his smoky eyes, and made her touch the sun-burned crinkles that deepened at their corners. Then the voluptuous pleasure filled her completely and she clung to him with all her strength as they rose, flying, into the sky on the bright blue bird.

Afterward, they simply lay together, sated, tangled in each other's arms. Tay fell asleep. Dreams and more dreams drifted on the still, hot air of the afternoon, and Emily dozed and let them fill her head. She dreamt of Tay holding her like this every day of the rest of her life, of him declaring that he loved her.

The slow, pulsing beat of a drum began, back at Uncle Kulli's place, and scared the dreams away. It advanced on her and Tay, marched across the campgrounds and the meadow, burst through the thick trees and into their private cove. It found them.

Emily twisted out from beneath Tay's arm

and sat up, reached for her clothes and started putting them on. Tears rolled down her cheeks to the drum's merciless beat.

Emily pretended not to know when Tay woke, but the minute he opened his eyes she felt them, warm on her skin. Warm and inviting. But she would *not* turn around. She *could* not. If she looked at him, if she even caught a glimpse of his face, she would go right back into his arms.

She jerked her dress on over her head, frantically, as if it were protective armor. She stuck her arms through the sleeves, pulled it down around her waist, and began to work at the buttons. Oh, if only she could've gone without waking him!

"Where are you going, *ammi ohoyo pisa aiukli?*"

Her shaking hands froze. And her treacherous bones melted.

I'm not your fair woman, Tay. I can never be your woman.

However much it needed to be said, though, she couldn't say it. Saying it would make a travesty of this irreplaceable afternoon. This afternoon that would have to sustain her for all the rest of her natural life.

So instead she said, "You need to be going, too. Uncle Kulli said this morning that you're to lead Starting Dance, and the drums have started."

"You wouldn't find yourself in tears so often if you'd make a habit of giving your deep feelings more free rein."

She whirled around and came up on her knees, facing him, holding her dress together where she'd stopped with the buttons. "I just *gave* free rein to my feelings, and look where it's got me!"

"Where?"

"Betraying my best friend! My friend who would do anything for me, my friend who is already sick at heart!"

He lay there, looking at her, a perfect statue of a man, but one made of warm copper instead of cold marble. Unabashedly naked, he just lay there, watching her with his incredible silver eyes.

"Cotannah has nothing to do with what happened between us here today."

"How can you *say* that?" She flung out her hands in exasperation, then grabbed at her bodice when it gaped open again. His gaze followed her gesture, then came to rest on her breasts, a gaze so hot with possessiveness that, even with her hands over the opening of her dress, her bare flesh felt branded.

"I say it because it's true."

"It is not and you know it."

"Cotannah will know that it's true once she has gotten over her surprise."

"Cotannah will never know this. *Think*, Tay! Do you want her to go through the rest of her life believing that something is *wrong* with her, that she's unclean because the bandits stripped her dress off and touched her, that they and that awful headmaster in Arkansas abused her because of something *she* did?"

He just lay there, watching her with his all-knowing eyes, which were darkening, hardening, by the minute. "We can convince Cotannah that she's wrong, that she isn't thinking straight."

Slowly, as if she were moving against the force of rushing water, Emily lifted her hands and finished buttoning her dress. She wouldn't let her gaze fall from Tay's accusing one.

"It seems to me that you're awfully quick to urge me to throw over the only best friend I ever had," she said as coolly as she could. "What about saving your People? What about your election?"

He ignored that. "I'm not promised to Cotannah," he said quietly.

"Well, I'm promised to *Lee*!" Shocked by her own words, she looked down at the bare finger on her left hand. Not until that moment had she thought of Lee.

"But you don't love him."

She ignored that.

"It's a strange thing to me," he said in that rich, rolling voice of his, "that you can even think about Cotannah or Lee at a time like this."

"A time like what?" she demanded stubbornly.

"A time of lovemaking between us."

Lovemaking. Oh, dear God, yes, they had been making love. Love that had already been born in her heart.

"Are you sorry?" he asked softly.

She turned away, tears stinging her eyes, and

reached blindly for one of her combs, holding back her tumbling hair with the other hand.

"Are you sorry?"

Now his voice was granite, pure smooth rock like his gray eyes when she looked at him again. He knew she had lied. He was giving her another chance.

Help me now, Lord, she prayed. Help me make him believe it. For the sake of many, many people, this must end now.

"Yes! Yes, I'm sorry beyond measure we ever touched each other!"

He swept his gaze away from hers, reached for his breeches and pulled them on, stood up with his back to her to fasten them. As if she hadn't already seen him naked. As if she weren't kneeling right there, this very minute, with the wonderful, tantalizing scent of him all over her.

The beat of the drum sounded steadily and Emily stayed in place, rooted there by her lie.

"Listen to me," he said suddenly, harshly, turning on her. "You have got to understand that you are not God. You can't manage everybody's feelings and you can't make everybody happy."

Fierce, unendurable pain sliced through her and she lashed back at him. "Well, you think you're God, too! You think you're responsible for who lived and died during the War!"

Shocked, *stunned*, by her own cruelty, appalled beyond belief that such terrible words had come out of her mouth, she scrambled to her feet, wheeling away from him, frantically trying to gather all her disheveled hair in one hand and fasten it on top of her head with the other.

Her heart cracked, all the way up and down. Oh, Lord. Oh, dear God, how could she have said such a deliberately hurtful thing? The blood in her body drained out through her feet and onto the ground.

"I'm sorry," she whispered, and she made herself turn around to face him. "Oh, Tay, I'm so sorry. I have no idea how I could say that."

He looked at her, his eyes like silver swords. "Perhaps you're learning," he said in a hoarse, hollow voice she'd never heard before. "After all, you certainly don't try to make *me* happy, do you?"

Her whole body was empty inside now, her heart gone, nothing but a hole in its place. She tried not to, but she watched every motion of his beautiful body, stiff now with fury and hurt, as he bent down and picked up his shirt. When he had put it on, he looked at her again, with his eyes picking up the frosty blue of the appliquéd pieces that formed a yoke across his wide shoulders instead of the brilliance of the shirt. His voice was hard when he spoke, hard but very quiet.

"It doesn't matter what we did or what we tell each other. Ultimately, Miss Emily, we're the kind who do our duty."

"Yes," she whispered, her throat nearly closing with relief that they could agree before parting. "You must save the People, Tay, and I must keep my promises."

She turned and fled.

All she wanted, *all*, was to be alone to hurt, to become accustomed to this constant pain, which went far too deep for tears. But the instant she opened the door to her room in Uncle Kulli's house and flung herself inside, Cotannah cried out.

"Mimi! Oh, Mimi, what in the world has happened? What's wrong?"

Emily stopped stone-still with her hand on the doorknob as Cotannah turned from the mirror and rushed to her. She reached out to her friend, and Emily submitted to a brief hug before guilt drove her to break away. Guilt and panic. What could she say? Was she so disheveled that Cotannah could see what she had been doing? Why, oh, dear Lord, *why* wasn't Cotannah outside at the celebration?

"I thought you'd never come," Cotannah said, following her to the bed where she collapsed into a heap. "But I had no idea something terrible had happened. Mimi, *what is it?*"

I have just lain with the man you think you love, the man you want to marry.

It might salve her conscience to blurt out the truth, but she couldn't claim that relief. It would destroy Cotannah.

"I—I—" Emily stuttered.

"Did someone hurt you? Did you have an accident? Look, oh, Mimi, let me get some water. You have a terrible scratch on your cheek that's all bloody!"

"The t-trees," Emily muttered. "I was run-

ning through the t-t-trees." Her mind searched
frantically for a reason. What could she tell
Cotannah that was big enough to explain her
being in such a state? She stalled for time to
think. "Wh-wh-why aren't you still out at the
c-celebration, 'Tannah?"

"Maggie gave me your message, so I was
dying to know what Tay said when you talked
to him about . . . me. I waited and waited for
you to come back, but I couldn't find you in the
crowd and I decided you might've come here to
the room for something."

Cotannah turned and ran to the washstand,
talking over her shoulder. "Did you see Tay?"

The question was like a knife to Emily's
heart.

Cotannah poured water, splashed a cloth in
it. "Well, did you?"

"Y-yes. H-he's going to talk with you
s-sometime soon."

"Do you think . . . Was I right about why he
isn't courting me?"

"No!" Emily cried, half sitting up to look at
her friend, frantic to atone for her sins by
freeing Cotannah from her fears. "No, 'Tannah, he never even thought of any of that." She
let her head drop back to the bed and pulled a
pillow into her arms for comfort.

"Well, did he say why he hasn't come calling
on me?" Cotannah said, running back to the
bed with the wet cloth.

Emily closed her eyes. She absolutely could
not go on with this charade. She could not. But
she did. "No," she said, shaking her head back

and forth in agony. "He just said he'll talk to you."

"Thanks, Mimi," Cotannah said with a heartfelt gratitude that multiplied Emily's guilt. "Thank you for talking to him for me. It greatly relieves my mind."

Emily threw one arm across her forehead. She wished she could crawl under a rock and hide forever. "I'm glad it relieves you, 'Tannah," she said.

"Now move your arm so I can get to this scratch on your face, and tell me why you were running through the trees," Cotannah said. "Was something chasing you?"

"No."

Cotannah began dabbing gently at the bleeding scratch. "You weren't playing with the twins, because they were with Maggie."

Emily sighed. Cotannah would never give up, and if the situation were turned around, neither would she. Best friends cared about each other.

"I was running from my own thoughts, 'Tannah, my own feelings."

There. That was honest enough.

But the inevitable question followed.

"What thoughts and feelings?"

"I . . . I can't marry Lee." She had no idea where that came from, but the instant she blurted the words, Emily knew they were true.

"What!" Cotannah stopped washing her wound, a horrified look on her face, her eyes wide with shock. "Why not?"

A terrible weariness, one that had nothing to

do with the distance she had run so fast, washed over Emily. A weariness that had nothing to do with Tay, either. "I don't love him."

Tears welled in her eyes, rolled down her cheeks. They stung terribly when they hit the scratch.

That was good. That was wonderful. That pain could serve as a tiny distraction from the agony raging in her heart.

"Did you get a letter from him?" Cotannah spoke in the overly patient tone of a mother speaking to an unreasonable child.

Emily closed her eyes again. "No. I just finally admitted to myself that what I've been thinking is true: Lee and I don't have a passion like Maggie's and Cade's. We really don't have a passion at all." Her tears came thicker and faster. "I d-don't think I'll ever marry, now," she said.

Cotannah dropped the washcloth and knelt beside the bed to put her arms around her. "Of course you will," she soothed.

"I can't talk anymore now," Emily said. "I want to be alone for a while."

"Then you shall be," Cotannah said decisively as she hugged Emily again and then got to her feet. "I'll put a dab of ointment on your face and then I'll go back outside where Tay can find me."

"Tell Maggie and Mama that I don't need anyone."

"I will." Cotannah found the salve and came back to her. She spread the ointment gently on Emily's wound and then dropped the tube in her hand. "You need to sleep, Mimi," she said. "Tomorrow we can talk about this some more."

When she was gone, Emily pushed to her feet and ran to lock the door. She turned around and threw her back against it, then, as more tears flooded out, she slid down into a crouch on the floor and covered her face with both hands.

Cotannah said they'd talk more tomorrow because she'd sensed there was much that Emily wasn't telling her. In three years they had told each other everything, shared every hope and dream and feeling, and now that closeness would be no more. Always, always now, there would be a secret between them, and Cotannah would sense it just as Emily had known when she was worrying over her secret fears. Now their friendship was changed forever.

And the one with Tay was over, she thought, with the great hollow feeling growing and growing inside until nothing was left of her but the shell of her skin. She and Tay could not possibly be friends now that they had been lovers.

She had lost Lee, too. She couldn't marry him, she could not be so dishonorable after she'd been with Tay—and she didn't *want* to marry him. She never had; she knew that now.

And Katie! She had lost Katie, too—she would never be her little girl. Fresh tears poured out and ran between her fingers covering her eyes. She could still smell Tay on her hands.

Oh, dear God in Heaven, how would she ever live without him now? The memory of this afternoon would have to sustain her through all the long years. She loved him so. Oh, dear Lord, she loved him so.

But Mama and Maggie and Cade, Cole, and Miranda would have to be enough for her now. The five of them and her pupils would be all she would have. If she couldn't have Tay, she wouldn't marry anyone.

No, she would never marry now. She would never have children of her very own. And poor little Katie would be so hurt!

What an irony! What a bitter, bitter irony: She, Emily, Gentle Emily, who always tried to make everybody happy, was ripping people's hearts out, left and right.

Including Tay's.

She went completely still. She had hurt him horribly when she'd said she was sorry they had ever touched each other; hearing those words had nearly killed him.

She knew he loved her.

She wrapped her arms around her knees and rocked from side to side in agony. Tay loved her; he had told her that with every inch of his body, with his eyes, with his wonderful, magical hands.

A tiny keening sound came from her throat as she swayed miserably back and forth. She could still feel Tay's hands, every single place they had touched her. She could still feel them and she always would.

But she would never hear him tell her in

words that he loved her because of the awful things she had said to him, the lies she had told and the cruel way she had mentioned the horrendous burden he carried from the War. Never, ever, had she deliberately hurt anyone like that, but somehow, since the first moment she'd laid eyes on him, Tay had always made her behave in ways that were totally out of character for her.

Like this afternoon's tryst in the woods.

She dropped her forehead onto her bent knees and went still again, laughing a small, bitter laugh. That was the greatest irony of all. Tay unleashed the wild woman in her, he turned loose all the deep feelings inside her that growing up in her father's house had taught her to hide so well.

And now she had no use for them because she was trapped forever by her bounden duty.

Chapter 17

E mily took to her bed and stayed there for three days and nights, pleading dizziness and pain in her stomach. It was true: Her whole body hurt in sympathy with her shredded heart, and she was light-headed from lack of sleep and too much thinking. The whole family seemed to doubt her, though—it was so unlike her to be sick *or* to isolate herself that they could not stop questioning her and they would not leave her alone. Cotannah didn't offer to sleep in another room when she returned from the celebration that first night—or from any of her many visits to the campground during the next few days. Instead, she sat on the side of Emily's bed and told her all about seeing and visiting with Tay's auntie Iola, whom she hadn't seen for years, and the other long-ago friends she'd run across again. A time or two she had exchanged a few words with Tay, she said, nothing of importance, and he hadn't asked to court her, but at least it was something. They hadn't yet had a chance to really talk, she confided—there were always too many people wanting Tay's attention—but she knew if he'd told Emily that he would talk to her, he would find a time soon.

Maggie and Mama came constantly, offering diagnoses and soup. Pansy brought herbal cures. The twins brought flowers they had picked from Uncle Kulli's garden. Cade brought strong coffee he brewed for her himself.

Finally, early on the fourth morning when the twins crawled into bed with her and prepared—with great excitement—to be treated alongside her by the medicine man Uncle Kulli was sending for, Emily threw back the covers and got up. She might as well. The rest of her life would have to be lived without Tay in it, so she'd better start learning how.

She sent the children to bring Mama and Maggie, then sat down at the dressing table to pull a brush through her hair. One glance in the mirror told her she looked dreadful—her eyes looked like two burnt holes in a blanket, and her color was gone, completely gone. She might have been deathly sick for a month.

Well, she would tell everybody why and get on with her life. She was tying her hair back with a piece of Cotannah's ribbon when her audience arrived. She took a deep breath to fortify herself and then turned to try to smile at them. No matter what it took out of her, no matter how much acting she had to do, she would convince them that there was only one reason she looked like this. Maggie and Mama already had guessed she was sick at heart instead of in body.

"Mama, Maggie," she said, as they burst through the door, thrilled that she had summoned them. "Please sit down for a minute. I have to tell you something before I lose my nerve."

It was true. A part of her, the big part of her that desperately needed a home and security, was terrified to do this. But her heart refused to give her a choice. "I know I've been worrying you all sick and I'm sorry."

Cotannah appeared in the doorway, and Emily waved her in. "I've taken off Lee's ring," she said, "and when we go home I'll give it back to him. I've decided I can't marry him."

Mama stared, dumbfounded. Maggie looked surprised but not shocked. "Why have you decided this?" she said.

"I-I-I just know I don't love him as much as I should love a husband."

As much as I love Tay.

Maggie's blue eyes looked straight into her soul, searching it. Emily's insides constricted.

Mimi, it seems to me that you're reacting a bit strongly to Tay Nashoba.

She had said that the first time Emily had ever danced with Tay. She must not guess anything about Tay now—for all their sakes, she must not.

"T-t-truly," Emily stammered, "I haven't even missed Lee at all, I've hardly thought of him since I've been away from him. I know I don't love him."

"Pshaw!" Mama said, dropping down to sit on one of the beds. "You've had a whole different world here in the Nation to take your mind from Lee. Love isn't thinking about someone every minute, every second."

Yes, it is. Oh, yes, Mama, it is.

But what she said was, "Well, whatever love is, I don't have enough of it for Lee to live with him for the rest of my life. I'm writing to him today and I'm writing to Katie." Her voice broke on the little girl's name. "I only hope he can keep his job and he and Katie and I can all live on the ranch as friends."

Mama was shaking her head in disbelief. "You were always, always, my most sensible daughter," she said. "I don't know what's come over you, Emily."

Love, Mama. Love for Tay Nashoba.

"I'll have my teaching and my pupils and Randy and Cole to love," Emily said, talking more to herself than to them. "And all the rest of you. I'll be f-fine."

"Well, don't talk as if you'll *never* marry!" Maggie cried. "Texas is full of tough, handsome men."

But the one tough, handsome man I want will be far away in the Choctaw Nation.

Just thinking that nearly killed her. But she pasted a semblance of a smile on her face and got up to go to her mother and sister and the friend she had betrayed, holding out her arms for whatever comfort they could give her.

Tay started looking for Cotannah the minute he stepped down off the podium that afternoon. It was unconscionable of him to have waited three days to talk to her when he knew she was truly suffering under her misunderstanding of his feelings, but those three days had been like three years of torture to him. They had drained him of strength and filled him with pain in its place until he hadn't been able to cope with anyone else's additional hurt.

Well, whether he felt like it or not, today he had to talk to her. At least he could release her from her agony of thinking that the touch of those bandits had made her forever unclean.

He lifted his hand in greeting to his auntie Iola, who, along with Uncle Kulli, was still applauding his speech, and stepped around a chattering knot of Joe Burton supporters to get a better look at a girl he had glimpsed.

"Cotannah!"

She turned to look at him with such a pure happiness coming over her face that it sent waves of guilt rolling through him. What a cad he had been! He would tell her now, in the gentlest way, that he could never court her, never love her except as the little sister she had always been to him.

They worked their way toward each other through the milling crowd.

"Come walk with me, 'Tannah."

She turned toward the line of trees that marked the creek. "Want to go down by the water?"

Dear God in Heaven, no. I'll never be able to go there again.

"Let's go over by Uncle Kulli's yard fence so we can smell the honeysuckle."

She chattered to him about being back home in the Nation as they made their way through the crowd.

"You seem to have come back to your old self," he said, smiling down into her upturned face.

"Yes, I have."

She looked up at him eagerly. *I'm well now,* her eyes seemed to say. *Well enough for you to come courting me.*

He must get to it, get this over with. "Emily tells me—" he had to stop and swallow to try to rid his throat of the lump that had come when he said her name; he could not say it again "—that you're worrying about my reaction to . . . the bandits' abusing you. That I might be put off by that or think that it was your fault. That's not true, Cotannah. I've never thought about it in that way at all."

She smiled up at him, adoration in her eyes. "Mimi said that you told her that, and I am so *glad,* Tay!"

"Don't ever, ever think that getting kidnapped was your fault, 'Tannah. I can't fathom thinking any less of you for such a reason—no sensible man would.''

As if *he* were a sensible man!

She tilted her head in her old coquettish way and slipped both her hands into the crook of his elbow. And she waited. Expectantly.

Yes. There was definitely a tension of waiting there between them. She was waiting for him to ask to court her, now that her main worry was out of the way.

Cotannah, I can never come courting you, honey. I can never love you except in the way I love you now—as a sister and friend.

He opened his mouth, but he couldn't say it. Her eyes were shining so that he couldn't bring himself to douse their light. The world was already too full of hurt. She had already been through too much for a girl of eighteen years.

But he was a man of thirty-five years, and he knew that letting her put her hopes for the future in him was even more cruel. "I'll always love you like a sister, 'Tannah . . .''

Then a sudden bitterness took him. Why didn't he just go on and add that he would try to *learn* to love her like a wife? Why didn't he salve both her loneliness and his and just make a match right now that the Nation would love?

Because somehow, some part of him couldn't give up on Emily, even if she *was* sorry that he had ever touched her. Even if she didn't love him more than she loved Cotannah. Or her loyalty to Lee. A pain stabbed through him that left him physically weak. Oh, what he would give if he didn't love her so!

Cotannah laughed and squeezed his arm. "I don't know what I would've ever done without you. You were my big brother when Cade was off having his Wandering Year."

He grabbed the opportunity to talk about something else while they strolled along in the shadow of the sweet-smelling honeysuckle vines. Thank goodness they weren't roses to remind him of Emily.

"Cade as a settled family man is the most amazing sight I've ever seen," he said.

The topic distracted Cotannah, but nothing helped him. The fragrance of flowers, no matter what kind they were, filled his heart with the memory of Emily.

That evening, after actually falling into a true sleep for most of the afternoon, Emily dressed for the dance. She had no choice—everyone expected her to join the festivities, and she could not hope to escape them. Also, she needed to go where Tay would be; she couldn't avoid him forever.

But when she had put on her best lavender gown trimmed in matching lace to give her courage, when she had walked with Cotannah out of Uncle Kulli's house into the sultry early dusk, she changed her mind. She didn't want to see Tay, she *couldn't*, not ever again, unless she could call out his name and run into his arms.

The drums and the dancing and a round of speech-making had started early in the after-

noon and had gone on until suppertime, which
was just about over. A lull had fallen before the
evening dances—people were finishing their
meals at the long tables and on picnic blankets
or sitting around on the grass visiting. The
aromas of spicy pork and beef roasting in the
pits and of beans, greens, and hominy soup
cooking in huge iron pots filled the air.

Emily took a long, deep, shaky breath. She
could smell the pines in the mountains, too, on
the slight breeze, and the cooler air of the
night. She would smell everything, look at the
people, and listen to the unfamiliar music playing, and forget about Tay. She wouldn't even
think about him anymore.

She tried not to look for him as she strolled
through the meadow campground, but her
blood raced in anticipation anyway, and her
eyes roamed in and out of the shadows and the
summer twilight that lay over the crowd, stopping her heart as they touched on each tall,
broad-shouldered man. None was Tay.

Disappointment, so bitter she could taste it
on her tongue, formed a knot in her throat as
she walked along beside Cotannah.

She made her legs keep moving, made herself smile vaguely whenever Cotannah smiled
and waved at someone she knew. But again she
was searching for him, trying not to let Cotannah notice, trying not to know it herself.

"Look, there's Tay!"

Startled, Emily stopped and followed Cotannah's frank stare.

He was standing beneath a tall pine—hadn't

Cotannah said his farm was named Tall
Pine?—relaxed and entirely at ease, his shoulders and one heel propped against the trunk
and his hat pushed back on his head while he
talked and laughed with the half dozen men
gathered around him. He stood out among
them as the moon would in the dark sky a few
minutes from now. Her heart crashed against
the wall of her chest.

Oh, yes, there he was.

Tonight he wore a pale gray shirt to match
his eyes, or maybe it was white, made to look
gray by the lengthening shadows. It shone like
silver when he made a sweeping gesture with
his arm.

All around him the meadow looked peaceful
and serene, with the smoke curling up from the
campfires and the people moving slowly back
and forth and the breeze waving the branches
of the trees along the creek. It all looked so
peaceful compared to the turmoil in her heart.

She would enjoy it and not look at Tay again.

But then someone spoke to Cotannah and
took her attention away, and Emily's treacherous eyes drifted to him again.

He was more dressed up than she had ever
seen him. His tall black hat had two long white
feathers tied to the hatband, his shirt had fancy
appliqués across the shoulders just as those of
almost all the other men did.

Streamers tied to his beaded belt swung at
his side when he moved, long ribbons of blue
and maroon, white and silver, with ornaments
tied in them at the bottom, brushing his knee.

He looked handsome, festive, and very happy, laughing with his friends, there in the center of his People.

And she felt unbearably lonesome.

Maggie and Cade and Mama were here somewhere, Cotannah was right here by her side, but she felt lonesome. Cotannah was speaking Choctaw to the older woman who had hailed her.

When Emily turned to her she switched to English. "Come on, Mimi, I want you to meet Tay's auntie Iola."

Cotannah pulled her over to sit in a straight, cane-bottomed chair, one of two empty ones facing two that were filled with plump, older women. Both had twinkling dark eyes; Tay's aunt had a thick braid wound around her head.

After the introductions, both women smiled at Emily and then set in to quizzing Cotannah. Had Tay been courting her? Had she been encouraging people to vote for him? Didn't she feel much better, now that she was home in the Nation again?

They went on and on, always somehow subtly touching on the subject of Tay and Cotannah. From time to time, when she least expected it, Emily caught Auntie Iola's button eyes darting over to her.

"Did you see Tay is wearing the *eskofatshi* I made him?" the other woman, Hattie Tubbee, asked Cotannah.

"I saw it. It's beautiful."

"What is it?" Emily asked.

"The beaded belt," Hattie said proudly. "I

used the crossed sticks and the coiled serpent because Tay Nashoba is the only one running for Principal Chief who will keep the old traditions." She slapped her fat knees and threw back her head to laugh. "Tay, he told me I should've used the road and the circle because it'll be a long, hard journey for him to keep this ornery People unified."

Auntie Iola and Cotannah laughed, too. Emily had no idea what was funny.

Someone struck a beat on a drum then, and began to sing a slow, plaintive song.

"Yo he le, yo he le, ka yo wa . . ."

"Time to think about dancing," Iola proclaimed, and heaved herself to her feet. She slapped Emily on the shoulder. "Come and dance with us," she said, as she waddled away with Hattie.

"That invitation didn't sound too cordial to me," Emily said dryly when they had gone.

"Oh, she meant it," Cotannah said. "Iola will like you just fine unless you try to settle down and move into the Nation. She and her husband—and half the rest of the tribe—have been going around here for months raving that white intruders are going to be the ruination of the Nation.

"Come on, Mimi. When we get to the Stealing Partners Dance I intend to steal Tay if he doesn't steal me, and maybe then we can talk some more."

Just the sound of his name made Emily feel his arms around her. Suddenly she could barely hold herself up to walk along beside

Cotannah. "Some more? So he *did* finally call on you?"

"No, we talked this afternoon after the Principal Chief candidates were done with their speeches. He said not to ever think that getting kidnapped was my fault and that he could not fathom thinking any less of me for such a reason. Oh, he was so sweet to me, Mimi!" She smiled dreamily. "I just know he'll make a courting call on me soon. He really hasn't had much of a chance to since we arrived here, and I got my good spirits back again because the Board of Governors has met every night this week and we've had the speeches every day and all."

She beamed at Emily as they walked slowly on again. "If it weren't for you talking to him about me, and telling me what he'd said, I'd still be moping around thinking that he couldn't stand me . . ." She slipped her arm around Emily's waist and gave her a hug. "Thanks, Mimi. You're a true friend."

Oh, yes. If that's true, 'Tannah, you don't need any enemies.

But of course, she didn't say it.

When they reached the large, packed-down circle that was the dance ground, men and women were already forming a long double file of dancers, men on the outside, women on the inside, and beginning to move in a counterclockwise circle.

"Don't join in when the dancers answer the singer," Cotannah said as she and Emily stepped into the women's line. "In the Starting Dance, only the men and boys sing."

Emily made a noncommittal noise in answer because she wasn't sure exactly what Cotannah had said. Tay was walking toward the dance ground with his powerful stride, making the long, colored ribbons on his belt swing with a furious rhythm. He and the men were still talking, and they took places in the men's line without ever once glancing at the women's.

Emily forced herself not to look at him, set her gaze on Cotannah's feet so she could see what to do. But it didn't really help. She could taste his mouth and feel his hot eyes on her.

Her knees went weak at the thought. How could she live the rest of her life with him ignoring her like this?

One of the men, the leader, sang out a short phrase, which the other men and boys repeated, and the dancers started moving at a brisk, trotting step. The singer sang another phrase and the others answered in the same minor key. Emily managed to move her feet as Cotannah did and the circle turned, taking her with it, taking her around to where she felt someone's eyes on her. She glanced up. Auntie Iola was staring straight at her with her eyes narrowed, her small, moccasined feet never missing a beat.

The loneliness overwhelmed Emily again. For some reason, Iola and Hattie didn't like her; she had sensed it the moment she sat down with them. Suddenly everything—the music, the dancing, the singing, even the sweet smoke from the wood cookfires—seemed alien to her. She wished this were fiesta instead, back on Las Manzanitas. Fiesta, where Tay had danced with her and held her in his arms.

Where she would never be again. At that moment her whole body ached to extricate herself from the circle and run, simply run, forever, to escape that truth.

The singer stopped and the moving circle came to a halt. The dance was over and full dark had come; no one but 'Tannah would notice her going now, so she turned to tell her. But she couldn't say it. Tay was here, very near, so how could she go? Right over there in the corner of her vision she glimpsed him, head bent, talking to someone, his white feathers glinting against the black of his hat.

"Oh, Mimi, stay close to give me courage," Cotannah whispered, pulling Emily along to get into the new line of dancers that was forming.

Emily's stomach tied itself into a knot. She must go, and go now. She couldn't bear to see Cotannah with Tay.

Yet she would have to. One day, before she could escape from here, Tay would announce he was going to marry Cotannah, and then she would see them together all the time.

The dancers began to form a single file this time, with men and boys at the head of the line, then women and girls behind them. The singing started and everyone joined hands: Cotannah grabbed Emily's right hand in a trembling grip, and a girl of about fifteen whom she hadn't met took her left one. They all began moving counterclockwise again, but doing a different step this time: toe-heel left, toe-heel right. More and more spectators began to drift over to stand around the dance ground and watch.

Suddenly those bystanders gave a great whoop of delight and Emily looked up to see that one of the male dancers had darted out of line to run back toward the women and girls. She smiled. It was Cade, who made a great show of running up to Maggie and snatching her out of line. All the onlookers hooted and yelled advice, in Choctaw and English, as he took her into his arms and swung her around like a square dancer. Then he pulled her close and took her with him to his place at the head of the line while his audience shouted rowdy approval.

The dancing continued. Emily turned her head so as not to look at Cade and Maggie and not to see Tay in the line only a few men behind them.

Another man must have darted out of line, because the spectators let out another round of calls and laughter. She didn't want to see it. Instead she kept on looking down the line of women and girls to the lights glowing back at Uncle Kulli's house. Soon, after Tay stole Cotannah away, she would go back there, find Sache, and take a long night ride.

So what if she didn't know the lay of the land in the dark? She didn't care if she got lost and never came back.

She sensed someone behind her the instant before big hands clasped her waist. Tay's hands. She knew at the first touch.

He swung her around in the square-dance step and then ran with her to his place in the line. She kept moving, somehow, only because his powerful arms and hands held her up and moved her like a puppet.

"Be ready," he said, bending near enough to brush her hair with the brim of his hat. "When the next one steals a partner, we're getting out of here."

She couldn't answer, couldn't think, couldn't know what to do except whatever he told her to do. Moments later, a woman broke out of line to steal a man, and then men and women both began stealing people willy-nilly from the non-dancers, and a great confusion of squealing and whooping and laughter filled the air. Tay pulled her arm through his and they turned and ran, escaping like naughty children into the night.

Chapter 18

He took her east across the open meadow, not south toward the creek.

"Tay!"

"What?"

"What are you *doing*?"

"Taking you to see the moon rise."

She was gasping for breath, more from shock at what they'd done than from their run. "I cannot believe this."

He laughed. "See the pines up there on top of that little hill? We'll have a great view from there."

Cotannah thought you were going to steal her, not me.

But she couldn't say it. She could not bear to even think it because the wild woman in her was rising. She would live this time with Tay on this sweet summer night. She would live it, every moment.

"Come here," he said. "We're liable to miss it."

He swept her up into his arms then, and carried her away from the noise of the dance, from the people, from everything behind them. With a long sigh, she laid her arms around his neck and looked, just looked, at his heart-piercing face beneath the shadowy brim of his hat until he ran up the gentle rise with her and sank to his knees in a bed of needles fallen from the spicy-smelling pines.

"There you go," he said. "We got here just in time."

That whole hillside shimmered in silver light. The moon looked close enough to touch: a huge full melon of a moon riding low and heavy in the dark night sky.

"Oh, Tay . . ."

A primitive cry from somewhere nearby stopped her. It started as a high wail, long and drawn out, and then came back down slowly, one little singing note at a time, rising and falling again, covering the hill like the moon-light and striking, like the moon, straight at Emily's heart.

"Our friend the song-dog," she whispered.

"With his salute to the rising moon."

Tay rocked back on his heels and pulled her close, held her against his hard chest with his arms crossed in front of her.

"He makes this whole night perfect," Emily murmured.

"Well, now, not that I'm jealous, but I was hoping you'd say that about me."

He nuzzled her neck as he murmured to her in his sensuous drawl, and she leaned into the caress, cradling his head in the hollow of her shoulder. He pressed one light kiss against her skin and then another, his lips wet, the tip of his tongue importunate and bold. Excitement shot through her, hot and trembling, and turned her around in his arms.

She closed her eyes as he laid her back on the thick, soft pine needles without ever stopping his steady, hungry, demanding little kisses, moving them around to the arch of her throat, then down into its hollow.

"I thought I could not live these past few days without you." He said it with such a vulnerable conviction that her heart broke open.

"Oh, Tay! I nearly died without you, too." She whispered the words while he devoured her face with his smoky eyes. "I'm so sorry, so *terribly* sorry, for all the cruel things I said to you . . ." His lips were coming closer and closer to hers. ". . . the . . . last time . . ."

His mouth triumphantly took possession of hers and his thumb traced the low, lacy curve of her dress, his hand hovering maddeningly over her breasts. He broke away suddenly, slipped the gown off her shoulders and down to fall off her arms and free her.

"Pretty woman," he said, his voice rough with wanting, "pretty woman in lavender lace. My fair Emily."

She was lost then, and gone, gone into the moonlight and the night, carried away by his hot, greedy mouth, which tried to lave both her swollen breasts at once, held together in his wild, hard hands. She reached for him and undid the buttons of his breeches, one at a time, brushing him with the backs of her fingers until he groaned and cried out.

"A person can't choose who they love," he said, his breath coming ragged between each word, "and now you know it. After tonight you'll damn well know, too, that you belong to me."

She narrowed her eyes and stared into his chiseled chieftain's face, thrown into stony relief by the moonlight. "Prove it," she said, her voice rasping low. "Prove it to me now."

And he did, without speaking a single other word. He gave a tortured groan and kissed her until her breath was gone. He melted her bones right into his arms, he made them one being to float up into the dark and then into the pathway of the shining silver moonlight. The sharp fragrance of the pines mingled with theirs and the voice of the song-dog came again, telling of something lost and something found, something from far away and long, long ago, from a summer night before time began.

Afterward, they lay for the longest time without moving, unwilling to let even a breath of air come between them. They didn't speak for even a longer time, not even when, finally, Tay rolled to his side and lay stroking her hair.

"Cade told me your betrothal is broken."

"Yes."

"Good. It's about time." His hand cupped her chin, tilted her face up to look at him. Moonlight slanted through the branches and lit the hard line of his jaw. "We will tell Cotannah together," he said. "She'll get over it. Sooner than you think, she'll get over it and she'll understand. Emily, don't feel guilty. I'm not the right man for Cotannah. She needs someone younger, someone to match her spirit."

Emily sighed at the thought of her friend. "Perhaps you're right. She's getting a lot of her old spirit back already."

"You two will still be friends. You'll see."

She lay looking at him, so heartbreakingly handsome in the silver moonlight. "But what about the People?" she asked, and the worry that was weighting her down came heavy into her voice. "They're talking against white intruders. They're expecting you to take a Choctaw wife."

His gaze drifted to his fingers, which were still playing in her hair. "They'll get it over it, too."

He sounded entirely sure and serene. But when his eyes met hers again a shadow passed across them, a shadow from the moonlight or a shadow from inside him—which, she couldn't tell.

Cotannah's arms and legs felt wooden, her throat cried out for a drink of cool water, and her head swam from all the noise, but she didn't stop dancing. She couldn't. If she stopped, if she walked off the dance ground even as far as the row of chairs where Aunt Ancie and her friends were sitting and watching, Tay would never come back to dance with her. He was only gone now, with Emily, because he needed to talk to her as a friend. If she stayed right there and danced every dance, even if she had to keep dancing until midnight, he would.

"Tinsanale Hitkla!"

A man out in the middle of the dance ground shouted the name of the next dance, the Wedding Dance, and the lines of men and women began breaking up to form couples. Maybe Tay was just there, out in the meadow; maybe he would come back onto the dance ground now and be her partner.

She turned toward the center and glimpsed a tall, broad-shouldered, black-hatted young man striding toward her. For one instant her heart leapt up and turned over, but he didn't really walk like Tay, he wore a black shirt instead of pale gray, and as he neared her she saw he was a stranger. From what she could see of his face by the moonlight, he was passably handsome. Not as handsome as Tay, of course, but his features were hard-chiseled and strikingly Indian.

He stopped directly in front of her. The drum rolled, the player struck the claves, and the man reached out and took both her hands as called for by this dance. His hands were broad and callused and so strong, they seemed to lift her off the ground.

The song began and, around the whole circle of couples, the men danced forward, the women danced backward. Draw back left, step— draw back right, step. The circle moved slowly, counterclockwise, then the tones in the song changed and the women danced forward, the men danced backward. In this song both men and women were supposed to answer the lead phrase of the singer as he beat time with the claves—Cotannah could hear the couples on each side of them singing—but neither she nor this mysterious man who was her partner sang at all.

She felt weightless through the whole dance, as if the man were carrying her just above the earth like a feather, using only the power of his strong fingers. How could that be? They weren't touching in any other way. He looked at her, though, all the time; she could feel the heat of his eyes and see the flash of them beneath the brim of his black hat.

When the drum and the claves and the singing stopped and the dance was over, he stood over her and looked at her some more. His stance was easy but ready, his feet set apart, his heels dug in. She retrieved her hands, but he stayed there, standing very still, facing her, his head cocked to one side as if she were there to be stared at.

She could have walked away and she thought she would do that, but instead she tilted her chin up at him and looked back challengingly.

"Who are you?" she said.

"Thank you for the Wedding Dance," he said. "We'll do it together again sometime."

He spoke in excellent English, but with the trace of an accent that said it was not his first language. His voice was deep and easy—and very, very sure of his own proclamation. And something about it was . . . well, possessive.

That was the only word to describe his manner: It held an air of possessiveness.

She tightened her jaw and stared back, trying to see up into his face in the shadows.

"Don't put your heart into looking forward to it," she said tartly. "I was waiting for someone else when you walked up to me—a man I've loved for a very long time." Her heart constricted at those words.

Her dance partner said nothing. He didn't go away and he didn't stop looking down at her. He wasn't even responding to her challenge, for he seemed to think that she'd been put here on this earth for him to do with as he pleased. And at this moment, what pleased him was to look at her.

"I'm as good as promised to him," she said coldly.

"What does 'as good as' mean when it's attached to a promise?"

His low drawl was insolent, his words insulting.

And a terror. They struck too close to the doubts that tormented her.

"You have no *right* to question me! And I'll never dance with you again, so get away from me!"

Furious, she whirled on her heel and left him.

But there he was, right behind her.

"Stop looming over me like some great, black crow," she cried, half turning to spit the words at him. "Get away from me, I said!"

He fell into step beside her instead.

"For such a proud one to love a man for such a long time—"

She cut him off. "You don't know anything about me!"

"I know you didn't dance with me like a woman in love with some 'as good as promised' other man."

Stunned, she stopped in her tracks in the middle of the crowd, dancers and nondancers milling around, visiting and laughing all over the dance ground. This conversation was too strange!

"What are you talking about? I didn't dance with you 'like' anything. I didn't even dance encircled by your arms. I barely touched you!"

"You touched me."

There it was again—that flat, imperturbable, *irrefutable* tone. Well, by thunder, *she* would refute it.

She opened her mouth, but the man dressed in black held up a commanding hand silencing her. Her heart raced with fury, struck harder against her ribs than the drummer had struck the drum.

"You danced in perfect harmony with me," he said. "Your body moved with my body in the natural flow of the night. Your spirit touched my spirit in the song."

"It did not!"

"Which did not?"

"None of it! None of what you said. And it never will! My body will never move with yours!"

Embarrassment flickered beneath her roaring

anger as she realized how that sounded—but he hadn't picked up on the possible double meaning of her remark. Instead, his laconic answer was even more appalling.

"On the contrary, Cotannah Chisk-Ko," he said, "someday you'll seek me out."

Then he turned on the heel of his boot and vanished into the crowd.

The sounds of the singing and the drum stopped as Emily and Tay came back into the meadow. By the time they reached the dance ground, it was a scene of cheerful confusion with people heading for the food-laden tables or to chairs and blankets to rest or to friends to visit. Immediately an older man standing in a tightly knit group of men spotted Tay, raised his arm, and motioned for him to come and join them.

But she couldn't let him. She couldn't let go of his hand, unable to bear him out of her sight. She couldn't think what she should do or where she should go without him—she was coming back into the real world after having been to Heaven.

She stopped in her tracks and drew in a long, shaky breath. "You go on," she said. "I'm just going to find Maggie . . . or Mama . . ."

But she didn't really want them. All she wanted was a quiet spot where she could sit and think about Tay. And where Cotannah wouldn't see her for a little while yet.

He squeezed her hand. "I'll find you later."

Emily wandered around the edge of the

dance ground, weaving in and out among the
people drifting in every direction, and ended
up walking toward the honeysuckle-covered
fence that separated the meadow from the yard
of Uncle Kulli's house. Someone had spread
some blankets there and then had gone off and
left them.

Whoever it was wouldn't begrudge her, she
thought, and she'd get up and leave if she saw
anyone heading her way. Gratefully she sank
down and then stretched out on her back in the
shadows, looking up into the sky where the
big, silver moon was riding higher now.

Could it really be true that she and Tay
would spend the rest of their lives together?
Could it be *true*?

It was true that their love was bigger than
them, so strong nothing could stand in its way.
Cotannah would get over it, she really would,
after the first shock of the news wore off. And
she would be happy for Emily—someday.
Someday when she had seen that their passion
was an irresistible force, a force beyond their
control.

Someday when she had found a passion like
this for herself with the man she was destined
to find.

But oh, how horrible it would be to tell her
the news! Her stomach constricted and she
threw her arm over her eyes. She had to do it,
though. Tay had been sweet to offer to help, but
his presence would embarrass Cotannah and
make the situation worse.

No, she had to tell her by herself and she had

to do it tonight—as soon as she and Cotannah
returned to their room in Uncle Kulli's house.
Tay had been right. Sometimes she had to
think of her own happiness, and this was one
of those times, for she couldn't sacrifice the rest
of her life and Tay's for the sake of Cotannah's
feelings no matter how much she loved her.
Thank goodness 'Tannah wasn't nearly so vulnerable now as before.

Emily dropped her arm to her side and just
lay there, watching the moon, letting it carry
her drifting off into the memories of their
lovemaking. Then she set herself to try and
glimpse one picture and then another of her life
with Tay as she caught sight of each star
struggling to come out and be seen in the
bright wash of moonlight. Oh, and their *children*! If only they could have lots of children,
boys and girls both!

She shivered a little, despite the heat of the
late-summer night, and sat up, scooting around
to lean her back against the wood rail of the
fence, huddling into the fragrant honeysuckle
as she hugged herself, holding her dearest
desires to her heart. Tay and lots of children.
She could never ask for, never dream of, anything more.

The sudden sound of Tay's voice paralyzed
her. "Here's your lemonade, Auntie," he said.
"Now, what did you want to talk to me about?"

"You and women," Auntie Iola's brisk voice
answered. "You steal the white girl for your
partner and you leave the dance ground with

her, yet you know Cotannah is waiting for you."

There was a heartbeat of silence.

"I know the whole Nation expects me to marry her."

"It's more than expect, it is necessary. And Kulli and the Board of Governors and everybody else who wants you to win this election, they all are beginning to worry mightily."

"They should worry about their own problems."

"This *is* their problem. If you are defeated, Tay Nashoba, this Nation is on the road to losing everything. The People need you desperately—you know it well."

Tay said nothing.

Iola pressed again. "It is mightily important for you to have a Choctaw wife."

"I know it would renew the spirit of the People."

Tay used his smooth, placating tone to pacify his aunt, but Emily knew him now. Beneath the calm surface of his voice she could hear a rushing river of pain.

She wanted to will her heart out of her body to go to him, to comfort him. It would never return. Her blood stopped running, never to start up again.

It had been pathetically foolish on her part to hope for one minute that she could marry him and live with him for the rest of her life. His People had had a hold on him for a long, long time, and he well knew that keeping them together, keeping their identity, was a responsibility no one else could fulfill.

We're the kind, Emily, you and I, who always do our duty.

Even if he weren't the only candidate for Principal Chief who could save the Nation, his auntie Iola and his other relatives, who were so adamant about white intruders, would never accept her. She knew, from living on Las Manzanitas with Cade and Cotannah, Aunt Ancie and Uncle Jumper, about the closeness of the Choctaw extended families. If Tay married her, he would never be close with his relatives and friends again.

Therefore, eventually, he would come to hate her, no matter how much he might love her now.

Tay and Auntie Iola exchanged a few more remarks—Emily's mind simply refused to take them in—and then she heard the swishing of footsteps moving away through the grass. They sounded very close compared to the striking of the claves and the beating of the drum that had started up again on the dance ground.

Tay wasn't gone, though. She sensed his presence. Auntie Iola had walked away, but Tay had not moved.

Tay. The love, the only love, of her life.

Yet she must end it. This was the time. Here in the shadows, away from the crowd, as quickly as she could, she must end it. Waiting would do nothing but make the pain deeper— although at this moment that seemed entirely impossible.

Somehow she moved, made some sort of motion that rustled in the honeysuckle vine and caused it to tremble along the fence. She never knew how, but by the time Tay saw her she was standing, her feet braced apart, one hand holding on to the fence to keep her upright.

"Emily! Darling! What in the—"

She held up her free hand to stop his sensuous voice. Her hand shook horribly. Her face must look like a ghost's in the moonlight, for she was sure the blood was never going to flow in her veins again. She felt cold as death.

"I'm telling you good-bye, Tay," she said, forcing the words out in a rush. "Good-bye, forever."

"No! You can't . . . What did you hear? Iola . . ."

"Iola is right," she interrupted in a voice so calm she scared herself. "And no matter how much I love you, I won't come between you and your People."

"The People will love you as much as I do—"

"No. They'll never get the chance, for I'll be living on Las Manzanitas."

"Married to Lee?" he asked in a voice like warm velvet, a voice that said he already knew what she would answer.

"Not married at all. I have never made love with any man but you, Tay Nashoba, and I never will."

He took a step closer. "Then you can't leave me. You're a passionate woman, Emily."

She stepped back so he couldn't touch her, back into a cloud of sweet fragrance from the honeysuckle vine, which always from now on would smell bitter as gall to her. If she felt his magic hands on her, even once, even in a lightly brushing touch, she would melt from a frozen statue into a hot pool of tears.

"I am passionately in love with you," she said softly, barely daring to move her lips because they ached so, longing for his kiss. "And I will always be. No one else will ever do."

"And I love you more than life itself."

"You do now," she said, speaking as intimately, as quietly, as he had done, "but you would come to hate me just as much."

"Never." He stood like a mountain directly in front of her now.

"Let it go, Tay. Let *me* go. Don't tempt me anymore, please don't, and don't ever touch me again."

"Never."

His calm broke her control into pieces.

"Yes!" She screamed it at him, then turned and ran along the fence before he knew she would move, glancing back at him when she paused to climb up and throw herself over onto the house side of the rails, voluminous skirts and all. He was standing where she had left him, still watching her.

He would give her time to calm down, to absorb what Iola had said, and then he would talk to her again. She knew that because now she knew him so well.

But she would surprise him. She would never see him alone again.

If she did, he would touch her and she would crumple into his arms; she would end up married to him and then she would have to see the love in his eyes turn to resentment and then to hate. She had seen enough of that in her parents' marriage, and she would never let it happen to her. No marriage at all was far better than a marriage like that.

She ran across the wide, moonlit yard and into the back door of the house without speaking to anyone, ran through the hallway and up the stairs without letting the tears come. Never. She would never let Tay touch her again.

But when she was locked in the room alone, when she had lit the lamp and was looking into the chifforobe mirror to see the shell of a woman that she would be from now on, she heard the small voice of irony in the back of her mind telling her that at least she no longer had to dread breaking the news of her and Tay to Cotannah. Then she turned her head and saw something that shattered her resolve not to let him touch her again.

It was a braid, a tiny, perfect braid, tied with a small, silky feather from his hat. He had woven it into the side of her hair while they lay on the hilltop together, listening to the song-dog in the moonlight.

Chapter 19

Nothing helped the hurting. That was the thing that Tay could not believe. Running in the early morning didn't even slow the pain; throwing himself into the work of the Nation couldn't hold his mind from Emily; talking to tribal members about the election; thinking about becoming Principal Chief. Everything only added to the terrible, lost feeling that was now his constant companion. That and the ferocious, unrelenting anger.

She had *lain* with him twice! She had made love with him, body and soul, with all the apparent sincerity of a life-giving angel, and then she had treacherously parted with him on the excuse that *he* did not love *her* enough to make a marriage last!

Three days had passed. He thought about that as he finished his morning run with a frantically fast ascent of the steps to his front veranda and collapsed onto a woven-cane chair. He would never be able to find the courage to live out one year, much less the rest of his life, at the snail's pace of these last three days.

Never. Not with this exquisite pain gnawing away at him every second of every endless minute.

Breathing heavily of the humid morning air, he threw his head up and stared blindly out across his yard. God help him and God help the Nation. He couldn't let the identity of his People and everything they had worked for, everything the elders died for on the Trail of Tears, go to ruin over a woman, now, could he? Especially not a woman who didn't love him enough to marry him, to have faith that their love would endure.

But people married for reasons other than love every single day of the year, and anyone who thought differently was a naive fool. Even Maggie and Cade, who were wild about each other now, had married for lifesaving practicality and only later come to find their love. He had been right to go to Texas to marry Cotannah in the first place, to help him win the election, and he had been unforgivably stupid to even quibble about the fact that he didn't love her as he should love a wife.

How many men loved their wives in any way, even with the warm regard he felt toward Cotannah? And Cotannah, at least, by God, loved him. At least she'd said she did for ten years, and it'd be an ingrained habit by now.

He got up so fast that he left the chair rocking crazily and strode toward the front door, jerking it open, fast. A man couldn't just sit around and bleed to death from a wound to the heart. A man had his pride.

Crossing the oak-floored entry hall, heading for the stairs, he bellowed for his houseman, who had been heating water for Tay's bath when he left at first light to go on his run.

"Dexter! Have Peter saddle my horse!"

The answer came from upstairs, from where Dexter, no doubt, was filling the tub. "Yessuh! Right away, suh!"

But Dexter was still there, puttering at laying out Tay's fresh clothes, when Tay charged into the room.

"What are you doing? Go see that my horse is saddled."

"Gonna storm, Mistah Tay," the old man said, his wrinkled face collapsing with worry. "My dreams tol' me sure: Gon' come a bad storm."

"It may," Tay said, stripping the buckskins from his legs. "It's so humid and hot that I'm pouring sweat, and I had to stop running twice because the air's too heavy to breathe."

"Right! Tha's right!" the old man cried hopefully.

"But I don't care if it comes an early blizzard," Tay finished. "I'm going to Uncle Kulli's place as soon as I'm dressed."

Moaning with worry, Dexter went to find Peter while Tay plunged into his bath, fortified by the decision he'd just made. He simply *would* not live in pain like this.

After he bathed and dressed in his very best traditional shirt, after he was mounted and ready to ride, Dexter tried one more time.

"Peter say he gon' leave the best hosses

stabled till the storm blow past," he confided as he handed Tay his reins.

"Fine," Tay said. "Tell him that's just fine."

He had no more than ridden down the driveway and out onto the road when he admitted that Dexter was right. The sun was drifting in and out of some low-hanging clouds—they didn't look so bad—and there wasn't much wind, just a little bit of breeze now and then. But the birds were too quiet, the woods along each side of the road were too still. It was a good thing he had only five miles to go or he might show up to ask Cotannah to be his wife with his clothes wringing wet, looking a wretched sight. Cotannah wouldn't care, though; she loved him no matter what condition he was in.

Cotannah was a beautiful woman—the way she carried herself was fantastic, almost majestic, really. She would be a wonderful wife for the Principal Chief. And he *would* win the election. He was not about to accept even one more loss in his life.

And he was not about to live alone anymore in that big house. It needed children running through its rooms and laughter echoing from its beams. He was sick to death of silence.

He lifted his horse into a short lope and moved on toward Uncle Kulli's place and his goal. He wanted to get there quickly and have the thing done, but he didn't want to lather the horse.

Pulling out his handkerchief, he mopped his brow. The morning, the sky, the woods, were

all closing down around him like a giant's fist;
it felt like something had to burst open, something had to change, and soon.

He chuckled bitterly to himself. Mother
Earth herself was in sympathy with his misery;
she, like he, was ready to explode, *tukafa*. He'd
be lucky, very lucky, if he reached Kulli
Hotema's before the storm hit.

Emily looked at the clock when she woke.

"Yes, it's the middle of the morning," Cotannah said briskly. "You've already lost the best
time of the day."

*What I've already lost is the best man in the
world.*

Groggily Emily sat up to try to get away from
that thought. Cotannah threw the covers off for
her.

"Maggie sent me to get you up and bring you
to the storm cellar. Hurry if you don't want
everybody to see you in your night shift."

Emily groaned. "No. I'm not going! Cellars
smell like mildew."

"Better that than blowing away." Cotannah
turned and ran to the armoire. "I'm getting my
mother's locket," she called back over her
shoulder. "If you have any treasures in here,
better take them. Hurry, Mimi!"

Emily swung her feet to the floor and stood
up. "Lee's ring," she said dully, padding across
to the chifforobe where she'd put it away
among her clothes. "It was his mother's, he
meant to give it to Katie, and I'll feel even
worse if I can't even return it to him."

Now, *that* was a laughable thought. How could she possibly feel worse? She already felt so bad, so sore in her spirit and so miserable in her mind, that she'd probably feel better if the wind did blow her away.

A gust rattled the window promisingly and sudden raindrops slapped the upper glass panes and the wood of the floor.

"Hurry! You girls come on, right now!" Maggie appeared in their doorway, her arms full of folded quilts. "Don't take time to dress, Mimi. Grab a wrapper and come on."

The back door slammed.

"But I can't . . ." Emily muttered.

"Now!"

Maggie spoke in her most compelling voice, the voice that Emily had been obeying since she was five and Maggie was four, so Emily did as she said.

Cotannah tucked the locket into her bosom, closed the window, and ran to take part of Maggie's burden. Emily ripped her wrapper out of the armoire, stuck Lee's ring into its pocket, and followed them out of the room and down the hall. They ran down the back stairs.

The rain was gusting harder now, and small hailstones beat against the house. By the time they got to the back door and opened it, hail was piling up here and there on the ground.

"It has never failed in all my life," Emily said crossly, "that every time I've *ever* gone to the cellar, I've gone right out into the worst of the storm."

Maggie grabbed her arm. "This isn't the worst of it," she cried. "Thank goodness Mama and the twins are already there!"

"Where's Cade?" Cotannah yelled over the sound of the rising wind.

"Out watching for twisting clouds like all the other silly men," Maggie yelled back.

Then they couldn't talk anymore because the wind pulled them out into the rain and hail so fast they couldn't even shut the door behind them.

"Run!" Maggie cried. "Run!"

The rain slashed through their clothing like cold, sharp needles and the wind snatched at their hair. Emily couldn't see anything, so she just held on to Maggie and ran, reaching back with her other hand to pull Cotannah along. The wind and the rain were so blinding and the hail so punishing, she hadn't a hope of lifting her head.

Every scrap of breath left her, but she kept running, pulled on by Maggie's unrelenting grip, pushed from behind by the wind's terrifying force. After what seemed like a lifetime of cold and wet, thunder and lightning, a light appeared right in front of them and she, Maggie, and Cotannah fell into the arms reaching up for them.

A crash, a terrible, grinding crash, rolled behind them as a bolt of lightning split open the world. Then the cellar door slammed on their heels and shut out the storm.

The smells of kerosene lamps, wet cloth, and wet skin hung heavy in the sudden silence and

mingled with those of the onions and potatoes
stored in bins. Somebody pulled her down
onto a bench—Mama, it was Mama—and
murmuring voices finally penetrated the water
in her ears. Someone pressed a handkerchief
into her hands and she wiped her streaming
face.

"I need a towel," she said when she could
see. "I'm soaked."

"Here, Mimi," Maggie said and threw
one of the quilts to her before she spread the
other out on the floor for the children. "If
you'd get up of a morning so you could wear
clothes . . ."

Everyone laughed a little, but just politely.
Every face in the lamplight was furrowed with
worry, even Randy's and Cole's.

"Those men ought to be in here with us!"
Maggie whispered frantically. "I don't know
how long it can take for them to warn everybody!"

But the twins heard her and immediately
began to wail. "Papa? Where's Papa? I want my
papa!"

Maggie went to comfort them, and her wet
embrace changed their wails to shrieks of cold
discomfort. Cotannah laughed and teased
them, Ancie offered them dry towels, and
Mama Harrington reached into her knitting
bag for small sweets to distract them.

Emily stared at them silently, for a terrible,
frightened feeling was taking her into its grip
and a cry was echoing in her head.

Tay? Where's Tay? I want my Tay!

Somehow—she could never have said how—she knew that Tay was nearby. It was more than the fact that she'd seen him from her window every morning for the last three days, riding onto the campground to talk to his people. It was a knowing in her bones and her flesh that terrified her.

Please God, let Cade and Tay come in, bring them in, *now*.

But it was too late.

The wind stopped. Even through the heavy slab of the cellar door, the silence echoed. The rain stopped. The hail stopped. There was no thunder, no more splinterings from the lightning.

Then it came: the huge, rushing roar, the driving, pulsating noise of a fast-moving tornado, and the closer it came, the more air it sucked out of the cellar. There was none left to breathe. The air was gone. The lights of the lanterns went out.

The children didn't even whimper, nobody moved. Nobody moved, nobody spoke. It stayed there, roaring above them, forever.

Then, at last, it was gone. Silence fell over them, held them down a moment longer, and then its grip broke under the spattering of rain.

Maggie and Emily were at the door in an instant, unfastening the hook and pushing at the weight of it with their shoulders. They lifted it enough for sunlight to show around its edges. Cold air came rushing in.

Cotannah came to help and the three of

them started climbing the steps steadily, one behind the other, pushing with all their strength until they stood the door straight up onto his hinges and it fell backward onto the soggy grass. Mama and the children, Aunt Ancie, and everyone else in the cellar came climbing up the steps behind them.

"Ohh, dear Lord," Mama murmured.

Aunt Ancie set up a high, keening sound, and another woman joined in.

"Our people in the camp!" another one cried.

"It hit the *camp!*"

Debris lay strewn everywhere, much of it in small pieces, most of it unrecognizable. However, some things were left whole: a two-wheeled buggy, apparently unscathed, rested in the limbs of a large oak tree near the house. Emily looked at it long enough to realize what it was, and then she looked past it, her straining eyes searching the landscape for Tay.

The back porch had been torn off the house, but its brick steps were left standing, starting in a bed of roses, leading up . . . up to nowhere. At their foot a small group of men stood in a loose knot looking down at something. Cade was kneeling . . .

"Look, Maggie, there's Cade!" Mama called, over the sound of the rain that was falling gently now.

"Papa! Papa!" Cole and Miranda screamed.

"Somebody's hurt!" Cotannah said.

"It's Tay!" Emily cried.

Emily knew. It was Tay who was down, and she had to get to him this instant. She had to talk to him, tell him she'd been wrong. She had to have these minutes with him and all the rest of the minutes that either of them would live.

No. He wasn't dead and he wasn't going to die, either. She would not let him die before they'd even had a chance to live together.

She started running over the rubble and through it. She stumbled and fell, and nearly fell again. She cut her hands on something when she tried to brace herself, then she lunged up to her feet and started running again. By the time she got to Tay, her heart was roaring and spinning in her chest like the tornado, and Tay was lying as still and quiet as the air at the center of it.

"No! No! Tay!"

She couldn't even catch her breath from the run because she had to keep calling to him or he would die. He wasn't already dead, but he needed her to live.

He was lying perfectly still while Cade and the others bent over him. She pushed in between Uncle Jumper and a man she didn't know to throw herself across Tay.

"Tay, I was wrong, I was wrong! Listen to me, I love you, Tay. I love you. Ever since I told you to leave me alone, I thought I would die."

Her hands were so numb, she could hardly make them move, but when her fingertips touched Tay's face they came alive again, alive to the feel of his prominent cheekbone, to the line of his hard-angled jaw. As alive as her whole soul was to the fact that she loved him.

"You can't die," she cried, trying frantically to find the pulse at the base of his throat. "I won't let you. I will *not* let you die!"

Help. She needed some help here. A doctor. What she needed was a doctor.

"Get a doctor." She tossed back her hair and took her eyes off Tay for one heartbeat to glance at Cade. He was still kneeling on Tay's other side. "Cade, can you get a doctor?"

There! Her forefinger found his pulse, felt the beating of his heart and clung to it.

"He's alive," she cried, dropping from her knees to her bottom and scooting closer to him through the cold mud to try to gather his head and shoulders into her lap, bending close to his ear to call, "I love you, Tay. Can you hear me? Tay, I love you."

He was so heavy she could barely move him, but she cradled his head in her lap, bent over him to shield his face from the cold, soaking rain. Help. She had to have help.

"Somebody help me pick him up," she cried. "We have to get him somewhere dry!"

She looked for Cade again, but he was gone, and what she saw was Cotannah's stricken face.

They stared at each other with the rain running down over their faces like buckets of tears. Cotannah wasn't crying, though—her eyes were dry. Dry and wide and burning with shocked betrayal.

"I-I-I'm so sorry, 'Tannah," Emily stuttered. "I didn't m-mean to t-take him away from you. I-it just h-happened that I-I s-started t-to love him. H-he loves me, too."

Cotannah just looked at her.

"P-please, 'Tannah . . ."

"Don't talk to me, Emily."

She called her Emily, not Mimi. She might never call her Mimi again. They would probably never be friends again.

A terrible, helpless feeling rolled through Emily and crushed a corner of her heart. That would be horrible, she would grieve about it forever, but what could she do? Her love for Tay could no longer be denied.

She and Cotannah just looked at each other, neither of them saying any more. Silence hung over them for a long moment. *Neither* of them was crying, Emily thought; she couldn't believe neither of them was shedding a tear.

Some pain was too deep for tears.

Then Tay moved his head in her lap and everyone and everything else vanished as she cradled his face in her shaking hands.

"Tay! Tay, it's Emily," she cried. "Wake up. You were hurt in the tornado."

"When the porch flew off, one of the posts hit him across the head," Uncle Jumper said sorrowfully. "I slipped and fell on the way to the cellar, and he bent to pick me up or it would have missed him."

"Don't blame yourself, Uncle," Cade said. "All of us should've taken shelter earlier."

Uncle Jumper ignored that. "It should have

hit me," he mourned. "Tay took the blow instead of me."

Several voices answered him, and Emily glanced over her shoulder to see a whole crowd of dazed faces looking down at her. Half the Nation, it seemed, had gathered around.

Tay moved again and then opened his eyes. They were glazed at first, uncomprehending, but he smiled at her, and a heartbeat later the smile was real.

"Emily," he muttered and lifted one hand to caress her hair. "I've got to get up."

"You're hurt. That might make it worse!"

"No. I only got knocked out. I've been hit harder in a stickball game."

Everyone cheered at that lighthearted sally. He sat up to the sound of a great, happy buzzing of voices, and then, to Emily's sheer consternation, stood up without ever letting go of her hand. The mischievous grin that she loved played across his mouth in spite of the fact that he had to set his feet wider apart to keep his balance on the wet ground. She stepped closer and tried to help support him, but he held her at arm's length.

"It took a sharp blow to the head to bring me to my senses . . ." he said, speaking loud enough for everyone nearby to hear.

Once again, everyone laughed.

"But I'm telling you now, Emily Harrington, that I'll never let you get away from me again. I love you and I intend to marry you."

The laughter died.

"We've stayed apart too long," she said,

looking into his handsome, mud-streaked face, unable, totally helpless, to look at anything else. "But wh-what about your p-people . . .?"

She didn't need to ask: A shocked silence had fallen over the crowd. A cold silence of betrayal.

Chapter 20

A fresh breeze picked up and moved through the tree limbs above their heads, shaking down some leaves and small pieces of debris. They rattled on the wide brim of Uncle Jumper's hat. A baby began to wail over in the campground. And all around Tay and Emily, the sullen mutterings began, the words clear enough to hear, but the voices muffled enough to remain unidentified.

". . . thought he wanted to limit white intruders."

". . . supposed to be betrothed to the Chisk-Ko girl."

". . . preserve the old customs . . ."

Anger boiled up in Tay like water in a pot, filling his head with a steaming pain. What did they want from him, anyway? Every minute of every day of his life, and then his very soul on top of that?

"If you want me to be your Principal Chief, then elect me," he said, tightening his grip on Emily's shoulder. "But I won't live my life for that, not anymore. I've denied my love for

Emily for too long. We've lost too many days we could have had together because we were both trying to do our duty, both thinking of what example I should set for the Nation if I was going to be preaching that marrying inside the tribe is best."

He looked around, from one familiar face to another. Hard eyes glared at him. No one answered him.

"Now I know that I should not have said such a thing to begin with—we can't choose whom to love, no matter what effect that love might have on other people. Love comes to us unbidden."

Emily made an incoherent, joyous sound. He dropped his hand from her shoulder and put his arm around her waist as she stepped closer to him.

"So now," he said, "I ask you to remember our long tradition of welcoming the white wives and husbands of members of the Nation. From the earliest times, we have had the custom of honoring each person's choice of partner no matter what color skin that person might have."

"That's right," someone said.

One person, one voice of support for him. But he didn't care. He didn't care if there were none.

"Each person has to deal with his or her own destiny," he said. "And this woman, Emily Harrington, is mine."

He waited, jaw clenched, for a challenge, for a denunciation, for a proclamation that such a

turncoat should never be elected Principal
Chief. In one way, it would be a relief. In
another, it would tear him apart.

But now, either way, he could survive and go
on. Now he had Emily standing by his side.

Together they waited, but no one said a
word. The silence came back, gathered
strength, and held.

"Hey! We need help," someone shouted
from the campground. "It'll take more men to
lift the trunk of this tree. We've got a woman
trapped here."

That cry dispelled the mood and the crowd
and the very thought of anything but the
practical consideration of the damages done by
the storm. People turned and started moving to
help.

Tay took a step forward, too, before Emily's
arms came around him. She wasn't trying to
hold him back, though; he knew that instinctively.

"Go," she said, "but promise me you'll be
careful. That was a hard blow to your head."

"It's a hard head, darlin'."

He gathered her close and held her against
him, in spite of the mud on them both, letting
the rose/rain fragrance of her hair fill his
nostrils, taking a long, deep breath of her scent
to sustain him. Their wet bodies stuck to each
other and clung, warming each other.

How had he ever lived all those long, lonely
years without her? How had he survived? One
thing he knew, he could never live without her
again.

"Go find some dry clothes," he said. "The temperature's dropping."

She smiled up at him. "What about you?"

"I'll come in in a little while."

She loosened her arms and stepped back, smiling up at him. "I'll find some of Cade's clothes for you," she said. "Don't be gone any longer than you have to."

"Right," he said and touched her face before he left her.

Night had fallen before Cotannah had to be in the same room with Emily again. All day, while they worked at finding blankets and dry clothing for the people on the campground, while they cooked and served hot food and helped nurse the injured, she had pretended that Emily did not even exist. She intended to keep doing that until this horrible ache went away, even if it took a whole moon or more.

She *had* to do that. If she thought about losing Emily, if she admitted to herself that her only friend, the person she trusted most in the whole world except for Cade, had never cared one whit about her, she would be so sad she would die. She couldn't deal with it all at once—right now she was making herself know that Tay was lost to her, that *he* had never loved her, and that was all she could bear.

Thank God it was only the women here, and the men were still working in the campground by the light of the fires. It'd also be more than she could bear to be in the same room with Emily and Tay both.

"Cotannah, you aren't eating a bite," Aunt Ancie said. "You'll collapse if you don't—you've worked like two mules today."

"I can't."

Not with Emily the traitor sitting at the same table with me.

But she wouldn't say it. Not if holding the words in her throat choked her to death right here in front of everybody—she would keep her pride since now that was all she had.

"'Tannah," Maggie said, and the sympathy in her voice nearly brought tears to Cotannah's eyes. "Are you getting sick? Did you wear that wet dress too long this morning?"

"No, I didn't. And I'm *not* sick." Her voice, full of fury, echoed in the big room. "I'm fine," she said in a calmer tone.

After all, poor Maggie couldn't help being Emily's sister.

"You don't need to do anything else today," Uncle Kulli's daughter, Martha, said. "We've already fed the men, and the rest of us can go see about the people who are hurt another time tonight without you having to do it."

"Why don't you try to eat a few of your grape dumplings so you'll have something hot in your stomach and then go on up to bed?" Aunt Ancie said.

Every single one of them had spoken to her in the tone they would use with a very fragile, hysterical child. Every single one of them was feeling sorry for her because she'd been jilted and made a fool of right in front of the entire Nation.

Fury overcame her need for pride and snapped the last threads of her control.

"Because I have to find another bed," she cried. "I'm certainly not going to share a room with *her* anymore. If you all are so understanding, surely you can understand that!"

She pushed back her chair, jumped to her feet, and leaned across the table to glare down at Emily. For the first time since they had both knelt over Tay's unconscious body, she actually *looked* at Emily. It made her stomach turn, made her heart hurt. How could she ever have thought that Emily cared two figs about her? Emily met her gaze with her eyes full of tears.

"Don't try to fool me with your false tears," Cotannah said icily. "I know now that everything about you is false—most especially your friendship."

"That's not *true*," Emily cried with such pain in her voice that Cotannah almost believed it was real.

But she wouldn't give an inch. "Oh, but it *is* true. Friends don't steal each other's beaux, friends don't sneak around behind each other's backs and get themselves secretly betrothed to men who belong to their so-called *best friends*."

Emily stared back at her, her eyes glazing over with tears and two spots of high color springing up in her cheeks. Then she stood, too, and opened her mouth to speak. But she dropped back down into her chair as suddenly as if someone had hit her behind the knees.

"I-I'm hurting, too, Cotannah," she said.

"I'm h-hurting so b-bad that I can't even stand up."

"Oh, Mimi!" Maggie said sadly. "And, Cotannah, dear, I . . ."

"Leave us, please," Emily said without taking her eyes from Cotannah. "Please, Maggie. We have to get through this sometime, and it's better to do it now."

So Martha scooted her chair back and said, "Ladies, let's give these two some privacy."

Dimly Cotannah was aware that the others were leaving the room, but only at a distance. Everything in the whole world had seemed at a distance from her ever since she'd heard Emily and Tay declare their love. Life was all terribly removed from her now except for that exact memory, which was part of every breath she took, which kept repeating itself over and over again in her head.

I love you, Tay, I love you.

I love you, Emily, and I intend to marry you.

Those words, and the looks on the faces of the two people she had thought loved her most, would forever be etched in her memory.

Therefore, she would never have another love. Nor another friend.

"Cotannah," Emily said, speaking in a stranger's shaky voice. "I never meant to hurt you. All I did was follow my heart, and I tried as hard as I could not to do it."

It was hard for Emily to look at her; Cotannah knew her so well, she could see the guilt and discomfort trying to make Emily look away. Too bad she hadn't known her well enough to see that she was stealing Tay.

"I have loved Tay Nashoba all of my life. I told you that, I told you everything. I trusted you."

Emily's gaze strengthened and her shoulders straightened. "I did not betray your trust. I simply fell in love with Tay."

"And you made him fall in love with you."

"No. That was not in my power. And, Cotannah, it wasn't in your power to make him fall in love with you, either, no matter how much you believed that you could. Nobody can force anything to happen when it comes to love."

"I wasn't *trying* to force it."

"You were only trying to live out what you believed was meant to be," Tay said.

Cotannah clapped her hands to her cheeks and froze. Tay was here. She could not bear to turn and look at him.

He walked on into the room, his bootheels ringing on the hard oak of the floor, walked steadily around the end of the table.

Of course, he would go to the other side and sit by Emily. Now it was two against one; he had come in here to defend sneaky Emily. Bitterness rose in her throat like a terrible bile.

But he didn't do as she expected—he stopped where he was. Then he looked at Emily, just *looked* at her, and she looked at him. Watching them made Cotannah's blood drain. He didn't need to go sit by Emily, he didn't need to touch her, he didn't even need to speak to her; that look was enough.

Love. There it was, connecting them: That look was love.

She fought the empathy that sprang up in her without warning. And she fought the admission that crept into the back of her mind: She had known this, somewhere, deep down, she had known it at least since they'd left that dance together.

Tay pulled out the chair in front of him. "Sit down, Cotannah, please," he said, "so I can sit."

"Manners," she said, and she stubbornly continued to stand, "manners are even more important when a person's deepest feelings are involved. You should have had good enough manners to have told me at the very beginning that you loved each other."

She made herself look up into his gray eyes. He was so handsome, so treacherous, so *lost* to her, that her pain sharpened and twisted until it sliced her heart into narrow ribbons.

"Yes," he said simply, "we should have."

"We didn't because we didn't want to hurt you, Cotannah," Emily said. "But to hurt you early on would have been less painful than this is now."

"You made such a fool of me, both of you," she said as images and memories flashed back through her mind. "There I was, poor, silly, inexperienced girl, thinking that you, Tay, wouldn't come courting me because the *bandidos* had sullied me in your eyes."

She had to stand stiffly in her place so that her brittle body wouldn't break into a thousand pieces, but she did dare to turn her head enough so that she could see Emily.

"And you, Emily, you led me to believe that you loved Lee. You led me to *hope* that Tay would still marry me someday."

"We never meant to fall in love with each other," Tay said, "but we were drawn together from the start."

"We fought it," Emily said, "but it was too strong for us. 'Tannah, we love you, we don't want to hurt you, but ours is a love that can't be denied."

That was true, Cotannah thought grudgingly. She could see that.

But she didn't *want* to see it—somehow it only made her angrier and more sad.

"You betrayed me."

"We didn't mean it that way!" Emily cried.

"Cotannah, you're so young," Tay said. "I've always loved you like a little sister and I always will."

It wasn't fair. This simply was not fair. It made her so *mad*.

"I already have a big brother."

"Then I'd like to be your friend."

At the sound of the word, Emily burst out crying, and Cotannah felt hot tears begin to form in her own eyes.

"How *could* we all be friends now, after what you've done? How could I trust either one of you ever again?"

Her savage tone hung in the air; the words echoed in the big room.

"We only hope you can find a way," Tay finally said. "For example, you might remember that you and I had no promises or betrothal between us."

"Hah! You knew how I felt, what I thought you meant by coming all the way to our Texas ranch."

"Yes," he said, "and I knew the whole time I was there that I should tell you that the moment I saw you, even though you were all grown up into an extraordinarily charming and beautiful woman, I knew in my heart that my brotherly love for you would never change into any other kind."

"You *should* have!"

"I'll always regret the fact that I didn't."

Strained silence filled the room again, and then Emily spoke as softly as Tay had just done. "I don't want to lose you, Cotannah. You're like a sister to me."

"How sweet! I'm like a sister to both of you! Somehow it seems to me that you've both treated me more like an enemy than a sister!"

After a moment, Tay spoke. "We can't stop loving each other. And we can't undo what is done. We've made mistakes, but with your best interests in mind, Cotannah. Now it's up to you to decide how things will be in the future."

Yes. Of course. Great. Now that her life was in shambles, she held all power over the future.

But sarcastic thoughts were no comfort. Hurting Tay and Emily in revenge was no comfort.

"I . . . love you both . . ." she said brokenly, and although the words nearly choked her, they were true, sadly true.

She swallowed hard. They would not see her cry; she would not let them. Holding back the tears, forcing calm into her voice, she started over again.

"I love you both, but you've betrayed me. I can't be your friend right now." She turned away from the sight of them and ran from the room.

Tay felt sick inside as he watched her go. Sick and utterly helpless.

"There's nothing we can do except give her time to get used to us together," Emily said, using a napkin to wipe away her tears.

She got up and went to Tay. He turned, took two long strides, and pulled her into his arms.

"You're my comfort," he murmured and brushed back her hair to lay his cheek against hers, to nuzzle the soft, warm spot beneath her ear. "Oh, Emily, you're my soothing strength."

"I know," she said, "I know. And you're mine. We'll have to keep telling each other that someday Cotannah will understand and she'll feel warm toward us again. We have to believe that."

"I do believe it."

The scent of her, roses and warm woman, touched the strings of tension that were holding him together, just the scent of her eased his muscles, eased his mind. He pressed his lips gratefully against her warm skin, but she didn't turn her face to find them with her mouth. She only held his head still with one soft hand, held his cheek securely against hers.

"Cotannah isn't the only one upset about our love," she said. "Your people, Tay. Your people don't want me to be your wife."

"They'll come around," he said, praying as he said the words that it would prove true. "Give them time to get to know you and love you, and they'll come around."

Two days later, Emily believed that Tay might have been right about the People coming around to accept them as a couple, because Auntie Iola, of all people, sent word for Emily to come visit her at her home that afternoon.

The note sounded so friendly that an ardent hope sprang up in Emily's heart. She certainly would indulge Auntie Iola and she would try her hardest to win her over—then, perhaps, the whole tribe would follow! As she hurried to dress in her best summer day dress and its matching bonnet, she tried to imagine what the visit would be like.

Tea and tea cakes and lemonade, probably, with the two of them, Tay's aunt and Tay's betrothed, sitting and talking on a cool porch—a conversation that would be the beginning of the melding of their two families, and of the healing of them both. For Tay's was not the only family upset by the coming marriage.

Cade and Maggie were understandably torn between Emily's happiness and Cotannah's despair, and Mama was frantic that Emily

would be staying in the Nation, far away from
Las Manzanitas. Somehow, though, even if she
and Cotannah were never friends again, the
rest of them would manage to remain close;
instinctively Emily knew that. Auntie Iola,
however, was a whole different story—and
today if she could form a bond with *her*, the
whole tribe might follow.

She sent Pansy to ask Joshua, the young
Choctaw orphan Uncle Kulli had taken in, to
hitch up a horse and drive her to Iola's, and
then she set herself to concentrate on the
reason for Iola's invitation as she put up her
hair. Probably, after thinking about Emily and
Tay for two days, after seeing them declare their
love in the wake of the tornado, Auntie must
have decided that their marriage was inevitable, that she might as well accept it.

Or, more likely, Tay had gone to talk to her,
and she had promised her nephew—who was
clearly one of her very favorite people—to give
Emily a fair chance. If only she could show him
the invitation and ask him! But he was gone, no
telling where, on business for the Choctaw
Council, and he wouldn't be back until after
dark.

Every step of the way on the three-mile drive
through the hot sunshine to Iola's house, Emily
prayed that Iola would come to like her, or at
the very least, approve of her. If the People
would accept her marriage to Tay, it would
make his life so much better, for he needed
them and his work for the Nation in a deep,

elemental way, almost as much as he needed her.

As Joshua turned the horse and gig off the road and into a neat yard, bordered all around with flowers, Emily saw Iola's short, round figure standing on the porch, stolidly waiting for her. She smiled. Today she would ask Auntie Iola to tell her some stories about Tay's childhood.

And the next time she saw Iola's friend, Hattie Tubbee, she would ask all about the bead designs and their meanings. Soon she would know what the road and the circle and the coiled serpent signified, and she wouldn't feel like such an outsider.

"I wait for you, Miss Emily?" Josh asked, proudly using the English he was learning.

"Whatever you wish, Joshua. I'll be here visiting for an hour or two."

"That cool shade there is where I go."

"Fine. Thank you."

He brought the horse up short at the foot of the three low steps as Auntie Iola walked to the top of them.

"So," she said, as Joshua jumped from the driver's seat to help Emily step down. "You have come to see me, have you, girl?"

The words were innocuous enough, but there was something in Iola's tone, an edge to it, that definitely could not be called welcoming. It sounded more . . . challenging. It froze Emily's foot to the ground, but when she looked up into Iola's round face the woman was smiling broadly and her dark eyes were bland.

"Yes, I've come to visit you, Auntie Iola. Thank you for the invitation."

The woman gave her one of her sharp glances when she called her "Auntie Iola." Emily's hopes sank. But what else could she call her? She knew no other name.

"All strangers need to get acquainted," Iola said. "Wouldn't you say that is true?"

Emily nodded in agreement instead of speaking, for at that moment Joshua drove, with a great rattling of wheels, away toward the shade. Iola shooed Emily toward the door as if she were a chicken, Emily thought. She didn't take her hand or her arm, she didn't touch her.

But she spoke cordially enough when she said, "Come in, do come in."

Emily stepped from the bright afternoon sunlight into the dimness of the house ahead of her hostess. She blinked. The three-mile ride in the sun must have addled her brain; she must be having hallucinations. She thought she had seen several women, a lot of women, sitting around the perimeter of the room.

When she opened her eyes and looked again she saw they were real. Real but silent. Silent and staring contemptuously at her.

Chapter 21

What is this? Sudden panic weakened Emily's legs and filled her with a terrible urge to turn around and run right back outside, screaming for Joshua to bring the gig and take her back to Uncle Kulli's.

She stiffened her spine and took another step into the parlor. Dear Lord, there must be twenty-five of them!

Obviously she had been wrong. Neither Auntie Iola or the People had come around to accepting her and Tay—instead, they had set a trap for her. Iola came in behind her and broke the silence.

"My friends want to talk to you," she said with an even harder edge in her voice. "They didn't have a chance to visit with you the night of the dance."

Because you, shameless white hussy that you are, lured my nephew away from us and out into the dark to be alone with you.

That unspoken judgment echoed from the cold walls of the room. How could it be so cold in here when outside it was so humidly hot?

"Well, it seems we'll have a chance to talk now," Emily said. "How thoughtful of you to invite all of us here."

Her sarcasm was only bravado, though, and all of them knew it. Her heart was pounding as if she were running away from a pursuing hungry bear.

"Sit," Iola ordered briskly, and placed a chair, a straight, cane-bottomed kitchen chair, at the back of Emily's shaking knees.

Her legs gave way and she sat, trembling inside as if suffering a chill. Lifting her chin took a monumental amount of strength, but she did it and she forced herself to look at the faces turned toward her from every direction so they could see that she wasn't afraid of their petty machinations.

Yes, Hattie was here—but she certainly didn't look in the mood to explain Choctaw symbols. And two other women with whom Emily had spoken in the aftermath of the tornado were sitting like stones, glaring at her.

Then, as she glanced on around the rough circle, her stomach tightened and her heart nearly stopped. Cotannah. Oh, dear God, Cotannah was here.

Tears stung her eyes. How could she participate in this? Had she, instead of Iola, been the one to arrange it? How *could* she resort to such an awful revenge?

Hattie Tubbee led the charge. "How do you cook *Lokchok-Ahi?*"

Emily's jaw dropped. So. It was to be an

inquisition, then, to point up her inadequacies to be Tay's wife. There was so much hostility in the air that she wouldn't be surprised if, at the end, they stoned her.

And Cotannah. Cotannah, who once would have risked her life to save her friend, would probably throw the first stone.

Lord! She wanted to cry. She wanted to drop her head into her hands and cry. How could they be so *mean*? She had no earthly idea what a *Lokchok-Ahi* was.

"Ch-chop it up and b-boil it in water."

The sudden stillness told her she'd lucked onto the right answer.

"What about *Kantak*?"

"Th-the same way."

"Ha!" Hattie shouted, and the others began shaking their heads and making low, sullen noises of disapproval.

Beads of sweat broke out on Emily's upper lip, but inside she felt even colder.

Iola walked heavily across the floor in front of Emily without a glance at her and sat down in the only empty chair in the room, a high-backed armchair next to Hattie. She settled herself in it with her plump hands flat on the arms and her feet barely touching the floor.

Hattie and Iola by the window seemed to keep all the fresh air blocked out of the room, as completely as if they had closed it. Emily could barely breathe.

"Any woman who will marry a *Mingo* of the Choctaw Nation must know how to cook *Kan-*

tak," Iola said, speaking pompously as if imparting a great, secret truth. "And that woman also must know how to feed his heart and his spirit as well as his body." She gave Emily a long, stern look. "Tell me, what would you do if ten hungry families came out of the mountains and camped in the yard of the Chief, your husband?"

"I would feed them."

Emily gave that answer straight from her heart without hesitation, without a stammer. A slight change flickered over Iola's round face—she knew sincerity when she heard it. But she wasn't about to admit that.

"For how long?" she asked suspiciously.

"For h-however long I had f-food to share."

"And in return?"

"They could h-help to grow that food. The Choctaw Chief I will marry has a farm."

There. She had stuttered, but determination rang in her voice.

"You will marry him. Ha!" Hattie said derisively, and the rest of them started those bitter, scornful sounds all over again.

Sweat came out on Emily's forehead, too.

Another woman, one of the ones she had spoken with on the campground, a woman with a face wrinkled as a dried persimmon, took her turn.

"At the great fish fry, what color paint do we use to mark the people who are allowed to stay and take part?"

Emily blinked and tried to stare her down,

although her pulse was racing with a wildfire of fear. This humiliation was totally insane. What else did they plan to do to her?

"H-h-how could I possibly kn-know s-something like that?" The words burst out of her in an angry cry, and she turned and looked directly at Cotannah. "This is totally crazy, Cotannah," she said. "What in the world does it prove?"

Cotannah only stared at her, not the slightest sign of recognition on her face.

"It proves you are not Choctaw," Iola said, "and not right to marry Tay Nashoba. He needs an Indian wife who can observe the traditions and who can make a safe home for him, not a white one who will nag at him to take sides with her white people who own the railroad."

"And the intruder cattle," Hattie said.

"And the mining camps," the wrinkled woman said.

"And the liquor for sale."

"The organized gangs of cattle and horse thieves that steal from us are mostly white people."

"All white people stick together to make money," Iola said, nodding wisely. "They love money and jewels. They are greedy. Greedy."

"Tay Nashoba's wife needs to farm like other Choctaw women," Iola said. "The Principal Chief must have freedom to ride out and see to his people. *You*, white girl, *you* would be afraid to stay on the farm alone, and you could not manage the work and the farmhands."

They all laughed at that and then began making a low, ominous, rumbling sound that caused chill bumps to spring up on Emily's arms. She looked around the circle as much as she could bear, but did not see a friendly eye anywhere.

In spite of the heavy summer heat, she had gone so cold inside that she would never get warm. What a fool she had been. What an utter, simple *fool* to fall for Iola's friendly invitation to visit her and be tortured! The People would *never* come around; she had better get used to that idea right now.

"No doubt you cannot—" another woman began.

Hattie interrupted mercilessly. "She says she would feed the hungry at Tay's farm. But I think she is too greedy for that. She will take Tay *away* from his farm and from us to live in the white world. She will try to make him forget us."

"He will *not* forget," Iola cried. "He will remember and he will long for his home in the Nation. He will be miserable."

"And the Nation will be miserable, too—lost to the white intruders without him," Hattie replied as if they were reciting a responsive reading.

"She does not care about that," a young woman taunted. "She only cares about herself. She is white and she likes money; I can tell by looking."

"Th-that is not t-true!" Emily cried, turning

to look at Cotannah again. "T-tell th-them it's
not t-true!"

But Cotannah only looked at her through
huge dark eyes set in a beautiful mask of stone.

Emily sprang to her feet. "You sound like a
flock of guinea hens chattering and fussing,"
she cried. "And you make just as much sense.
Not one of you knows what you're talking
about. Have you ever thought that I can *help*
Tay and the Choctaw Council when they bargain with the white businessmen because I
might better understand the way those men
think? My father was a white businessman."

She stepped around behind her chair and
grasped its wooden back for something to hold
in her hands, something to hold her back from
running toward her tormentors and smashing
her fist into the first hard, smug face she could
reach. They all continued to stare at her from
around the circle, but now she caught a glimmer of surprise in their eyes.

"And I can help the Nation, too, by working
with the teachers in your schools. You want
your children to be educated and to be able to
survive in a white world. I know that because
Tay tells me you Choctaw have twice as many
schools as any of the other Civilized Tribes."

She took a deep, steadying breath and made
herself meet one woman's gaze, then another's.

"I am a teacher and I love my work. I've
taught many Spanish-speaking children on our
ranch in Texas to speak and read and write in
English. I can help your children do the same.

Also, I can help prepare the students that you send to college in the States."

Her heart was thundering and she willed it to calm while she waited a moment for her words to sink in. "You say that I would be afraid to stay alone at the farm," she said, "and I might be. But I would do it and I would learn the farm work the same way I learned to help Maggie and Cade with the ranch work at Las Manzanitas."

She paused and fought the urge to look at Cotannah. "I would also face any dangers here in the Nation the same way I faced the bandits who attacked our ranch in Texas. I was terrified, but when they stole Cotannah and would have carried her off to Mexico, I risked my life to help Tay save her."

That seemed like bragging on herself, but these taunting women might as well know she was no coward. And if it made Cotannah ashamed of her own petty behavior today, all the better.

"I'm not greedy either," she said, speaking more quietly now that she had their breathless attention. "I don't need money or jewels or anything else the white world has to offer. I don't care to live in that world, and neither does Tay."

She stood up very straight and took in a deep, long breath. The need to cry was still with her, but it was fast retreating as she thought of her love for Tay. She stared right back at them all through eyes glazed with unshed tears.

"I know how much Tay loves you all—although, at this moment, only God knows why he does—and I would never expect him to live anyplace but here in the Nation."

They were listening. They honestly were listening. A great gust of confidence swept through her.

"I want to help Tay in all the ways I've told you, and I want to be his comfort. I want to be his peace and happiness. If you're honest, you'll admit that he has needed that for a long time."

The room fell into a silence so complete, she could not even hear them breathing. She was strong now, strong enough to overcome them all. Her love for Tay was making her strong.

"Tay tells me that I am his soothing strength," she said softly. "And he is mine. I am the love of his life and he is mine."

Her eyes were clear now and she looked from one rapt face to another, all around the room. "If I felt, for one moment, that the best thing for Tay would be for me to leave him, I would do so. If he told me that he wanted me to go, I would go."

She stood very still and listened to her own words floating in the air, echoing from the walls now, instead of the hateful, hurtful ones the others had spoken. All of them there were listening to her words; they were all thinking about them, testing them for truth.

Suddenly Tay's voice rolled through the room. "You do well to listen to Emily. She tells you the truth."

Emily's heart took flight and she whirled to see him. Yes, he was here in the flesh.

He walked to her with his great, strong stride and stood on her other side, placed his big hand at the small of her back, pressing the palm of it intimately against her. It warmed her blood and her bones. Now she would never be cold again.

"I got wind of what you all had planned," he said, looking at Iola, then at Hattie, "and I rode fast to Emily's rescue." He smiled down into her eyes, and suddenly the world seemed brighter. "Then, when I stood outside the window and listened, I heard that Emily could rescue herself."

He glanced around the room again. "I'm asking you to open your hearts to everything that she has told you. Remember, too, that I have been loyal to this Nation with my heart's blood and all of my strength for my whole life. I always will be."

He paused, and Emily felt tension vibrate in him. "I may owe you for being loyal to me and I may owe you for the results of the decisions I've made, during the white man's Civil War and in the years since, but you do not own my soul. This is the woman I love and this is the woman I will marry."

For an endless, silent moment, Emily thought that nothing either of them had said had made any difference, that nothing had changed. Then Iola heaved herself out of her chair and came toward them, Hattie following.

In an instant it seemed that every one of the women was on her feet, gathering around her and Tay. Many of them were teary-eyed now, and they were murmuring best wishes and comments about such a great love, such a great romance, as they surrounded the two of them and took them into the fold.

But it wasn't until Tay and Emily were leaving, walking across the porch with their arms around each other, following Auntie Iola, who was going ahead calling for Joshua to bring the gig, that Cotannah spoke to them. She slipped out the door behind them, and when they turned, she met their eyes only briefly before hanging her head.

"I'm sorry I had anything to do with . . . this," she said, gesturing toward Iola's parlor. "I am forever grateful that you both rescued me from the *bandidos*, and I don't want you to think that I'm not."

"We know you are," Tay said. "No need to say it."

"I do need to say that I still love you both," Cotannah said. "But I can't stay in the Nation. I'll go home with Maggie and Cade when they go."

Then Cotannah was gone and Auntie Iola was walking them to the gig where she hugged them both before Tay tied his horse to the back of it and they climbed in.

"Tell Kulli Hotema that I will visit him tomorrow," Iola said.

Tay laughed as Josh drove them away.

"That puts my mind at rest," he said. "Now we know that Uncle Kulli is sure to accept you, too."

Emily smiled and scooted closer to him, into the safe haven of his arms.

During the two weeks left until the election, Emily was amazed that she could feel as if she were becoming a whole new person altogether and, at the very same time, that she was freer and more open to simply being her old, true self than she had ever been. Tay's love gave her both of those perceptions because he loved her so entirely for herself, yet he changed her into someone new by helping her become part of his land and his People.

He showed her every corner of his farm, Tall Pine, nestled in a curving bend of the Kiamichi River with the hills rising majestically behind the rambling, two-story frame house that his parents had built beneath a lone pine tree when they came west from the Old Nation. He took her on long rides in the beautiful purple mountains that surrounded it and taught her to open all her senses to every cedar and pine and sweet gum tree, every bobwhite and scissor-tailed flycatcher bird, every deer, every coyote.

The sight of a song-dog never failed to cause them to look at each other and smile, leaning from their saddles to kiss. They spent whole, long days wandering in the woods and riding along the ridges where they could look for miles out across the endless, rolling mountains and into the sky.

"Tay, darling, I love this so," she said, as they

dismounted one morning and walked, arms entwined, to a whole stand of pines where they would sit in the shade. "But this is the fourth day in a row that we've done nothing for your campaign. What if Burton wins? What if he's up to something that we don't know?"

"Next week," he said as he reached with his free hand to touch her face, "for the last few days, I promise, we'll really work at getting elected."

"Am I still a detriment to you?" she teased. "Are you wandering around in the woods with me instead of asking for votes because you've lost all hope of winning?"

He chuckled. "No, after you set Iola and Hattie straight and won *their* hearts, I have no hope of losing. We'd better enjoy this time alone because once I'm Chief, there won't be much of it."

She smiled up at him as they sat down on the bed of pine needles. "So? How come now you're so sure that you're the winner?"

"Because you love me."

Then he pulled her down to lie beneath him, to hold her closer than the sun was to the sky, to kiss her senseless in the cool, cool breeze that blew high above the rest of the world.

And during that next week, too, the last week when, true to his word, Tay spent every waking hour working to get elected, Emily still had that new, trembling sense of excited well-being. Always, since the first horrible tirade of her father's that she could ever remember, she had felt a responsibility on her shoulders: to make peace, to try to make everyone happy. On the ranch she had felt, whether school was in or not, that she must do all she could for her students. Now, for this short while at least, other people took on all the duties and made the peace for *her* benefit; others stepped forward to teach *her*.

Hattie and Auntie Iola insisted that she sit beside them for the speeches; then, when Tay stepped down and started off to ask for votes all across the increasingly crowded campground, they insisted that she stay with them and accept some instruction. More and more Choctaw were coming in from the hills to stay at the campground until the election took place, and most of them were full-bloods—she must know a few things in order to win their respect, they told her.

Emily complied, although she suspected that their plump, round faces, which looked so solemn and serious, concealed more curiosity than concern. They knew *some* things about her now, after the harrowing trial they had put her through, but Maggie and Cotannah had said that they had bombarded the two of them with questions about Emily while she was out roaming the hills with Tay.

She smiled to herself. These two were the dowager queens, she was the interesting newcomer in their society, and they were determined to know more about her than anyone else did.

"First we take you to help at my daughter's

cookfire," Hattie said, pointing through the thinning crowd around the speaker's platform to a fire near the long communal tables. "Soon it will be time to feed your hardworking man."

They all got up and carried their chairs with them, Emily walking in the middle.

"Always cook good food and lots of it," Iola instructed as they made their way toward the fire Hattie had indicated. "And if a worrisome thing has happened that day, never tell it to your husband until after he has eaten."

"I will. I won't," Emily said, and the last of her lingering bad feelings toward Auntie Iola vanished.

Iola truly did love Tay, and now that she knew how deeply he and Emily loved each other, she wanted to help her in every way she could. Iola had raised him and she'd only been acting like a protective mother when she'd tested Emily, Tay had told her. She had had no other children and she'd been terrified that Tay would be lost to her forever, swallowed up by the white world, which she didn't understand.

Now she was determined that Emily would understand Tay's world. At the cookfire, all the women working there gathered around to answer the questions they had thrown at Emily at Iola's house and to show that they hoped she held them no ill will.

Hattie's daughter, Tulla, showed her some *Lokchok-Ahi*, both cooked and raw, explaining that it was a root, which some called mud potatoes and which tasted not unlike them. *Kantak*, although also a root, was not cooked at all the same way—it was the big-headed root of a stickery vine, and a person had to peel the root, slice up the inside of it, and spread it on the housetop to dry. Once it dried, it had to be beaten as corn is beaten into meal until it made flour. Tulla had made fry bread from it and showed Emily how to drop the little pillows of dough into a pot of boiling fat to fry.

While it cooked, they talked about their schools and what they wanted for their children and asked shy questions about Emily and her students on Las Manzanitas. She talked eagerly about her work as they all drifted over to the table with a platter of the hot, golden fry bread. They sat around one end, dipping the pieces in honey and eating the delicious morsels. Emily marveled as she glanced around at the group that had taken her in—it seemed impossible that only a few days earlier she would have sworn that could never happen. She truly felt almost like one of them.

"No one has explained the great fish fry to me," she said. "And why some people are marked with paint and allowed to stay and others aren't."

Iola shrugged as she dipped another piece of fry bread. "Some people aren't supposed to be there that day, that's all."

"According to whom?"

Iola ate the bread before she answered. "The signs."

The other women murmured agreement.

"Just on *that* day," Tulla said. "Another great

fish fry day, that same person might be invited."

"But who does the inviting? What *kind* of signs?"

Iola shrugged again, and Tulla looked puzzled. Hattie spread her hands helplessly in the face of such ignorance.

"Dreams," she said, "like those of going to *Nanih Wayia*, signs of being called without voices, without words."

The others nodded agreement and looked at Emily as if now, surely, she would understand.

"But *always* no expectant mothers," one young woman called Sophie said.

"Yes."

"Never on great fish fry day."

"That is right."

Then they all gave a final nod as if they had explained the subject thoroughly. They carried on with their eating and chattering.

No, Emily mused as she took one more piece of the fry bread. She was not quite one of them after all. Not yet. Maybe not ever. But they had taken her in, and that was what mattered for Tay.

Chapter 22

On Election Day Emily woke with her head still filled with a dream. She sat straight up and opened her eyes to the gray predawn light, then reached behind her to stack some pillows against the headboard at her back. In the dream she and Tay had been married ten years and they had been surrounded by children. Beautiful children. They still loved each other beyond reason, and he was still serving as Principal Chief.

So. Probably it was an omen that he would win the election today.

But she didn't feel happy. Something else had been in the dream, something to give her this low pounding of a headache in her temples and knot of dread in the pit of her stomach.

She saw the smiling faces from her dream again and then she knew. The oldest girl of hers and Tay's had had Katie's face. Her name had been Katie.

The familiar blow of guilt and regret struck her heart. She drew up her legs and threw the sheet up over her shoulders before wrapping her arms around her knees, rocking a little to comfort herself. Dear, sweet little Katie! Had the news that Emily wouldn't become her mother after all, that she wouldn't even be coming back to Las Manzanitas, devastated the poor darling?

And had it hurt Lee terribly? He was a good man, he meant well, he had truly loved her in his way. And he had been through so much—a hard childhood, the death of his wife, the loss of his own ranch, and then trying to be both mother and father to Katie while he worked so much to keep his job and make them a permanent home.

If only he would answer her letter. If only she could know that they would be all right and that they didn't hate her! She had rewritten the message over and over to try to bring the least hurt to them both, but maybe she could have done better. Maybe she should write again.

Suddenly she wished she had someone to talk to, someone to show the letter to and ask an opinion. Instinctively she glanced at the bed on the other side of the room, the empty bed that had been Cotannah's, and then she quickly closed her eyes. What a travesty that would be—to show Cotannah her letter to Lee!

Another familiar sadness rolled through her. She would never share anything with Cotannah again. Since that day at Iola's house, Cotannah had stayed away from her and Tay as carefully as if they had the plague. Maggie said Cotannah was still here in Uncle Kulli's house, but Emily had not even glimpsed her in all these two weeks.

She opened her eyes. If she had to give up Cotannah's friendship for Tay's love, she would do it. She had already done it, in fact, and now she would try to put it out of her mind.

She threw off the sheet as fast as she'd thrown it on and leapt out of bed to pad barefoot across to the desk. She fumbled in the top drawer and found the copy of the letter she had sent to Lee by special messenger the day after the tornado. Unfolding the paper and holding it near the window didn't throw enough light on it, so she lit the lamp.

Dear Lee,

As you can see, my hand is shaking so badly that I can hardly hold the pen to write this hurtful message to you. I know, however, that the longer I wait, the worse it will be for you and Katie and for me. Lee, I have fallen so deeply in love with Tay Nashoba that I cannot possibly ever leave him. He loves me, too, and he has asked me to marry him, which I will do very soon.

I know that you saw my attraction to Tay from the beginning, and now I'm glad because this won't come as a complete shock to you. I'm sorry—so sorry—though, to bring you pain.

And I cry because this will hurt Katie, too. Oh, Lee, I hope she won't start to believe that

*every mother or prospective mother she ever
has will end up leaving her! That would just
break my heart! Please explain to her that that
is not true and please read her this message:*

*Katie, darling, I won't be your mother after
all, but I do love you very much and I always
will. I won't be coming back to live on Las
Manzanitas, but maybe we'll see each other
again someday. Please study hard for whoever
is your new teacher. I'll never forget you.*

*Oh, Lee, I hope that soon you will love
someone new. You are a good, kind man and
I'll always appreciate the time we had together. Also, I'll always be honored that you gave
me your mother's ring. Cade and Maggie will
safeguard it and bring it back to you.*

*I'll never forget you, either, and I hope that
with the passage of time we can still be friends.*

Emily

She let the wrinkled page fall. If Lee had sent
a reply, she should be receiving it soon. If she
could know how he and Katie were taking the
news, she thought she could let them go completely from her heart.

For a long time she sat looking out the
window, watching the sun come up and redden
the sky and the land. Her new land. Below her
the campground was coming alive with people
stirring up fires and bustling about getting the
tables and chairs ready for the officials to sit
and record the votes in their poll books, and

others running in all directions on errands. Tay no doubt was out for his morning run at his place, but he was coming to Uncle Kulli's for breakfast.

Just the thought of seeing him in the next hour set a quick excitement thrumming in her veins. This was Election Day, the first day of the rest of their lives together. Win or lose! Surely Tay would win: All the talk for the last two or three days had been that he would.

But Election Days could be wild and violent, he had told her, and Burton could have some dirty tricks up his sleeve—lately he had confined himself to the same old litany of complaints about Tay with no new charges, and that wasn't characteristic of him. Emily's personal theory, which she had gotten from Auntie Iola, was that Burton knew he would be beaten and he didn't want to call any more attention to himself.

Pansy came in then with warm water for her basin, and Emily jumped up and began to dress. Soon she and Tay would be dressing together, talking over their plans for the day— whatever happened today, from now on, she and Tay were going to be together! Her heart pounded like a hammer on stone at the thrilling thought of waking up beside him every single day.

As soon as she was dressed and her hair was up, she ran downstairs and out onto the porch to wait for him to ride in. Cade and Uncle Kulli were already out there, standing in the yard, talking to a half dozen men. Some others came across the lawn to join them, and soon she realized from the tone of their voices that something had happened.

She ran down the steps and started toward the campground, angling her path to go near them, near enough to catch Cade's eye and perhaps ask him the news or at least to overhear what had caused the excitement. However, before she was halfway there, hoofbeats sounded in the driveway and she saw Tay's big white-gray horse.

Watching him come toward her made her remember the first time she'd watched him ride in, that early June evening at Las Manzanitas. June. And Election Day in the Choctaw Nation was always the first Wednesday in August. Two months. And she needed him so in her blood and her bones that it seemed impossible she had lived for twenty-three years before she knew him.

He smiled when he saw her and touched the broad brim of his white hat.

"There he is!"

"He's here. See what he has to say for himself!"

The cries came from the campground while everyone there, it seemed, began to drift away from their fires and their tasks to flow in an inexorable tide in Tay's direction.

He rode up to Emily and stopped, leaning into one stirrup to reach down and touch her hair.

"Good morning, *holitopa*," he said, his voice a low melody beneath the noises of the crowd, his eyes bright with meaning for her, only for her. "I've been thinking about you."

He felt the same way she did, she thought, with a mighty lift of her heart: He couldn't wait, either, for them to wake up together every day. She covered his hand with hers for a moment, then he sat back in his saddle and watched the people coming, listening for what they had to tell him.

Suddenly Emily realized that Candidate Burton was one of the men in front. He was so disheveled, she hardly recognized him—his shirt was on lopsided and it was torn, his face showed a bloody scratch, his hat had a hole through the crown.

"There's the ambushing coward!" he cried, pointing at Tay. "He tried to kill me at sunrise while he was out on his *morning run*, and I'm not the only one who says so!"

Several people surrounding him set up a chorus of agreement, shouting that they were willing to tell the story.

"Shoot your opponent on his way to the election," one of them cried, "and you don't have to worry about losing."

A tense silence came down over the crowded yard, and people fell back to leave an open line of fire between the two candidates for Principal Chief. Burton's hand hovered just above the pistol he wore.

Horrified, Emily whirled and looked at Tay.

His rifle was in his scabbard, as always, but he had no handgun today.

Yet guns seemed to be the furthest thing from his mind. He was sitting his horse, completely relaxed, looking down at Burton as if this were a performance staged solely for his amusement. After a long moment he smiled.

"Now, let me get this story straight," he drawled. "Are you saying that *I* put that hole through your hat?"

"You know damned well you did," Burton said. "And your second shot creased my face! Look! It's still bleeding!"

Tay chuckled, his low, rich chuckle that rolled out over the people like an invitation to enjoy all of life with him. "Wouldn't you say it's a little early for you to be on your Election Day drunk, Burton? That's pushing it, even for you."

Several people laughed. Burton's face folded into a ferocious scowl, and for a moment Emily panicked, expecting him to draw the gun.

"I ain't drunk. You've gone too far this time, Nashoba. Five people rode with me on the road at dawn, and we all seen you running away."

"How'd you tear your shirt?" Tay said.

"Chasing you through the woods, and you know it."

Tay shook his head in amazement; his lips turned up at the corners in the barest smile. When he spoke, though, his voice held a hard, dangerous edge. "I shoot at you *once*, Joe, never mind twice, and you've passed over, brother.

Everybody in the Nation knows I hit what I target."

Several voices rose to agree to that. Many people nodded.

Suddenly, as easily and offhandedly as if there were no dispute whatsoever, Tay stood in his left stirrup, threw his leg over, and stepped off the horse.

"I'd never shoot at you, though," he said. "You can rest easy, Joe. Life's too short and there's too few Indians."

That brought laughter that started in a shout of delight and swelled into a roar that filled the morning air. He won the election in that moment, Emily thought. He was the Principal Chief.

His supporters immediately surrounded him, but Tay walked straight to Joe Burton, clapped him on the shoulder, and held out his hand. After a moment's hesitation, and a sheepish duck of his head beneath his damaged hat, Joe took it.

Cheers and laughter erupted again and the day became one long celebration. Periodically riders or runners came in with the poll books with their records of voters' names, numbers, and choice for Principal Chief from the election precincts where people who didn't come in for the big gathering had voted. No tally was to be announced, though, until late afternoon when they all had come in and had been tallied.

Around noon a rider appeared who at first was taken for another election messenger but who turned out to be bringing a letter from

Texas. From Lee. Emily's hands shook a little as she opened it.

Dear Emily,

I had an awful feeling when your coach rolled out of here that early morning that I'd never see you again. Yes, ma'am, I did sense the feeling between you and Tay from the first, and somehow a part of me knew that even the ring wouldn't hold you. But I tried my best and that's a cold comfort to me now. I can't help but pity myself some. I wish you happiness, anyhow, for if ever anyone deserved it, that person is you.

Katie is well. She says to tell you that she'll always love you, too, and that she won't cry at school in front of the other children because that would make them cry, too.

> *Respectfully yours,*
> *Lee Kincaid*

Tears filled her eyes as she folded the letter and put it away in her pocket, but then she looked up at Tay.

"I love you, *holitopa*," she said, and the words took her sadness away.

This time she had done right to make herself happy instead of someone else. All afternoon Tay didn't leave her side.

Finally, as the moon was rising, the three judges of the election proclaimed the votes all counted. Tay led her by the hand across the campground and kept her beside him as they stepped up onto the low platform. The judges joined them, and one of them raised his arms to signal quiet for the announcement. All the noise of hundreds of people died away.

"The winner of the 1874 election for Principal Chief of the Choctaw Nation is *Tay Nashoba!*" he shouted.

The People gave a long cheer and then fell silent again, waiting for Tay to speak.

He stepped forward, taking Emily with him. "I am honored that you have trusted me with this office," he said. "Every sun that shines and every moon, I will do all the good I can do for all of you and for my beloved Choctaw Nation."

Everyone listened expectantly for more, but he had nothing else of a political nature to say.

"Now, there is something I will do for you even before we break this camp and part to go back to our homes all over this Nation. I will invite you to a dance and a feast of celebration all day tomorrow here on this campground."

A few people cheered at that, but most sensed, as Emily did, that he hadn't finished.

"The celebration will be for winning this election, yes," he said, "but it will also be for the wedding which will happen here tonight beneath this moon." He turned to Emily and spoke even more solemnly. "That is, if my bride will agree to that."

Emily's heart stopped.

Then he smiled that smile of his that could

charm a fox from its lair. "Emily Harrington,"
he said, "will you marry me tonight?"

She smiled back at him with her heart so full,
she thought she couldn't speak. But she could,
without a stutter and so loud and clear that
everyone there on the campground could hear.

"Yes. Yes, with all my heart, I will marry you
tonight, Tay Nashoba."

And then she *couldn't* speak because he was
kissing her passionately in the new silver
moonlight.